HAZARD IN CIRCASSIA

Historical Fiction by V. A. Stuart
Published by McBooks Press

THE ALEXANDER SHERIDAN ADVENTURES

Victors and Lords
The Sepoy Mutiny
Massacre at Cawnpore
The Cannons of Lucknow
The Heroic Garrison

THE PHILLIP HAZARD NOVELS

The Valiant Sailors
The Brave Captains
Hazard's Command
Hazard of Huntress
Hazard in Circassia
Victory at Sebastopol

For a complete list of nautical and military fiction published by McBooks Press, please see pages 253–255.

THE PHILLIP HAZARD NOVELS, No. 5

HAZARD IN CIRCASSIA

by

V. A. STUART

McBooks Press, Inc.
Ithaca, New York

Published by McBooks Press 2004
Copyright © Vivian Stuart 1973
First published in Great Britain by Robert Hale & Co.
Also published under the title *Hazard to the Rescue*.

Cover: "Reporter After Inkerman," 5 November 1854, *The
Illustrated London News*. Courtesy of Mary Evans Picture Library

Library of Congress Cataloging-in-Publication Data

Stuart, V. A.
  [Hazard to the rescue]
  Hazard in Circassia / by V.A. Stuart.
    p. cm. — (The Phillip Hazard novels ; #5)
  Originally published: Hazard to the rescue.
  ISBN 1-59013-062-6 (trade pbk. : alk. paper)
  1. Hazard, Phillip Horatio (Fictitious character)—Fiction. 2. Great
Britain—History, Naval—19th century—Fiction. 3. British—Russia
(Federation)—Circassia—Fiction. 4. Great Britain. Royal Navy—
Officers—Fiction. 5. Crimean War, 1853-1856—Fiction. 6. Circassia
(Russia)—Fiction. I. Title. II. Series.
  PR6063.A38H395 2004
  823'.92—dc22

2004005298

Distributed to the trade by National Book Network, Inc.,
15200 NBN Way, Blue Ridge Summit, PA 17214
800-462-6420

Additional copies of this book may be ordered from any
bookstore or directly from McBooks Press, Inc., ID Booth
Building, 520 North Meadow St., Ithaca, NY 14850. Please
include $4.00 postage and handling with mail orders. New York
State residents must add sales tax to total remittance (books &
shipping). All McBooks Press publications can also be ordered
by calling toll-free 1-888-BOOKS11 (1-888-266-5711).
Please call to request a free catalog.

Visit the McBooks Press website at www.mcbooks.com.

Printed in the United States of America

9 8 7 6 5 4 3 2 1

AUTHOR'S NOTE

With *the exception* of the Officers and Seamen of HMS *Huntress,* and of Colonel Gorak and his daughter, all the characters in this novel really existed and their actions are a matter of historical fact. Where they have been credited with remarks or conversations—as, for example, with the fictitious characters—which are not actually their own words, care has been taken to make sure that these are, as far as possible, in keeping with their known sentiments.

Extracts from official despatches and telegraphic communications are made from existing records, with the addition of the names of fictitious characters and ships only when necessary to add credibility to this novel, which is based on fact and *could* have happened as narrated.

The author thanks the Navy Records Society for permission to reproduce map from the Society's publications *Russian War, 1854* and *Russian War, 1855*—Captain A.C. Dewar, R.N., and D. Bonner Smith, also Commander W.M. Phipps Hornby, R.N., for technical advice on ships mentioned, most kindly and generously given at her request.

The action of this story is based on the despatch from Commander Sherard Osborn of HMS *Vesuvius,* published in *Russian War, 1855* (No. 74 Inclosure, dated 18th, May, 1855), see page 241.

Sir Colin Campbell remained in command at Balaclava—at Lord Raglan's request—when the *second* expedition to Kertch sailed from Sebastopol on 22nd, May, 1855, although he was himself most anxious to accompany the troops of his Highland Brigade.

FOR LADY ELIZABETH MATHESON

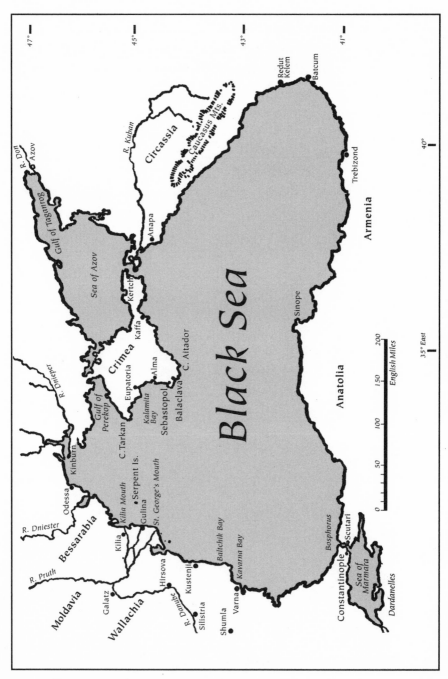

47°

45°

43°

41°

40°

35° East

Redut
Kelem

Batcum

Circassia

R. Kuban

Caucasus Mts.

Trebizond

R. Don

Azov

Gulf of Taganrog

Sea of Azov

Anapa

Armenia

Kertch

Kaffa

C. Altador

Crimea

Eupatoria

Alma

Sebastopol

Balaclava

Sinope

Black Sea

R. Dnieper

Gulf of Perekop

C. Tarkan

Kalamita
Bay

Anatolia

English Miles

0   50   100   150   200

Kinburn

Odessa

Killa Mouth

Serpent Is.

Gulina

St. George's Mouth

R. Dniester

Bessarabia

Baltchik Bay

Kavarna Bay

Bosphorus

Scutari

Killa

Hirsova

Kustenji

Constantinople

Sea of
Marmara

Moldavia

R. Pruth

Galatz

Wallachia

R. Danube

Silistria

Shumla

Varna

Dardanelles

PROLOGUE

At *precisely* one hour before sunset on 3 May 1855 Her Majesty's steam-screw three-decker *Royal Albert* weighed anchor and put to sea, flying the flag of Rear-Admiral Sir Edmund Lyons, Commander-in-Chief of the British Naval Forces in the Black Sea. Two Generals—Sir George Brown and the no less redoubtable commander of the Highland Brigade, Sir Colin Campbell—stood with the Admiral on her poop, watching as the men of the 93rd Highlanders, brave in their faded scarlet and tartan, mustered on the deck below for inspection.

The flagship was followed from the Fleet anchorage off Sebastopol by five other ships-of-the-line, all of them laden, as she was, with troops, including several thousand French infantrymen and a battalion of Turks. The liners were joined by fifteen frigates and gunboats, led by the *Miranda,* a steam-screw corvette of 14 guns, under the command of the Admiral's son, Captain Edmund Mowbray Lyons. Taking station in three lines, the two- and three-deckers in the centre, the Fleet set course in a north-westerly direction, as if making for Odessa, with the object of deceiving those enemy watchers who might have witnessed and, in consequence, be speculating as to the reason for this carefully timed departure.

A smaller French squadron, commanded by Admiral Bruat in his flagship *Montebello,* 120, slipped their moorings and steamed out of Kamiesch Bay shortly afterwards, also with a General—D'Autemarre—and a large contingent of troops on board. The French naval Commander-in-Chief, however, made no attempt to conceal his destination. Prior to sailing, he had ordered his captains to proceed at once to the pre-arranged rendezvous with their British allies, off the heavily fortified towns of Kertch and Yenikale, which, standing at the end of a jutting peninsula, guarded the entrance to the shallow, land-locked Sea of Azoff, to the east of Sebastopol. Here the combined force of some eleven thousand men—over seven thousand of them French—was to be landed at two points to the south of Kertch, from whence they were to advance, take the town by assault, and put its formidable gun batteries out of action. This would permit the entry of an Allied squadron of light-draught steam frigates and gunboats to enter the Sea of Azoff for the purpose of cutting the Russian supply routes to the Crimea and Sebastopol.

Throughout the long, bitter Crimean winter Sebastopol had held out against the pounding of the Allied siege-guns, despite casualties which averaged two hundred and fifty a day and which rose to six thousand at the height of a single day's bombardment. Such a feat would have been impossible had it not been for the constant stream of men, munitions, and food supplies entering the beleagured city from the north, where the road from Prince Gortchakoft's army headquarters at Bakshi-Serai lay outside the investing lines of the Allies, secure from attack by land or sea and far beyond the range of the cannon ringing the Heights to the south.

A survey of the coast had confirmed the existence of a military road, linking Bakshi-Serai and Simpheropol with towns on the shores of the Sea of Azoff, by means of which virtually all the needs of the Russian army in the Crimea were being supplied. In the six months since he had succeeded his former Chief, Vice-Admiral Deans Dundas, as Commander of the British Fleet, Admiral Lyons had advocated the launching of a combined naval and military expedition to seize control of the Sea of Azoff, and he had planned the operation down to the smallest detail, in the deeply held conviction that, if successful, it would shorten the war and starve Sebastopol into submission.

Once through the Strait, the gunboat squadron could maintain itself and go about its task unsupported, since the enemy had no ships in the Sea of Azoff capable of opposing the intruders. For this reason the troops, save for a small Turkish garrison, could be withdrawn after Kertch, Yenikale, and Arabat were taken.

It was a bold, well-conceived plan, and Admiral Lyons had pleaded for its adoption by the Allied High Command with all the fervour and eloquence he possessed.

Up to the last moment, however, General Canrobert, the French military Commander-in-Chief, had wavered—first giving his approval to the plans put forward by Admiral Bruat and then rejecting them. He could not plead any shortage of troops, since he had reinforcements already disembarking at Constantinople, amounting to a reserve corps of twenty-five thousand men, which would bring his total strength up to almost three times that of the British.

Finally, on 29th April, at a lengthy conference held at Lord Raglan's headquarters, he had, with extreme reluctance, agreed to contribute seventy-five hundred of his troops to the expedition, for a limited period of fourteen days. He had only then agreed to do so as an alternative to continuing the bombardment and assault on Sebastopol's Central Bastion, which had been urged upon him by Lord Raglan and his own General Pélissier, concerning the initial launching of which he had twice changed his mind in the course of a single week.

Admiral Lyons, pacing the poop of his flagship as she steamed majestically into the crimson glow of the setting sun, found himself thanking his Maker that the squadron was, at last, on its way. An eleventh hour change of heart by Canrobert had always been on the cards, but now, thanks be to heaven, it was too late for the French *Général-en-Chef* to have second thoughts. Forcing a smile to his lips, he walked slowly over to join the two British Generals on whom the success of the whole expedition would depend.

They could not have been better chosen, he thought. Both were Scots and, between them, they had more experience of the harsh realities of war than the rest of the British divisional commanders put together. Both men were in their late sixties, white-haired veterans who, as young officers, had served with great gallantry under the Duke of Wellington, in almost every battle of the Peninsular War. Sir George Brown had subsequently fought under General Ross in America; Sir Colin Campbell in India, under Napier and Gough—indeed, he had commanded a division at Chilianwala and Gujerat in 1849, although here, in the Crimea six years later, he merited only a brigade.

The Admiral's smile faded, as he reflected wryly on the rewards of nearly fifty years' distinguished military service when—as in the case of these two fine old soldiers—an officer had neither the money nor the necessary influence to purchase advancement in his profession. In the Navy, at least, commissions were not bought and sold and, although the right connections undoubtedly helped, promotion was not—as it seemed so often to be in the Army—the perquisite of the rich and titled, regardless of ability.

"Ah, Admiral . . . my congratulations!" Erect and soldierly in his immaculate frock coat, Lieutenant-General Sir George Brown turned from his rapt contemplation of the kilted Highlanders parading on the forward deck, a thoughtful frown drawing his bushy white brows together. Despite his sixty-seven years, he was a man of prodigious physical energy and—a martinet of the old school—was far from popular with the wealthy and titled younger officers, of the type who had been in the Admiral's mind, a few minutes earlier. He set, and insisted upon, a high standard of discipline in the Light Division he commanded, and was a firm believer in the efficacy of flogging, but the men, while they might complain of his severity and deplore his aversion to change, had nevertheless learnt to respect his personal courage and reliable leadership. They bestowed uncomplimentary nicknames on him behind his back, but having, at the Alma, recognized him for the competent professional soldier he was, they took a grudging pride in the demands he made on them and would have followed him anywhere. "Damme, you must be deuced glad," he suggested gruffly, "that we're at last headed for Kertch."

"I am," Admiral Lyons admitted. "To be honest, General, I expected—no, feared—right up to the moment we weighed, that one of Canrobert's aides would arrive with orders for us not to sail."

"So did I . . . infernal fellow! Incapable of coming to a decision and then sticking to it." Sir George Brown seldom minced words. "Poor Lord Raglan has a shocking time with him, just as he had with St Arnaud. Mind, I like Bosquet well enough, and Sir Colin"—he laid a hand on Sir Colin Campbell's thin, bowed shoulder—"has been trying to sing Pélissier's praises to me all afternoon. But damme, they're all the same, these infernal Frenchmen . . . one's just as bad as the other, in my view. I was happier when we were fighting against them and that's the truth!"

Sir Colin Campbell spread his hands in an indulgent disclaimer of this somewhat sweeping statement and observed quietly, "Ah, come now, my friend, we found the French worthy of our steel forty years ago—and they're not all tarred with the same brush as their present Commander-in-Chief. General Pélissier has a fine record and he was Canrobert's superior officer until they came to the Crimea, so I doubt if he'll let himself be overawed by anyone—not even the Emperor!"

Sir Colin's accent was strong and, listening to him, Admiral Lyons was reminded of another occasion when that dry, rasping Scottish voice had been raised to exhort the men of the 93rd to stand firm. They had been all that stood between the might of the Russian cavalry and the port of Balaclava, one misty October morning the previous year—two ranks of Highlanders whom Mr Russell, Special Correspondent of *The Times,* had described in his despatch as *"a thin red line tipped with steel"* . . . a dramatic but not inappropriate description.

"Remember, Ninety-third," Sir Colin had warned them, as they waited tensely for the expected cavalry charge, "There's no retreat from here—you maun die where ye stand, if need be . . ." and then, a little later, as some of the men started to surge forward to meet the advancing enemy, "Damn all this eagerness, Ninety-third! Keep your lines!"

The Admiral permitted himself a grim little smile, as he recalled the report of this incident which he had received from

Lieutenant—now Commander—Phillip Hazard, who had been present, on his instructions, his task to order the immediate evacuation of Balaclava Harbour should the 93rd fail to hold the line at Kadikoi.

Sir George Brown grunted. "God in heaven!" he exclaimed indignantly. "If it hadn't been for Canrobert, we could have walked into Sebastopol seven months ago, with scarcely a shot fired—and this infernally ill-conducted war would have been over by now! Damme, Colin, you know as well as I do that the Russians were ready to surrender the place to us after the Alma. They were routed and demoralized, they had no fight left in 'em and with the best will in the world, Korniloff couldn't have stopped us with his handful of sailors. But . . . Canrobert wouldn't have it. Land the siege-guns, he said, knock down their defences—an assault without a preliminary bombard-ment would be suicidal. He, more than anyone, is responsible for the ghastly losses we've sustained this winter, but in London they're blaming Lord Raglan for them." His voice rose in angry exasperation. "Unhappily for us, Canrobert com-mands the only army worthy of the name out here now—ours is pitifully inferior, both in size and equipment, as you also know—and so we're powerless to engage in any offensive oper-ation without the French. Even for this expedition, Canrobert has supplied three times as many men as we have and, the devil fly away with him, I would not put it past him to recall the whole lot within twenty-four hours of our landing! He's quite capable of it—don't you agree, Admiral?"

While privately sharing his fears on this score, Admiral Lyons decided that it might be wiser not to say so. "I earnestly trust not, General," he answered diplomatically. "Now that we have actually sailed with General Canrobert's troops aboard, it seems hardly likely that he can go back on his word—and he will have Lord Raglan to reckon with, if he does. Well . . ." He glanced skywards, inhaling the now dank evening air. "We shall change course as soon as darkness falls and there's a chance that we may run into fog tomorrow morning which—provided it is not too thick—will aid our enterprise. Let us go below to my quarters, shall we, gentlemen, and share the last of some excellent Madeira my son Jack brought out for me when he joined my flag."

They followed him to his spacious stern-cabin, but it was evident that Sir George Brown was not appeased.

"I don't trust Canrobert," he said. "I don't trust him any further than I can see him, 'pon my soul I don't." He accepted a glass of Madeira from the Admiral's nephew, Algernon Lyons, who was acting as Flag Lieutenant, and stared into it moodily. "Damnation, Sir Edmund!" he went on explosively. "I'd give six months' pay to know what's going on at the French headquarters at this moment—and I'm not a rich man, as heaven's my witness. Nor am I one who normally sets much store by premonitions, but I have to confess to you that I'm devilish uneasy."

Young Lieutenant Lyons regarded him in stunned surprise, as if afraid that he had suddenly taken leave of his senses, but the Admiral, aware that old Sir George was the last person in the world to allow his imagination to run away with him, heard him in frowning silence. Then, remembering his duties as host, he raised his glass. "Come, gentlemen," he invited. "Shall we banish our cares and drink to the capture of Kertch?"

Sir Colin Campbell was the first to respond. "Aye," he assented, with forced heartiness. "Aye, we'll do that, Admiral, and gladly. To the capture of Kertch!"

Glowering and reluctant, Sir George Brown rose to his feet.

"Very well," he conceded. "I'll drink to the capture of Kertch . . . and damnation to General Canrobert, if he *does* interfere with us; you know what the troops call him, don't you—Robert Can't. It's at least as apt as some of the names they call me!" He drank the toast and then lowered himself stiffly back into his chair. "I wish I knew," he added, under his breath. "Dear heaven, I wish I knew . . ."

CHAPTER ONE

T*he two* Allied squadrons which composed the expedition to Kertch came to anchor off Cape Takli in thick fog, some fifteen miles from the beach at Kamish-Bourno, at which it had been planned to set the troops ashore.

Phillip Horatio Hazard, commanding Her Majesty's steam-screw sloop *Huntress*, of 14 guns, stood with one foot braced against the weather hammock netting and his glass to his eye. Since sunrise, when the fog had started to clear, there had been a constant to-ing and fro-ing of boats between the *Royal Albert*, flying the flag of Rear-Admiral Lyons, and the *Montebello*, flying that of Vice-Admiral Bruat, and now he saw the French flagship was preparing to weigh anchor. Two other French ships, both frigates with troops on board, had already left the anchorage and set course, not, as might have been expected, for Kamish Burun, but to the south-west, as if their intention were to return to Sebastopol, and Phillip was puzzled.

The *Huntress* had been on patrol off the Circassian coast between Soujak and Anapa and, on instructions from Captain Moore of the *Highflyer*, senior British naval officer in the Strait, she had gone in company with the *Spitfire* to the rendezvous of the two Allied squadrons, in order to report the result of her observation of the enemy's movements, at first hand, to Admiral Lyons. The two squadrons had reached the rendezvous in the late afternoon and, soon after the arrival of the first ship, the fog had rolled in, shrouding the anchorage in a swirling white blanket of mist and causing some delay. Captain Spratt of the *Spitfire* had duly delivered his letters to the *Royal Albert,* but Phillip had not, as yet, been summoned to make his report. He had watched, in growing bewilderment, as a small French steamer had loomed suddenly out of the mist, coming from the direction of Sebastopol and, with scant regard for the danger of the prevailing conditions, had passed swiftly between the lines of anchored and still moving ships. Scarcely waiting until her own paddle-wheels ceased churning, she had sent a boat to the *Montebello* and shortly afterwards—although the fog was as dense as ever—the to-ing and fro-ing had begun.

The *Montebello's* barge had taken the French Commander-in-Chief, with his staff and what appeared, in the dimness, to be a number of army officers, to the *Royal Albert,* and Rear-Admiral Houston Stewart had followed them when the *Hannibal* came to anchor, an hour or so later. The boats had remained alongside the British flagship until long after the fog had been succeeded by darkness, and since sunrise—when the *Spiteful* made an unexpected appearance from Sebastopol— boats and barges had been going back and forth between the flagships, with both naval and military officers crowded into the sternsheets.

Now, however, it seemed to the anxiously watching Phillip, whatever sudden emergency had been causing the expedition's commanders such concern had been resolved, although with precisely what result it was impossible to say. Unless . . . frowning, he watched the *Montebello* cat her bower anchor, saw her screw start to rotate and, slowly and majestically, she moved out from the anchorage, her course—like that of the two frigates which had preceded her—south-westerly.

"She's heading back to Kamiesch!" A voice exclaimed at his elbow. Phillip turned, lowering his Dollond, as his brother Graham, now acting as his First Lieutenant, crossed the quarterdeck to join him. Since the restoration of his commission, Graham Hazard had been a changed personality, and their relationship—although, as Captain of the *Huntress,* Phillip still outranked him—had now been established on a new and happier footing. Not quite as it had been during their boyhood, of course . . . Graham was the elder by seven years, and those lost years, when he had drifted round the world, sometimes as an officer but more often as a seaman in the merchant service, had left their mark on him and, no doubt, would never be completely erased. But he was an efficient, conscientious, and very able First Lieutenant, under whose taut but always just administration the ship's company had shaken down in a manner Phillip had despaired of when Ambrose Quinn had been his second-in-command.

He shrugged and said, answering his brother's shocked observation, "So it would seem—and, by the look of things, the rest of the French squadron's about to follow her."

Graham lifted his own glass to his eye and subjected the slowly moving three-decker to a lengthy scrutiny. "No signal . . . nothing. That's odd. What do you make of it, Phillip? Surely the French can't be leaving us to take Kertch on our own?"

Phillip repeated his shrug. "At a guess, I'd say they were. The *Mouette* joined in the most almighty hurry last evening, just after you handed over the deck to Anthony Cochrane . . . she had her gig out and pulling across to the French flagship almost before she'd lost way. And I'm not sure, but I thought I recognized Fred Maxse in the *Spiteful*'s boat this morning, which suggests that Lord Raglan may have sent a despatch to our Admiral. He would scarcely have done that if all was as it should be, I'm afraid. Besides, you know General Canrobert, do you not? His indecision is becoming proverbial, so it's not beyond the bounds of possibility that he has changed his mind concerning the usefulness of sending a flotilla into the Sea of Azoff."

"Perdition take him!" Graham exclaimed. "At *this* stage, when we're in sight of our objective? I find it hard to believe— even of Robert Can't!"

"Nevertheless I very much fear he has," Phillip told him flatly. "As to the lateness of the hour, you surely haven't forgotten how he changed his mind when we had cleared for action, ready to bombard the Sebastopol sea forts, last October? I'd say that he's quite capable of countermanding *this* attack. He's never been in favour of it, according to Jack Lyons."

"By God, I hope you're wrong, Phillip!"

"So do I. But the fact that the Admiral has not yet summoned me to report on the Circassian coastal forts does suggest that there has been some change of plan and . . . as you can see"—Phillip pointed—"the *Lucifer* and the *Megère* are under way now. And Sedaiges of the *Lucifer* was supposed to be Jack's second-in-command, was he not?"

They watched in dismayed silence as the two French frigates, their decks swarming with blue-uniformed infantrymen, steamed past in the wake of the *Montebello*. Both had been designated to form part of the Allied steam squadron which, under Jack Lyons's command, had been under orders to enter the Sea of Azoff when Kertch was taken. This would just about break Jack's heart, Phillip thought. He and the Admiral had worked with such dedicated determination to ensure that the operation they had—as long ago as last December—termed "The Spring Offensive," should be carried out without a hitch when the time came. And now it was already May . . . he sighed, and Graham, guessing his thoughts, turned from his contemplation of the departing ships and gave a rueful shrug.

"I fear you are right, Phillip—there *is* something up. Dammit, I suppose it will be back to blockade duties and coastal patrols for us—if we're not ferrying troops—and we can kiss good-bye to any hope of action. I feel almost inclined to volunteer for service with the Naval Brigade on shore, if that's all that lies before us." He spoke with so much feeling that Phillip turned to stare at him in surprise.

"You're not serious, are you?"

"About volunteering for the Naval Brigade? Well . . ." Graham hesitated and then shook his head. "No, not really. I'm disappointed, even frustrated, at the thought of turning tail and leaving the enemy in undisputed possession of the whole of the Azoff coast. It's a natural reaction, and every man in this convoy will share it, I imagine, if that's really what we're going to do. But *is* it? Don't you think the Admiral might make an attempt to take Kertch without the infernal French?"

"He has too few troops," Phillip said regretfully. "I don't see how he can, alas, but . . ." He broke off as the Officer of the Watch sang out a warning from the port side of the quarterdeck.

"Signal from the Flag, sir." The young mate, Robin Grey, now confirmed in his acting rank and taking a regular watch, read the signal hoist with swift competence. "General signal for all Captains to repair on board, sir. Shall I call away your gig?"

"If you please, Mr Grey," Phillip turned back to his brother with a wry smile. "Well, we shall soon know, shall we not? I see Captain Keppel's smartly away"—he gestured to starboard, where the fine two-decker, *St Jean d'Acre,* of 101 guns, lay at anchor, dwarfing the clumsy, paddle-wheel steam frigates ahead and astern of her—"If anyone can persuade the Admiral to carry on without the French it will be Keppel! He must have had his gig in the water as soon as he got here, waiting for the signal . . . and Lord Clarence Paget is after him. With those two as advocates, we may see action after all."

"Indeed we may," Graham agreed, his expression more cheerful. They descended to the entry port together and, as the side party came to attention, Phillip lowered himself into his waiting gig, taking his place in the sternsheets beside the boat commander, Midshipman Sean O'Hara, who gave the order to cast off in a high-pitched treble. The fog was clearing quite rapidly now, with the warmth of the sun and a lively off-shore breeze and, as they joined a procession of boats all pulling in the direction of the flagship, O'Hara's sharp eyes spied a Cossack patrol, keeping observation from the high ground on the western side of the Cape.

"D'you see the bounders, sir?" He pointed, both tone and manner the cool, faintly contemptuous reaction of a veteran, to whom Cossack *videttes* were no novelty. At an age when most of his contemporaries were still schoolboys, the fourteen-year-old O'Hara—whose voice, to his impotent annoyance, had only recently started to break—had twice tried conclusions with roving bands of Cossack cavalry and had, on both occa-sions, distinguished himself. Phillip's mouth twitched as the youngster added belligerently, "They're in for quite a shock, sir, aren't they, when they realize that we intend to take Kertch?"

"It's to be hoped they are, Mr O'Hara." Phillip's reply was deliberately non-committal and the midshipman glanced at him in mute question, the eager light fading from his eyes when his glance elicited no further information. But he was too well trained to press the point, and only when he brought the gig alongside the *Royal Albert*'s starboard chains did he venture a diffident, "Good luck, sir," as an indication that, even if he did not understand the reason for his commander's evasiveness, he did not resent it. They would evidently need more than luck, however, Phillip decided, when he joined his fellow commanders in the Admiral's stateroom and glimpsed the glum expressions on the faces of those who had preceded him. The Admiral himself looked pale and strained; beside him, Sir George Brown, to whom command of the military part of the operation had been entrusted, was giving forcible vent to his feelings in a somewhat one-sided conversation with Sir Colin Campbell and Colonel Ainslie of the 93rd. Phillip caught the word "Canrobert" uttered as if it were an oath and then his attention was drawn to a group of senior officers of his own Service, who were subjecting Frederick Maxse—naval liaison officer to Lord Raglan—to a spate of questions which, apparently, he was unable to answer. Both Captain Keppel—his one-time commander in his midshipman days—and Captain Lord Clarence Paget of the *Princess Royal* were in this group and his heart sank as he heard the red-haired little Keppel say bitterly, "That's it, then. But I tell you, they'd run as soon as they saw our to'gallant masts above the horizon—they wouldn't stay to fight!"

There was a deep-voiced murmur of agreement, which died to expectant silence when Admiral Lyons moved to the head of the long table. "If you will be seated, gentlemen," he requested quietly. "I will endeavour to explain the situation in which we, most unhappily, have been placed. As some of you will have observed, General Canrobert sent a despatch steamer after us, with orders to Admiral Bruat to return to Kamiesch immediately, with the ships under his command and the troops they are carrying. The reason given for this change of plan was, I understand from Admiral Bruat, the fact that the

General received urgent instructions by electric telegraph from the Emperor Napoleon, requiring him to bring up the French Reserve Corps from the Bosphorus without a single day's delay." There was another loud and concerted murmur of shocked protest from the assembled Captains, but the Admiral, his voice stern and controlled, went on, "Needless, I feel sure, to tell you, gentlemen, we"—his raised hand indicated the two British Generals seated on either side of him—"we did everything in our power to persuade Admiral Bruat and General D'Autemarre to continue with us to the selected landing beach at Kamish-Bourno and, at least, set the French troops ashore, to enable us to take possession of Kertch."

"And they refused, sir?" Lord Clarence Paget asked incredulously. "They're returning to Sebastopol?"

Admiral Lyons bowed his head in reluctant assent. "I observed to them that General Canrobert had not sent us the text of the message from Paris, nor had he clearly defined it or ventured to say that Lord Raglan agreed with him in his interpretation of it. I assured Admiral Bruat that, were I in his place, I would unhesitatingly go on in the conviction that the Emperor, if he were on the spot and aware of our plans for this expedition, would undoubtedly command it. I observed, too, that it appeared from the statement of the officer who brought General Canrobert's letter that Lord Raglan had declined to write to me by him, which showed clearly that his lordship had no wish to see the expedition return. But . . ." he spread his hands in a gesture of resignation, "although the Admiral, after lengthy discussion, agreed to give the matter a night's reflection, he and General D'Autemarre came on board early this morning and they both said, to me and to General

Brown, that they considered it their duty to obey this order. Do not, I beg you, gentlemen, attach any blame to my gallant colleague. Admiral Bruat has worked heart and hand with me to bring about this enterprise and it was evident that his decision to abandon it was reached with extreme reluctance. As he reminded me during our discussion, he is entirely under the orders of the Commander of the French Land Forces and, although it was most painful to him, he deemed it his inescapable duty to obey the instructions received yesterday evening, since these came not only from General Canrobert but, in fact, directly from the Emperor."

Again there was a chorus of outraged voices, but Admiral Lyons wearily silenced them. "You remarked, my dear Henry," he said, addressing Captain Keppel, "that the enemy had but to see our to'gallant masts over the horizon and they would not stay to fight . . . and I should dearly like to put your contention to the test, believe me. Unhappily I have received a letter from Captain Moore, who, as you know, has had Kertch under constant observation since early in April. It was delivered to me this morning by Captain Spratt of the *Spitfire* and you may read it, if you wish." He motioned to his secretary, who laid the letter on the table in front of him. "There it is. In it, Captain Moore agrees with Colonel Desaint and Major Gordon, of the French and English Engineers, in thinking the moment very propitious for an attack, but all three officers recommend that it should not be undertaken with less than ten thousand men. And we have only two and a half thousand . . . in addition, a considerable portion of the French troops are being carried in our ships-of-the-line, as Admiral Bruat reminded me. He also reminded me that it was of the utmost importance to preserve our unity of action, and the good feeling which has hitherto existed between the two fleets and the two armies, and said that he took it for granted that we would not separate from him."

This time, his words were greeted by a stunned silence, which the Admiral himself broke. "Commander Maxse joined this morning in the *Spiteful*," he stated. "He placed in my hands a letter from Lord Raglan, which contained copies of a note addressed to his lordship by General Canrobert, and the text of the telegraphic despatch received by His Excellency from Paris. This last is in French, but I will read you its translation. First, however, I will read you part of Lord Raglan's letter to me . . . you have it, Frederick?" Lieutenant Cleeve, his secretary, obediently placed the letter he had asked for into his outstretched hand. Still in the same flat, controlled voice, Admiral Lyons started to read. *"I apprehend that if the French troops, which form three-fourths of your force, be withdrawn, there can be no chance of your being able to proceed on the expedition with a fair prospect of success and without incurring a risk which the circumstances would hardly justify.'* Gentlemen, I am regretfully compelled to agree with his lordship's assessment of the situation and so, too, is Sir George Brown, although Lord Raglan adds in his letter: *'Should you and Sir George Brown, however, after due deliberation, think it advisable to go on, and see the state of things with a view to taking advantage of any opening that may present itself, I am perfectly willing to support any such determination on Sir George Brown's part, and to be responsible for the undertaking.'"* He faltered suddenly, his voice losing its forced calm, and added, with unconcealed bitterness, "Sir George and I, aided and advised by Sir Colin Campbell, have discussed the situation endlessly and from every conceivable angle and, I tell you with deep regret, gentlemen, we have come to the conclusion that this expedition must be abandoned."

Once again there was silence. The assembled officers looked at each other in dismay; even when Sir George Brown rose to his feet and harshly confirmed the Admiral's announcement of their decision, no one ventured to question it. It was alas, all too evident, Phillip thought, that the decision was the only one possible in the circumstances. Two and a half thousand men—even if they included the splendid fighting men of the Highland Brigade—could not hope to drive an enemy numbering at least ten thousand from their prepared and well-armed defensive positions. He heard Captain Spratt, in response to the Admiral's request, confirm just how strong the Russians' defences were and then listened, in an unhappy daze, when the text of the telegraphic despatch from the French Emperor was read out. Beside him, young Lieutenant William Hewett, with whom he had shared some tense moments during the Russian attack on the Careening Ravine, which had been the prelude to the Battle of Inkerman the previous November, expelled his breath in a long-drawn sigh of frustration.

"Bully" Hewett, as he was affectionately known, had recently been appointed to his first command—that of the flat-bottomed, steam-screw gun vessel *Beagle,* of 4 guns—and his disappointment was understandable. The *Beagle,* by reason of her shallow draught, would have been one of the first ships to enter the Sea of Azoff had Kertch been taken, and her young commander, always in the thick of things, had been keenly looking forward to the prospect of taking her into action. "Now," he whispered glumly to Phillip, "there's to be no action. I'm beginning to wish that I'd stayed ashore with my Lancaster battery. Damn the French, I say!"

And this, it seemed, was the general feeling. The French, as usual, were to blame for the fiasco. Under General

Canrobert's command, it had so often happened that British plans for an end to the stalemate of the siege had been acceded to initially and then rejected that, although everyone was dismayed, few were surprised. There were one or two suggestions—the most pressing of these coming from Captain Keppel—that an attempt should be made to land what troops were available, after a preliminary naval bombardment of Kertch, but Captain Spratt's estimate of the depth of water in the Strait swiftly put a damper on even Keppel's enthusiasm. Phillip, called upon to make his report on the Anapa defences, did so very briefly, supporting Spratt's contention that the line-of-battle ships would be unable to approach close enough to their target, due to lack of water, to bring their guns effectively to bear.

"I am afraid, gentlemen, that further discussion of this unfortunate situation will be to no avail. We must retire before our enemy—General Canrobert has left us with no alternative," Admiral Lyons told them. He sounded very tired, but added, as his Captains rose, taking this as their dismissal, "Be assured, however, that I shall not cease to urge the Allied High Command to renew this expedition as soon as may be possible—within a week or two, if I have my way. The enemy can only look upon what has occurred as a feigned movement and they will therefore be less prepared for attack here, as elsewhere. Indeed, I cannot fancy anything so calculated to draw off his force from the main body of his army and thus aid other important operations—such as the French Emperor envisages—as for us to become masters of the Sea of Azoff." He laid a consoling hand on his son's shoulder and, for the first time since he had summoned the squadron commanders to hear his decision, his lips parted in a smile. "I thank you all for your patient forebearance. Good morning, gentlemen."

They started to file out, Phillip with them, when Algernon Lyons, the Flag Lieutenant, caught him by the arm.

"Don't rush away, Phillip," he said. "The Admiral would like a word with you. He's talking to Captain Keppel at the moment, but I don't think he'll be long."

Phillip waited and Jack Lyons, who had been standing talking to some of the officers of his light-draught steam squadron, recognized him and crossed to his side. "Well, Phillip, this is a sad day, is it not?"

"Indeed it is," Phillip agreed. "We can only hope that the Admiral will contrive to persuade General Canrobert of the urgent need for us to enter the Sea of Azoff."

"Don't speak to me of Canrobert!" Captain Lyons pleaded, an angry glint in his blue eyes. He was like his father, Phillip thought, taller, broader of shoulder, but with the same square-cut chin, firm mouth, and deep-set eyes. He had inherited his father's charm of manner, as well as his fine intellect and, at thirty-six, a senior Post-Captain with an enviable Service record, would almost certainly reach Flag rank himself in due course. Phillip had served under him in his first command on the China Station and their friendship was of long standing, dating back to the days when Sir Edmund Lyons had been British Ambassador to the Court of King Otho of Greece, a post he had held with distinction for fourteen years. "To think," Jack Lyons went on, "that we were within less than two hours' steaming from our destination when that miserable little despatch boat came up with us! If only the fog had fallen sooner, she might not have found us in time, for I swear, Phillip, had we set the troops ashore before Canrobert's instructions were delivered, Admiral Bruat would have permitted them to remain. He is the best of fellows, you know, and this operation meant as much to him as it did to my father. He was heartbroken when the decision to abandon it was forced upon him, but in the circumstances Canrobert left him no choice. If he had agreed to go on to Kertch it would have been held that he had disobeyed a direct order from the Emperor."

"I suppose it would. All the same . . ." Phillip shrugged disgustedly and the younger Lyons smiled, in rueful understanding.

"I know how you feel and how we all feel. However, *you* will not have to return to Kazatch with the rest of us, you lucky dog! My father has something else in mind for you which may relieve the monotony for a while."

Phillip's spirits rose. "You mean I'm not to go back to the blockading squadron?"

"So I was given to understand, although I know no details, beyond the basic fact that my father is anxious to make contact with the Circassian chiefs, with a view to organizing attacks on Soujak Kaleh and Anapa, aided by Turkish troops. It sounds as if it were to be a cloak-and-dagger mission of some kind and one very much after your own heart." Jack clapped a friendly hand on Phillip's shoulder. "After your exploits in Odessa last winter, my father naturally considers you well suited for the task. But come—the others are leaving, so he's free now and he'll tell you about it himself."

Phillip followed him eagerly and the Admiral, after taking affectionate leave of his son, seated himself once more at the head of the long table and motioned Phillip to a chair beside his own. A steward brought in a tray of coffee and set it down in front of him.

"Ah, Phillip, my dear boy—help yourself to a cup of coffee and, while you're about it, pour one for me, if you please. My throat is as dry as a bone, after all the cajoling and arguing I've had to do—alas, to no avail." Phillip did as he had requested

and he went on, "There is a service I should like you to perform, if you will, which may be of some considerable
assistance to me in my efforts to convince the French High
Command—and the Emperor—that this expedition to the Sea
of Azoff *must* be mounted again without delay. Have you the
maps I asked for, Frederick?"

"Yes, sir." His secretary spread out a map of the Circassian
coast and laid a sealed package at Phillip's elbow. "And the
orders for Commander Hazard, sir."

The Admiral thanked him and gestured to the map.

"Your orders allow you a fairly free hand, Phillip, but I'd
like to explain them before you go, so that you will understand
what I'm trying to achieve and act accordingly. I want you to
proceed at once to Ghelenjik and there make contact with a
Circassian chief by the name of Serfir Pasha—he has a Turkish
title but he's not a Turk. You were not with me when I made
a reconnaissance of the area last May, with part of the steam
squadron, were you?"

"No, sir." Phillip shook his head, "I was with the *Tiger,* sir,
when she—"

"When she ran aground in fog off Odessa and the enemy
blew her to pieces," the Admiral finished for him. "Yes, of
course you were . . . I had forgotten. Well, to give you a brief
resumé of our doings, we took Ghelenjik last May and left a
Turkish and Circassian garrison to occupy the place, after we
had repaired its defences. I had hoped then to enlist the armed
support of the Circassians against Anapa and Soujak Kaleh,
and I sent Captain Brock overland to Bardan, with a party of
Marines, with the object of persuading the chiefs—and, in particular, their paramount chief, Schamyl, who is a very able
soldier—to combine forces with the Turks. I wanted to gain
control of the whole coast, but"—he sighed—"Schamyl insisted

on waging his own campaign in Georgia which, I may say, he has done with conspicuous success. The others, although their hatred of the Russians is intense, told Brock that they could do little without aid—they asked for troops and munitions, and we had none to spare, unfortunately, and I had little success when I sought aid for them from the Turks. I did manage to obtain eight hundred troops from Selim Pasha, and with these we occupied Redoute Kaleh and Soukoum"—his long fore-finger jabbed at place names on the map—"which latter place is still held by a very gallant *naib* of Schamyl's, Mohammed Emin Bey, with about two thousand of his tribesmen." The Admiral went into details and Phillip listened occasionally, asking a diffident question.

"These Circassians are a wild, unruly, undisciplined people, Phillip," Sir Edmund Lyons warned. "They are robbers and freebooters, who have much in common with the Bashi-Bazouks—some of whom you may have encountered in the French camp. They fight bravely enough, but mainly for plun-der and as often among themselves as against a common foe, and they mistrust any leadership save that of their own chieftains. They have good reason to mistrust the Turks and especially the Turkish Pashas, whose generalship leaves a good deal to be desired and who, I have been told on reli-able authority, them with faulty rifles and out-of-date ammunition, with which to wage war on the Russians. Never-theless, they *have* waged war on them, sallying forth from their mountains to attack and harass supply columns and the like, with little help from the Turks. And they would have fought with us and under our command had we been able to leave even a token naval force with them last May—on the occasions when they did, we found them splendid allies. Captain Brock sent me a report on his dealings with them and

there's one from Captain Jones, of the *Sampson,* whom I left
at Soukoum Kaleh to repair defences. I've asked Frederick
Cleeve to prepare copies of both these reports for you, since
you might find them useful, and we are searching for an interpreter whom you can take with you."

"Thank you, sir," Phillip acknowledged gratefully.

"Don't thank me, my dear boy—you will need all the help
you can get. This is no easy task I am setting you, you know."

"I understand, sir. And I'll do my best, of course, sir, but . . .
what exactly do you wish me to do when I have made contact
with Serfir Pasha? Attack Anapa and Soujak Kaleh with the
Circassians?" Observing the Admiral's smile, Phillip reddened.
"I mean, sir, you—"

"In the now famous words of Sir Colin Campbell, 'damn
all this eagerness!' But it does my heart good to find you so
eager . . ." the smile was, Phillip realized, a kindly, even affectionate one and his momentary embarrassment faded as the
naval Commander-in-Chief went on, "No, Phillip, what I really
want you to do is to assemble the Circassian chiefs, with the
aid of Serfir—or, through him, obtain the promise of their support—and persuade them to join with a Turkish force, under
the command of Mustapha Pasha, who is coming to Ghelenjik
in a Turkish steamer within the next ten days. You need not
worry about Mustapha, he is one of the better Turkish generals and I am sending Commander Osborn in the *Vesuvius* to
meet him. We need a firm promise of concerted action from
both Circassians and Turks. If they could be induced to move
on Anapa and Soujak I believe that not only would the enemy
evacuate both places but that they might also withdraw from
Yenikale and Kertch . . . which would make our entry into the
Sea of Azoff very much easier. Even the promise of a move by
the Circassians against Anapa might enable me to shame

General Canrobert into reassembling this force, which has so shamefully had to be recalled. If you were able, in addition, to rouse the chiefs in the Kouban area to move on Yenikale, this too, would be extremely useful. But you have not much time, Phillip."

"No, sir. About ten days I think you said?"

The Admiral inclined his head. "Yes . . . perhaps a little longer. You will have to leave the *Huntress* to cruise off Ghelenjik, under the command of your First Lieutenant whilst you are ashore, but if, in order to offer encouragement to the chiefs, you consider it expedient to land some of your men I should not disapprove. You've no Marines on board, have you?"

"No, sir."

"Then we must try to supply you with at least some Marine Artillery and an officer. I shall also supply you with weapons and ammunition, to distribute among the chiefs—a case of Minié rifles to be included." Admiral Lyons smiled faintly. Turning to his Flag Lieutenant, who was hovering in the background, he issued the required instructions and then continued, "I think that's all, Phillip, except that if you see fit and believe such a manoeuvre necessary to impress the Circassians, take some of the leaders with you and fire a few broadsides at the Anapa batteries. Within reason, and, of course, without risking your ship, you may use your own discretion in this respect. The *Viper* will accompany the *Vesuvius*—if either you or Sherard Osborn have anything urgent to report, entrust letters to Lieutenant Armytage for delivery to me."

"Aye, aye, sir." Taking this as his dismissal, Phillip picked up the package Lieutenant Cleeve had prepared for him and got to his feet. "Thank you very much, sir."

His Commander-in-Chief eyed him with quizzically raised

brows. "I say again, I've set you no easy task and can allow you very little time in which to accomplish it . . . yet still you thank me! What it is to be young and eager, my dear boy . . . well, I can only wish you Godspeed and good luck. You can take the rifles with you, they're prepared. The Marines and your interpreter will be sent to you before we sail."

"Aye, aye, sir." Phillip stiffened to attention. "I shall hope to see you back here, with both squadrons, before long."

"I shall be back," the Admiral promised grimly. "Over General Canrobert's dead body, if necessary, for we shall never take Sebastopol and end this war until we control the enemy's supply routes from the Sea of Azoff—of that I am convinced. And we must end this war, Phillip . . . it is costing too much in human suffering to be allowed to drag on into another winter."

Phillip left him and found Algernon Lyons awaiting him at the entry port and his gig already alongside. "Your rifles and ammunition are aboard your gig," he said. "And—a bit of luck, Phillip—there's a Lieutenant of Marines called Roberts in this ship, who has volunteered to accompany you. He helped the Circassians to repair the defences at Soukoum Kaleh last year when he was serving under Captain Jones in the *Sampson*. He says he knows something of the country and a word or two of the lingo, so I thought you'd probably like to have him. I don't know him personally—he's only on passage with us—but he seems a sound sort of fellow."

"I'll be delighted to have him," Phillip assented. "Thanks for finding him, Algy. Is he ready—shall I wait for him?"

The young Flag Lieutenant flashed him a reproachful smile. "Commander Hazard, the difficult we do at once—the impossible takes a trifle longer! The Admiral only conceived the idea of sending you to Ghelenjik when the French left us high and dry, you know. Roberts is collecting his kit and choosing the men he'll be bringing with him, but as I only told him what was afoot about two minutes ago I'm afraid he won't have begun to sort himself out yet. Don't worry, though—I'm sure that you'll be anxious to return to your ship, so we'll deliver your Marines to you within the hour."

Phillip thanked him and, swinging himself through the entry port, descended to the waiting gig. He felt elated at the prospect before him. If it wasn't the action for which they had all been hoping, at least it promised excitement of a kind and a change of scene. Any change would be a welcome relief from the boredom of ferrying troops, or the no less wearisome but more exacting task of maintaining the blockade of the Russian Black Sea ports, in fair weather or foul. The *Huntress* had done little else for the past six months and the weather—he suppressed an involuntary shudder—had been almost always foul and invariably cold. Besides, the Admiral had given him permission to run in and fire a few broadsides at Anapa—his guns' crews could put in some useful practice, he thought gleefully, and it would raise the morale of the whole ship's company if they were able to open fire on the enemy, instead of keeping safely out of range of the coastal forts, as they were ordered to when on blockade duty.

Midshipman O'Hara caught the change in his mood and asked, greatly daring, "Sir, you look pleased . . . does that mean we're going on to Kertch without the French, sir?"

"No, that isn't on the cards, I'm afraid," Phillip answered. "Both squadrons are returning to Sebastapol . . . but we're not, praise be!" He said no more, but the boy brightened visibly and the gig's crew, reacting with that strange sixth sense all seamen seemed to possess, put their backs into their work, sending their small craft skimming swiftly across the anchorage to where the *Huntress* lay, rolling a little in the slight swell.

CHAPTER TWO

Back on board, Phillip lost no time in telling his watch-keeping officers of their new orders, which were greeted with cautious enthusiasm. The ships of the blockading squadron had been supplied with coal before leaving for the rendezvous at Cape Takli and Graham reported the *Huntress*'s bunkers virtually full, but her three-hundred-horse-power engines consumed coal at a prodigious rate, as Phillip had learnt from experience, and he decided to conserve his supply for as long as he could.

"We'll proceed under sail," he said. "The Marines and an interpreter have yet to join us but Algy Lyons promised that they would do so within the hour, so we'll weigh as soon as we've taken them on board. And"—he consulted his pocket watch—"I'll tell the ship's company what's in store for us, if you would be so good as to muster both watches aft before they're piped to dinner."

"Aye, aye, sir," Graham responded formally.

Lieutenant Lyons was as good as his word. The Marines—thirty men and an elderly sergeant—arrived fifty minutes later from the *Royal Albert*, bringing with them the remainder of the stores. Phillip took an instant liking to the tall, husky young officer in charge of them, who introduced himself as Nigel Roberts and expressed keen pleasure at the unexpected opportunity he had been given to renew his acquaintance with the

Circassian chiefs. The interpreter was less impressive, a swarthy, somewhat slovenly looking Turk, whose uniform had the appearance of having been worn both night and day and in all weathers, and whose manner was, to say the least, a trifle arrogant. He was an officer, he hastened to inform Phillip and, as such, entitled to a cabin and to take his meals in the wardroom. His claim was made aggressively, which suggested that these facilities had been denied him in the ship from whence he had come—the *Princess Royal*—of which he spoke disparagingly. Knowing Lord Clarence Paget as one of the most hospitable commanders in the Fleet, Phillip affected not to hear his waspish remarks and sent him below, under the escort of his steward, with instructions that he was to occupy a mate's cabin and mess with the warrant officers. Acting-Gunner Joseph O'Leary who, since his recent elevation to warrant rank, had ruled the mess with a rod of iron, could be relied on, he knew, to tame the overbearing little Turk and—since O'Leary was a stickler for cleanliness—probably also to prevail upon him to take a much needed wash.

He smiled to himself at this thought and turned back to the deck. Graham, he observed, had lost no time. He had picked up the lee anchor and heaved in to a short stay on the weather cable, with jibs set and foretopmen aloft, already laying out along the yards, loosening the foretopsail. Meeting Phillip's eye and receiving an affirmative nod, he sang out a string of orders. The waiting maintopmen went swarming up the shrouds and, as the maintopsail and courses were let fall and sheeted home, he brought the weather anchor to the cathead and ordered the head-yards braced around. There was little room to manoeuvre in the crowded anchorage, with several other ships also getting under way or preparing to do so. Graham, however, handled the *Huntress* with practised skill and her crew—almost all well-trained seamen now and proud of their ship—worked with a will, aware that they were being watched by numerous highly critical eyes.

The hands aloft—whose performance, Phillip noted with a keen sense of pleasure, could scarcely be faulted—came scrambling nimbly back to the deck, the maintopmen watching unobtrusively over Cadet Lightfoot, who had recently rejoined from the hospital ship *Bombay* at Therapia, after suffering a broken leg in a fall from the rigging. His twelve-year-old bones appeared to have mended perfectly and the fall had done nothing to shake his nerve; the boy bounded down the lee shrouds with the speed and agility of a small monkey, grinning cheekily at a grizzled seaman, who put out a hand in an attempt to slow him down.

"Trim sails for casting! Man port after braces and starb'd head braces!" Graham shouted, his voice and the boatswain's stentorian echo sounding above the thud of running feet on the deck planking, as the forecastle and after-men of the watch pounded, barefoot, to their stations. The sails started slowly to fill, the *Huntress* began to gain steerage way and Graham brought her head to port, bracing head- and after-yards in opposition, until she should have sufficient way on to answer to her helm. Ships with a screw aperture, like the *Huntress,* were harder to tack than those without: the water meeting a constant current coming from the lee side through the screw-hole, which had the effect of carrying the stern to windward at an angle from the line of keel, without touching the rudder at all. Graham conned her expertly and, with the after-sails filling, he called out a sharp order to the quartermaster to right his helm. "Of all haul! Brace up the mainyard . . . Square head-yards!"

By eight bells, when Anthony Cochrane came punctually

to relieve the deck, the ship was on course for Ghelenjik, running close-hauled on a freshening breeze.

"Hands to muster, sir?" Graham asked formally. Phillip nodded. "If you please. All hands, including the engineers and stokers."

"Aye, aye, sir. Bosun's mate . . . pipe all hands to muster aft."

The boatswain's mate of the watch put his call to his lips and, in obedience to the pipe, the men of both watches moved to the after part of the upper deck, forming up in their divisions, the divisional officers in front and the newly joined party of Marines, in their scarlet uniforms, to the right of the seamen. Last to make their appearance were the stokers, blue serge frocks hastily pulled over oil-stained undervests.

"Ship's company mustered, sir," Graham announced, as the men came to attention.

"Thank you," Phillip acknowledged. "I shall not keep them long, and Mr Cochrane may pipe the watch below to dinner as soon as I've finished." He gave the order to stand at ease and made his announcement as briefly as he could, explaining that the attempt to take Kertch and enter the Sea of Azoff had been abandoned and then going on to outline the purpose of their own mission, taking care to emphasize the importance of disciplined behaviour when ashore. "These people are our allies and we are calling on them in order to enlist their armed support against the enemy. The Admiral intends to put a steam squadron into the Sea of Azoff—he regards the operation as having been postponed, but not abandoned altogether. For this reason, he would like the Circassians, with some assistance from the Turks, to attack the Russian forts at Anapa and Soujak Bay, which are their last remaining strongholds on the Circassian coast. Both, and in particular Anapa, are well fortified and there are said to be in the region of eight thousand garrison troops in Anapa alone . . . so it will be quite a tough nut to crack."

"Are *we* going to crack it, sir?" an eager voice asked.

Phillip smiled. "We have the Admiral's permission to fire a few broadsides at the fort, lad, but . . ." his voice was drowned by a spontaneous cheer and he let this continue for a moment or two before raising his hand for silence. "We shall have to depend on an assault by land-based troops if the place is to be taken and occupied," he warned. "Which will mean a Turkish force due, I understand, to be sent over from Batoum in the next ten days, and as many of the Circassian tribesmen as we can prevail upon to join up with them. But don't worry, my boys—we'll have a hand in the attack if all goes well." There was another full-throated cheer and, looking at the excited, smiling faces about him, Phillip was satisfied that his announcement had raised the flagging morale of his ship's company. Young Lightfoot, momentarily forgetful of the fact that he was on parade, was dancing with delight, his dirk drawn; Acting-Gunner O'Leary's craggy face wore its familiar, gap-toothed grin; and Midshipman O'Hara emitted a spirited cheer of his own and flung his cap exultantly into the air.

In duty bound, Phillip reproved them. "That will do, Mr O'Hara," he said sternly. "Oblige me by resuming your head-gear. Mr Lightfoot, come to attention, if you please and remain so, until I dismiss you. I want the rest of you to remember that at no time is there to be undue familiarity with the native tribesmen . . . and their women are to be treated with respect. Is that clear? If any member of this ship's company is found in compromising circumstances with a Circassian woman, he'll have to answer to me—and I shall not go easy on him, what-ever his rank." A few faces fell a little as the implication of his words sank in and he went on, still sternly, "The success of our mission may well depend upon the manner in which you conduct yourselves. I shall expect all of you to behave with prudence and good sense. That's all I have to say." He caught Graham's eye. "You may dismiss the ship's company, Mr Hazard—including Mr Lightfoot."

"Aye, aye, sir. Ship's company, attention . . . dismiss. Mr Cochrane, pipe hands to dinner, if you please."

The pipe was sounding as Phillip made his way below. Normally he dined in his own quarters when at sea, the hour at which he ate being flexible but today he decided he would take dinner in the gunroom—which, in a frigate, accommodated all officers of wardroom rank—and he issued instructions to his steward. "How about the Turkish—er—officer, Higgins?" he asked curiously. "I did not see him on deck—was he satisfied with his cabin?"

Able-Seaman Higgins, a gaunt-faced man with seventeen years' service, who had joined the *Huntress* six months ago, after being hit by a shell splinter in the Naval Brigade's *Diamond* Battery, permitted himself a superior smile.

"He was revelling in it, sir," he answered expressively. "Told me 'e was a captain, sir, but it's my belief that 'e's no more an officer than I am. And I don't fancy the little perisher—beg pardon, sir, I mean feller—I don't fancy 'e's been to sea very often. Got 'is 'ead down right away, he did . . . said he thought it might come on to blow. When I left 'im, 'e was sleeping like a baby, sir."

"Sleeping, was he? Good Lord!"

"Yessir," Higgins confirmed. "I don't reckon 'e'll trouble the warrant officers much but I passed the word about 'im to Mr O'Leary, sir, just in case . . . and I'll keep me eye on 'im." He vanished briefly and returned with a steaming pot of coffee, which he set down at Phillip's elbow. "I thought you might care for this, sir, seeing you won't be taking dinner for an hour or so. Will that be all, sir?"

"Yes, that's all, thanks." Higgins was a good man, Phillip reflected, as he sipped his coffee—worth his weight in gold because he never had to be told what to do or have things spelled out to him. He had been a first-rate seaman, according to his record, and he made an excellent steward, always at hand when he was wanted and careful to keep out of the way when he was not. His wound, like Gunner O'Leary's, had left him with a bad limp but, although no longer fit to be rated a topman, this otherwise impaired him very little in the performance of his duties. Unlike O'Leary's, his service conduct sheet was unblemished; he had no serious charges against his name and could, by this time, have reached warrant rank, but he had apparently always refused promotion, content to remain an AB. He . . . there was a tap on the door of his cabin. "Yes," he called out, half-expecting Graham. "Come in."

Lieutenant Roberts entered diffidently. "I wondered if I might have a word with you, sir. If you're not too busy, that is."

"Yes, of course," Phillip assented readily. "I've been wanting a word with you, as it happens. Take a seat, Mr Roberts. Coffee? This has just been made."

The young Marine officer reddened under his tan seeming, at first, as if he were about to reject both invitations, but, after a slight hesitation, he seated himself. Higgins, without being called, appeared with a fresh cup and silently withdrew. "If you'd rather had a drink—" Phillip began but Roberts shook his head.

"No, sir, no, indeed. Coffee's most welcome." He accepted the cup his host poured for him and sat with it held awkwardly between the palms of his two big hands, his round, boyish face continuing to flood with embarrassed colour. He was a flaxen haired young man, with a slightly snub nose and a pair of ingenuous blue eyes, very tall and powerfully built. Phillip judged him to be about twenty-two or three, although his fair colouring made him look younger.

"Well, Mr Roberts?" he encouraged. "What can I do for you, pray?"

"I'm probably wasting your time, Commander Hazard," Roberts stammered, "But I . . . that is, sir, you—"

"Let me be the judge of whether or not you are wasting my time," Phillip said crisply. "Presumably some aspect of our mission troubles you?"

"Well, yes, sir, it does, But—"

"Then I should be grateful if you would tell me precisely what . . . and why, Mr Roberts."

"Yes, sir, I . . ." Evidently reaching a decision, the young Marine officer braced himself. "It was what you said just now, when you addressed the ship's company . . . about not permitting any familiarity with the Circassians. Does that also apply to me, sir? You see, I was with them for nearly three weeks at Soukoum Kaleh, when I was serving in the *Sampson,* and I made a good many friends among them—there and also at Redoute Kaleh."

"You helped to rebuild their defences at both places, didn't you?" Phillip asked.

"I did, yes. And they're remarkably fine people, sir. Not at all uncivilized, I assure you. They fight well and they hate the Russians, sir—believe me, they hate them—they welcomed us almost as deliverers and jumped at the chance we offered them to drive the Russian garrisons from the coastal forts. If we'd been able to land a few of our troops, even two or three thousand, the Circassians would have fought with us . . . Anapa would be in our hands now, sir, and probably Yenikale and

Kertch as well." In his enthusiasm, Lieutenant Roberts forgot his earlier embarrassment and talked on eagerly, describing the tribes he had met, their manners and customs, their fighting qualities, their courage, and Phillip listened with interest to his colourful account, conscious that the knowledge he was acquiring might well be extremely useful in the accomplishment of his mission.

"After we were recalled to the Fleet," Nigel Roberts went on, "the Circassians took a number of other forts, including Golovin and Navagnisk. The enemy evacuated both places, spiked the guns, blew up magazines and fortifications, but I understand that the Circassians repaired the damage and are still holding them. And—I know you'll find this rather hard to credit, sir—they also fitted out a small boat expedition, rowed across from Temriouk Bay, which is near the mouth of the Kouban River, to the Crimean shore, where they captured a couple of Russian gunboats. They manned the gunboats themselves and seized quite a number of grain boats and munition carriers before they were caught—that is to say, the Russians recaptured their gunboats but most of the Circassian crews managed to make their escape and—"

"You mean," Phillip interrupted in astonishment, "that they launched this boat expedition in the Sea of Azoff?"

Roberts inclined his head. "Indeed they did, sir. Imagine what they might have been able to do if we'd been in a position to land a small naval brigade to assist and back them up, sir."

The lad was right, Phillip thought, allowing his imagination brief rein. But this was the whole, regrettable story of the campaign up till now—because of the French insistence that all Allied resources must be concentrated on the siege and capture of Sebastopol. The flower of the British Army had perished at Balaclava and on the Heights of Inkerman and British naval strength had been severely depleted in order to furnish men and guns—and yet more men—for the prosecution of that costly siege. British fighting ships had been used as troop transports instead of for the purpose for which they were intended—to attack the enemy coastal forts, cut his supply lines and deprive him of reinforcements. French losses, in action and from disease, were higher in proportion to their numbers than the British, but Sebastopol still held out and General Canrobert, judging by today's fiasco, had no intention of changing his disastrous tactics. Only the despised and badly led Turks and, if young Roberts were to be believed, some Circassian brigand tribes employed the right strategy but so ineffectively and with so little attempt to co-ordinate their efforts that they, too, were dying in vain.

He smothered a sigh as Roberts came to the end of his recital and, setting down his still untouched coffee cup, turned to regard his new commander expectantly.

"So you see, don't you, sir, that I—"

Phillip cut him short. "I've no intention of restricting *your* contact with the Circassian guerillas, Mr Roberts," he said. "Your knowledge of them and, indeed, your previous friendly relations with them will be of immense value to us, I'm quite sure. The reason I issued a warning to the ship's company was, as you've probably realized, in order to protect the women, and if possible avoid any untoward incidents whilst my men are ashore which might cause trouble with the Circassians. They are Mohammedans, I understand, and their women are said to be very beautiful, so I deemed it advisable to make my warning a strong one."

"The Circassian girls are exceptionally beautiful," the young Marine officer confirmed. "So are the Georgians—"

"Georgians, Mr Roberts?"

"Oh, yes, indeed, sir—but they are Christians, of the Greek Orthodox Church. We met a number of them in Soukoum. They kept open house for us, in fact, and we . . ." Roberts broke off, once again pink-cheeked with embarrassment and, as if fearing that he might have said too much, he changed the subject, embarking on a lengthy description of the different races to be encountered in the coastal towns and the reason why many of them supported the Turkish, rather than the Russian cause. Phillip studied his face thoughtfully as he talked. It was a transparently honest face, but he came to the conclusion, something was still troubling its owner, although Roberts was obviously in two minds as to whether to tell him what this was. Interrupting a dissertation on the Armenians, he said flatly, "Mr Roberts, you will, I trust, forgive a rather personal question but—were you in any way involved with any girl you met on your previous visit to this area?"

"Involved, sir?" Robert's face was brick-red, but a look of relief spread over it. "Well, I . . . that was really what I came to see you about, Commander Hazard, only when it came to the point I . . . I couldn't bring myself to tell you. I was afraid you might think I had an ulterior motive for volunteering to join your ship and that if you knew, you might . . . well, that is—"

"That I might send you back to the Fleet?" Phillip suggested.

"Yes, sir. There is a girl . . . I mean, there was and to be honest, I was pretty fond of her. If circumstances had been different, I might even have . . . well, asked her to marry me. But as it happened, we got our sailing orders sooner than any of us expected and so . . . it didn't come to that, sir." Roberts spoke earnestly, his eyes meeting Phillip's without flinching. "I suppose you'll have to send me back?"

"Not necessarily, Mr Roberts. As I said, you could be very useful to us and I should be reluctant to have to deprive myself of your services. But I should expect you to conduct yourself with circumspection."

"You may rely on me, sir. I—"

Respecting his honesty, Phillip smiled at him. "I take it that the girl in question lives in Soukoum?"

Lieutenant Roberts inclined his head. "She does, sir, yes."

"My orders are to call only at Ghelenjik," Phillip pointed out. "Were you aware of that when you volunteered to join us?" Again the Marine officer nodded.

"Yes, I was."

"Yet you still volunteered?"

"I thought I might be of some use to you, Commander Hazard and I . . . well, I hoped I might be able to send a message to Soukoum. Or even that an opportunity might arise for me to go there."

"It's unlikely that there will be time for you to go there and back, Mr Roberts. We have only ten days." Roberts's face fell and, suddenly remembering his own feelings for Mademoiselle Sophie—who, in Odessa, was as far away from him now as any woman could be—Phillip relented. "If in the strict course of duty," he promised, "I require to send an officer down the coast to Soukoum or Redoute Kaleh, rest assured that you will be the officer I shall choose . . . provided that you can be spared, you understand."

"I understand and I . . . thank you very much, sir." Roberts rose, drawing himself to attention. "I'm very grateful. Forgive me for taking up so much of your time, sir."

"It was usefully spent," Phillip assured him. "I've learnt a great deal." He took out his pocket watch. "I am dining in the gunroom today, so I shall see you there in an hour's time, Mr Roberts."

"Aye, aye, sir," Roberts acknowledged cheerfully and took his leave.

Phillip had intended to occupy the next hour in a careful perusal of his orders and the report from Captain Jones of the *Sampson,* a copy of which had been provided for him but, try as he might, he could not concentrate on either for very long. His conversation with Lieutenant Roberts had stirred up old memories and he found his thoughts continually straying to Mademoiselle Sophie, as a vision of her small, sweet face—as he had seen it again in the Cathedral at Odessa—blotted out the closely written pages of Captain Jones's excellent but somewhat wordy report. They had bidden farewell to each other in her carriage when she had driven him back from the Cathedral and their parting, he reminded himself sternly, had been final and irrevocable. Had he not returned the ring she had given him, with the double-headed Imperial eagle cut into its magnificent stone, so that it might become the property of her then unborn child? His mouth tightened as he let his thoughts drift back into the past and, in memory, he heard the church bells ring out the glad tidings that a son and heir had been born to the widow of Prince Andrei Narishkin . . . *her* son, Mademoiselle Sophie's son, whom he had never seen and almost certainly never would see. And he would never see Mademoiselle Sophie again; he knew and accepted this now, without bitterness, and yet . . . Phillip shook his head dazedly, like a man roused suddenly from sleep. Why, he asked himself, in heaven's name why did she still hold his heart? Why could he not consign the memory of her to that limbo from whence it could no longer torment him?

He would not forget her, of course; the heart, as she had once told him sadly, did not forget but . . . he thought fleetingly of Catriona Moray and realized that, although he owed her his life, her memory possessed no power to hold him and had not been hard to banish from his mind. Perhaps this was because Catriona had never been quite real to him—she had never existed for him, in her own right, as a woman. She had attracted him initially because of the slight resemblance she bore to Mademoiselle Sophie and now, on that account, he could not separate her image from Sophie's, could not think of her as an individual. He sighed, the awareness of what might have been causing him a twinge of conscience. Where, he wondered, was Catriona Moray now? Had she returned to Scotland, to her grandfather's house, and was she living the life of a country gentlewoman among her Highland kinsfolk . . . and she, too, perhaps, with memories that brought her pain and could never be erased?

Sitting there, with his new orders in front of him, Phillip remembered what Martin Fox had said to him on the subject of Catriona and again experienced a pang of conscience. *"I should have liked to see her again . . . more especially since you told me that you had no serious intentions towards her yourself, Phillip"* . . . they had been almost the last words his dying First Lieutenant had spoken, and he had ended regretfully, *"Mine, I believe, might have been had she offered me any encouragement, for I held her in high esteem. Perhaps you will tell her so, if you write to her . . ."*

He had promised he would and had, in fact, done so, some weeks after Fox's passing, but his had been a brief, uninformative letter, telling her only the bare facts of the action at Eupatoria, in which Martin Fox had been fatally wounded. He had meant to write again, to pass on Martin's message in greater detail but, for one reason and another, he had not done so. He had received no reply to his first letter, which he had addressed to her care of old Sir Alastair Moray, her grandfather, and, uncertain of where to send the second letter, had let the matter slide. Feeling oddly guilty, he took out his pocket watch—which had been a gift from Mademoiselle Sophie—and again consulted it. The gunroom took its midday meal at two-thirty at sea and it was not quite a quarter to two . . . time enough to write a letter, although when he would next have an opportunity to despatch mail he had no idea. When the *Viper* joined them, probably. But he owed it to Martin to write . . . no doubt Catriona's grandfather would know where she was and would, in due course, forward his letter, if he again addressed it to Castle Guise.

Phillip reached for pen and ink and, having reached a decision, found that the words came easily and fluently, as he described the Cossack attack on Eupatoria and Martin Fox's courageous sortie in defence of the magazine. When it came to describing his friend's last hours, his pen moved more slowly and he was aware of a choking tightness in his throat, but he persisted and, when Higgins came to tell him that dinner was ready to be served, the letter was done, all three pages of it, the lines criss-crossing each other on the flimsy paper. He wrote the address, franked and sealed the envelope, and placed it in his letter-box, ready for despatch when next the opportunity should arise. His conscience somewhat relieved, he made his way aft to the gunroom to join his officers for the midday meal.

Ghelenjik was sighted during the latter half of the Middle Watch but Phillip decided to wait until daylight before entering the port. He was on deck at sunrise, to find himself looking out across the wide expanse of a beautiful bay, behind which rose a succession of mountain peaks, capped with perpetual snow. The lower slopes were thickly wooded, and precipitous cliffs guarded the eastern side of the bay, following its semi-circular curve to where a small town nestled in a hollow, at the foot of what appeared to be a rocky gorge. The fort, a square block-house pierced for guns and with bastions at the angles, stood on the cliff top above the town, covering both the gorge and the seaward approaches.

There were a number of fishing boats lying at their moorings alongside a wooden quay, several of which hoisted tall lateen sails and came out to meet the *Huntress* as, after exchanging salutes with the fort, she stood-in to the bay. The anchorage at Ghelenjik had been surveyed by Captain Jones and aware, from his report, that it was one of the best on the whole of the Circassian coast, with a more than adequate depth of water, Phillip instructed Graham to bring-up within hailing distance of the quay.

The fishermen, having inspected the new arrival and recognized the ensign she was flying, swiftly put their boats about and preceded her like a flock of white-winged gulls, skimming this way and that on the smooth, green surface of the water, their crews waving excitedly. They bounded ashore as the *Huntress* dropped anchor, eager to spread the news of her coming throughout the town and evidently did their work well for, when Phillip put off in the quarter-boat accompanied by Lieutenant Roberts, the Turkish interpreter and an escort of Marines, a considerable crowd had gathered on the sturdily built wooden quay to receive them.

It was a colourful and exclusively male crowd, the majority wearing sleeveless black jackets—fashioned from plaited goats' hair, according to Roberts—over gaily hued cloth blouses, trimmed with braid or embroidery and reaching to the knees. Voluminous pantaloons, leather-thonged sandals or boots and high caps of sheep or goat-skin completed this picturesque attire, and all were armed. Some had curved scimitars at their sides, others an assortment of evil-looking daggers thrust carelessly into the silk sashes which girt their waists and every man carried a long flintlock rifle and leather ammunition pouch slung from his shoulder. As the *Huntress*'s boat drew nearer, a big, red-bearded man, dressed in what appeared to be Cossack costume, sprang to his feet and, standing a good head and shoulders above his companions, fired his rifle into the air. This was the signal for a fusilade of shots and Phillip, realizing that the shots were intended as a welcome, crisply ordered his boat's crew to toss oars in salute, which was greeted by a roar of approval. When he stepped ashore, the red-bearded giant seized him in a bear-like hug, grinning widely.

"Ingealez?" he suggested. Phillip, still a trifle breathless from the huge fellow's exuberant embrace, inclined his head in wordless assent. The man fingered the hilt of his naval sword, bushy red brows raised in question. "For . . . fight?" he demanded, in pantomime, adopting a duelling stance. "Fight Muscovs?"

"Yes," Phillip assured him gravely, as his escort of Marines formed up at his back. "We have come to fight the Muscovs with you."

"Good!" the bearded warrior beamed. "Good, good!" This, it seemed, was the sum total of his knowledge of English and the Turkish interpreter, officiously waving him to stand aside, said that he was a Kouban Cossack. "They are poor, ignorant fellows, Commander Hazard—do not waste your time with this one." He spat his contempt. "There will be Turkish officers at the fort with whom we can speak."

"No doubt there will, Mr Aslam," Phillip returned coldly. "But I have been sent here to speak with Serfir Pasha, the Circassian chief, so perhaps you would be so good as to enquire where I may find him, if you do not wish me to waste time on underlings." He looked about him, his own smile echoing those on the handsome, light-skinned faces of the motley crowd thronging the quay. The plump little interpreter eyed him sullenly and he made a mental note that it would be unwise to trust him on his own, lest he endanger their relations with the local people with his strutting arrogance.

"Someone's coming from the fort now, sir," Lieutenant Roberts warned. He pointed to the cliff-top and Phillip saw two men on horseback who, after a brief pause to take stock of his party, put their horses to a gallop and came thundering down the steep slope in the direction of the quay. Both were superb riders and he guessed, from the chagrined expression on the interpreter's swarthy face, that they were not the Turkish officers he had expected but Circassians. Roberts confirmed his supposition as the two men drew rein and called out a greeting, before leaping lightly to the ground.

"They both look like Circassians, sir. I should imagine the elder of the two is in command of the fort."

"Then let us go and meet them, Mr Roberts," Phillip said. "Your men may stay where they are for the time being. Have them stand easy, though—this may take a little while. Mr Grey"—he turned to the young mate, who was in command of the boat—"carry on, if you please. Post a guard over the boat and those Minié rifles and let the rest of your crew ashore to stretch their legs."

"Aye, aye, sir," Grey acknowledged.

With Roberts at his side, Phillip went to meet the newcomers. Both, he saw, were as colourfully dressed as their compatriots on the quay and, apart from the fact that their cloaks and caps were of astrakan and less crudely fashioned than those of the townsfolk, only their authoritative bearing set them apart from the rest. One was in his late forties, the other a slim, athletic looking youth of perhaps twenty, with merry grey eyes and a very fair skin. Their close resemblance to one another suggested that they were father and son, the manner in which the crowd parted to permit them to pass that

one or both held a position of some importance in the com-
munity.

"Mr Aslam . . ." the interpreter came reluctantly in response
to Phillip's call. "Introduce Mr Roberts and myself to these gentlemen, if you please, and ask whom we have the honour of
addressing."

Aslam did as he was told, but the tone of his voice was less
than friendly. However, he received a courteous reply and,
turning to Phillip, he announced that the fort commander was
Najib Bey, and the youth his eldest son, Dafir.

"They are, it seems, in charge here," the interpreter added.
"The troops they command are of their own wild tribe, apart
from a few gunners of the Turkish *redif.*"

Phillip saluted and then held out his hand to Najib Bey who,
after a slight hesitation, wrung it with every appearance of
pleasure. The youth smiled but held back, subjecting the two
British officers and the corpulent Turkish interpreter to a wary
scrutiny before voicing a string of questions. His father
silenced him with a wave of the hand and interposed a question of his own.

"The young one asks if your ship has brought men and
arms to assist their struggle to drive the Muscovs from this
land," Aslam translated. "And both wish to know if more
English ships will come. Najib Bey further asks if your honour
has news of Mustapha Pasha. He says that he had word that
the Pasha would come some weeks ago."

Phillip phrased an appropriate answer, which Aslam
repeated in rapid Osmanli, and the eyes of both men lit up
when they learned that a visit from the Turkish commander
was imminent. "Now ask them, please, where I may expect to
find the Circassian chief Serfir Pasha. Say that I have an important message from my Admiral which must reach His
Excellency without delay."

The Turk repeated what he had said and again Phillip noticed a gleam of pleasure in the eyes of both father and son. The boy whispered to his father, who at first shook his head and then, evidently relenting, spoke quietly and at some length to the interpreter.

"Well, Mr Aslam, what does he say?" Phillip prompted impatiently when Najib Bey lapsed into expectant silence. The swarthy little Turk looked frankly apprehensive but he recovered himself and responded unhappily, "Serfir Pasha is with his troops in the mountains, sir, and if your message from the English Admiral can brook no delay, then you will require to go to him. He is, it seems, waiting to set an ambush for a supply train which the enemy are sending overland to Soujak. In the opinion of Najib, only your honour's personal intervention would bring His Excellency back to this place before he has achieved his objective, for he has planned the ambush for many weeks."

"I see." Phillip frowned. He hadn't bargained for this but he understood and could sympathize with Serfir Pasha's reluctance to abandon his carefully planned operation. By dint of question and answer, he elicited the information that the Pasha's camp was a full day's journey into the mountains, but that Najib would provide him with an escort of Circassian mountaineers led by his son and that, if he could be ready to leave within an hour, the greater part of the journey could be completed before dark, leaving only a short distance to travel the following morning.

"Your honour may take only two or at most three men with you," Aslam translated. "More than this number would, the Bey says, be too great a responsibility for his men to assume, since yours are not mountain-men and therefore will require assistance. He asks that fit men may be selected . . ." beads of sweat had broken out on his pale face, Phillip observed, and it occasioned him little surprise when the Turk went on, his tone pleading, "Commander Hazard, I am not a fit man, nor am I accustomed to heights—I become sick. Could your honour not dispense with my services? I should, without doubt, delay you and—"

"I'd gladly dispense with your services, Aslam," Phillip confessed. "But if I leave you behind, how can I communicate with Serfir Pasha?" The corpulent, unwilling little man would obviously delay him but it was essential that he should be able to convince the Circassian leader of the importance of the summons he brought for a meeting of all the chiefs, prior to Mustapha Pasha's arrival. He would be wasting his time if he made the long journey to the mountain camp and then failed— for lack of an interpreter—to persuade Serfir to return with him to Ghelenjik within the stipulated ten days. "There's no help for it—I'm afraid you will have to come."

Aslam, the perspiration now pouring down his cheeks, launched into an excited tirade in his own language, which the dignified Najib received with a polite smile. His answer, delivered with equal politeness, evidently offered a solution to his problem that pleased the Turk, for he turned back to Phillip with a relieved sigh. "Sir, there is a Polish officer, Kazim Bey, at the camp of the Pasha—he speaks French and, it is thought, English. There is with him his daughter, a young lady who has been educated in an Armenian convent school—she speaks French and Osmanli fluently and some English. In addition, Serfir Pasha also has a daughter with him, who has been educated in several languages. Who better to interpret your honour's message to His Excellency? Whereas he might doubt my interpretation, he would not doubt that of his own flesh and blood. Besides, sir, if you leave me here, I can make myself useful in your honour's service. I could go to other chiefs with His Excellency the English Admiral's summons and—"

Phillip cut him short. He glanced enquiringly at Roberts and the Marine officer replied to his unvoiced query, "I suppose he could be useful here, sir, because there will be other chiefs to summon, will there not? As to those Najib Bey suggests as interpreters, he probably isn't exaggerating . . . some of these girls *are* extremely well educated. The girl I told you about in Soukoum, sir, had also been brought up in a convent school and she spoke remarkably good French. The Polish officer is another possibility, of course, And if you do decide to leave Aslam here, it would enable you to take an extra man, who would pull his weight and be of more use to you in a tight corner than he would. It's rough going in these mountains, but my Marines, sir, would volunteer, I know, and I'd be glad to, if you—"

"I beg your pardon, sir," Aslam put in apologetically. "I have omitted to tell you that Najib Bey believes that it would be dangerous to take any of the redcoats with you. Sailors, he considers, would be better able to accustom themselves to the great height of these mountains, for it is in the nature of their work on board ship that they must climb aloft to tend the sails."

He was probably right, Phillip thought, but before he could say so Aslam went on, "The Bey asks that you permit the redcoats to take the places of the men of his garrison whom he will send with you. The fort is undermanned, sir—all who could be spared from its defence have gone with Serfir Pasha. He asks that your honour will give him also some of the new rifles you mentioned to him and that your Marines will give instructions in their use to his *redifs.*"

"He would seem to have an ulterior motive in not wanting your Marines to accompany me, Mr Roberts," Phillip said, his mouth twitching with suppressed amusement. "But I fancy I

had better accede to his request, don't you? It is not an unreasonable one, in the circumstances." Receiving Roberts's nod of
assent, he raised his voice, "Very well, Mr Aslam, you may
remain here. And tell the Bey, if you will, that I'm quite agree-
able to leaving him reinforcements and that he shall have some
of the new rifles. The rest I propose to deliver to Serfir Pasha."

Through the now beaming interpreter, he settled various
other minor details, including the provision of sheepskin clothing for his party, and then he made the formal request that
messengers should be sent to inform all other chiefs in the
area of the arrival of Mustapha Pasha, to which Najib readily
agreed.

"The Bey says," Aslam informed him, "that it would be
advisable for your honour to send for Mohammed Emin Bey,
who is at Soukoum Kaleh. He is—"

"I know who he is," Phillip returned. Again he glanced at
Roberts, whose nod of agreement was emphatic.

"Emin Bey is the most influential of all the Circassian
chiefs, sir—he is Schamyl's *naib,* and—"

"And you know him personally, do you not?"

"Yes, sir." Roberts's voice was devoid of emotion but his blue
eyes, as they met Phillip's, were suddenly bright. "I repaired
the gun emplacements for him at Soukoum and constructed a
blockhouse and earthworks, after the enemy destroyed the fortifications. But, sir, I—"

"Well, Mr Roberts? Would you not be the best messenger I
could send to Emin Bey, in the circumstances? I propose to
despatch the ship to pick him up and bring him here—it will
save time, since obviously the journey overland would take
longer. You should be back here as soon as I am, if not before."

Roberts drew in his breath sharply. "I thought you'd want
me with you, sir, and—"

"Mr Roberts, you are a Marine, a red-coated Marine," Phillip reminded him smilingly. "Unlike my bluejackets, you do not climb aloft to tend the sails, do you?"

"No, sir. But shall I not be required to command my men, when they're relieving the garrison of the fort?"

"The fort has a most efficient commander, I fancy—in any case, your sergeant is surely quite capable of instructing the Bey's *redifs* in the use of the Minié rifle, isn't he?"

"Yes, sir, of course. He is a very good N.C.O. and—"

"Then you will go to Soukoum, if you please, Mr Roberts," Phillip ordered formally. "My instructions from the Admiral are on board—read them before you land, so that you will know exactly what information you are to give Emin Bey."

"Yes, indeed I will, most gladly, sir." Roberts's voice was not quite steady. "Thank you, sir."

"You will not have more than a few hours in Soukoum," Phillip pointed out dryly. "So make the most of your time there, *after* you have spoken to Emin Bey. Now you had better detail your sergeant and six men for duty in the fort and march them up there, with a half dozen rifles. I shall return on board, to select my party and hand over command to the First Lieutenant. Carry on, Mr Roberts."

"Aye, aye, sir." Roberts saluted smartly and turned on his heel.

As he was being rowed out to the *Huntress,* Phillip gave careful thought to the choice of the three men who would accompany him. Grey's was the first name to come into his head but the young mate was gunnery officer and, in view of the possibility of an attack on Anapa, he decided that Grey—and with him O'Leary—might best employ their time in exercising the guns' crews. It was essential that the *Huntress's* fire should be accurately directed at military targets . . . Cochrane, then? As Second Lieutenant, Cochrane had his watch-keeping duties, of course, but Grey now took a watch, as did the master, so . . . Cochrane was the best choice. He was fit and agile, cool headed and completely trustworthy and, in addition, he spoke French.

As to men, the choice was almost unlimited. They were all good men, but the ones he took would have to be selected for their physical strength and stamina, since they would have to carry the case of rifles and the ammunition, which ruled out Higgins and half a dozen more, including his coxswain. Gunner's Mate Thompson was the biggest man in the ship's company and he, like Cochrane and O'Leary, had come from the *Trojan* . . . it had been he who had carried Martin Fox back to the ship, when he had received his fatal wound at Eupatoria. The best topman he had was a lad called Blythe, rated AB, who had been an Aberdeen trawler-hand but . . . Phillip hesitated, considering the merits of several others. He was still undecided when, after a preliminary exchange of hails, his boat came alongside the *Huntress* and the bowman deftly hooked on to the starboard chains.

"Wait for me, if you please, Mr Grey," he instructed. "I shall be going ashore again in about fifteen minutes. While you're waiting, have slings rove to enable the case of Minié cartridges to be carried, would you? Better have it hoisted aboard and work on deck—I want those slings to stand up to rough handling."

"Aye, aye, sir," Grey acknowledged. "And the rifles, sir?"

Again Phillip hesitated. The rifles were heavy and would make an awkward load but if he had them removed from their case and doled them out between the Circassians and his own men, they could be carried with much less effort.

"Break them out, Mr Grey, and make sure that they're correctly assembled and that each has a sling."

"Right, sir." Both Grey and the midshipman who was with

him watched, their eyes bright with curiosity, as their commander swung himself through the entry port. Phillip resisted
the temptation to tell them what was afoot, since he could take
neither with his shore party and, in any case, they would know
soon enough. Graham met him at the entry port and, at his
suggestion, followed him to his cabin. As he changed, he gave
his brother a brief account of the arrangements he had made
with Najib Bey and explained what he intended to do.

"I thought I'd take Anthony Cochrane and Gunner's Mate
Thompson with me—if you can do without them when you
take the ship to Soukoum Kaleh," he added. "The Bey was most
insistent that I should bring only men who are fit and accustomed to heights. This, in his view, ruled out the Marines—for
whom he then revealed that he had other plans . . ." Graham
smiled, when he enlarged on these.

"The cunning old devil! Obviously he likes the idea of
British redcoats pacing the battlements, armed with Minié
rifles. He's not expecting to be attacked, is he?"

"I don't think so. What about Cochrane, Graham? Can you
do without him?"

"Yes, of course I can. And Thompson's an excellent choice—
but didn't you say you wanted three men? Who is the third?"

"I'd thought of Blythe but I haven't made up my mind. Who
do you suggest?"

Graham considered the question. "You know you'll break
O'Leary's heart if you don't take him?"

"He couldn't manage with that leg of his." Phillip pulled a
thick, fisherman's knit jersey over his head and his voice was
momentarily muffled. "These mountains are pretty rough
going, according to young Roberts."

"And what about that leg of *yours,* my dear Phillip?" Graham
asked. His tone was deliberately light but the expression on

his face was concerned. "Will it stand up to rough going, you suppose?"

"My leg gives me no trouble now. It has healed perfectly," Phillip assured him. He donned a watch-coat, the oldest he possessed, and buttoned it with an air of finality. "My orders are to make contact with Serfir Pasha in person and to get him here in time to meet the Turkish commander—what's his name? Mustapha Pasha, who should arrive on or before the eighteenth of this month. It is, admittedly, unfortunate that the darned fellow has taken to the mountains but, since he has, I must go after him. There's no time to wait till he returns of his own free will, is there?"

"I would gladly go in your place," Graham offered.

"It's good of you, but no." Phillip laid a hand affectionately on his brother's shoulder. "You've had no more experience of mountaineering than I have and I can't leave anyone else in command of the ship."

Graham nodded regretfully. "Very good. Shall I warn Cochrane that he's to go with you?"

"Yes, if you please," Phillip assented. "And Gunner's Mate Thompson and, I suppose Blythe—unless you have a better suggestion?"

"There's Erikson," Graham reminded him. "The Norwegian . . . he's rated AB. An intelligent and well-educated lad, in the Lancaster gun's crew. I fancy he may have done some mountain climbing. Shall I find out?"

"Higgins can do that—you see Cochrane. We're supposed to be leaving in less than half an hour—Higgins, are you there?" The steward appeared in response to his shout and Phillip sent him in search of the two seamen. "They'll want the warmest clothing they've got and boots . . . and we'd better take rations for three days—no, four, to be on the safe side. See to it, will

you, please? And find out if Erikson has done any mountaineering—if he has, we'll take him."

"Aye, aye, sir." The steward departed on his errand and, left
alone, Phillip took his orders from the locked drawer in which
he had placed them and, after re-reading Captain Jones's report
with more attention than he had previously given to it, laid all
the papers in his personal log book and returned them to the
drawer. The key he put in his pocket to give to Graham. His pistol was also in the drawer but he left it there—a Minié rifle
would, he decided, be of more use to him and he would take his
Dollond. Ten minutes later, he was in the quarter-boat, on his
way back to the wooden fish-quay, with Cochrane beside him.

CHAPTER THREE

I *n spite of* Najib Bey's insistence that they must make an early start, Phillip and Anthony Cochrane, with the two selected men from the *Huntress*—Gunner's Mate Thompson and the wiry, fair-haired Norwegian able-seaman, Einar Erikson —were left cooling their heels on the quay for nearly half an hour. Then, to Phillip's relief, half a dozen Circassians made their appearance, bringing with them four baggage ponies and the promised sheepskin coats. By the time the case of ammunition had been strapped on to one of the ponies and a Minié rifle doled out to each man, six or seven more came from the fort accompanied by Roberts, who announced cheerfully that Dafir was also about to follow him.

"They've given my men excellent quarters, sir," the Marine officer added. "And they're hitting it off very well with the Circassian *redifs*. I've left Aslam to interpret for them for the time being—the Bey says he'll send him down the coast tomorrow with the Admiral's message. And he asked me to tell you, sir, that he thinks it probable that Mustapha Pasha will call at Redoute Kaleh himself, on his way here, because the garrison is Turkish and commanded by one of his officers."

Phillip thanked him and sent him back to the ship in Grey's boat, with instructions to Graham that he could leave for Soukoum whenever he was ready. To his annoyance, there was still no sign of Dafir and the *Huntress* had weighed anchor before the Bey's handsome young son came trotting unhurriedly to join him, mounted on a sturdy pony. The boy smiled but showed no sign of contrition, simply turned his pony's shaggy head in the direction of the distant mountains and, with a casual wave of the hand, invited the waiting men to follow him.

The cluster of wooden and stone-built houses and the bronze-domed mosque which constituted the town of Ghelenjik were soon left behind, Dafir—the only member of the party of seventeen who was mounted—setting a brisk pace. At first the going was comparatively easy and Phillip enjoyed the climb over a series of lush grassy slopes, the sun warm on his back and the scent of roses and jasmine borne to him on the gentle breeze. By noon they were walking through pleasant woodland, following the course of a shallow stream, beside which wild flowers and flowering shrubs of every description grew in delightful profusion. The Circassians, on reaching the stream, paused only to quench their thirst with a few mouthfuls of the clear, cool water and then plodded purposefully on, munching what appeared to be black bread and shallots, which, they took from their pouches and ate as they climbed. Quite soon the light green leaves of oak and elm, which had afforded them shade, gave place to the darker green of fir and pine, as the course of the stream became rocky and the path they were following steeper. It was also a good deal colder and Phillip was not surprised when, topping a rise, he found himself walking in snow. It was crisp and dry and they continued to make good progress, the mounted figure of their guide always a considerable distance ahead, leading them diagonally across a deep fold in the ground, from which nothing could be seen save a ridge of overhanging rock above them.

"Don't they ever call a halt, sir?" Anthony Cochrane asked

ruefully and Phillip, needing all his breath for the ascent, shrugged in answer. When they emerged on to the top of the ridge, the awe-inspiring sight of a precipitous peak, shrouded in snow, met their gaze, its summit hidden in cloud. To the left, a tree-grown crevice appeared to circle what they could see of the peak and, when Dafir turned his pony towards it, Cochrane exclaimed in dismay. "For heaven's sake! Do you suppose we're going up there, sir?"

Phillip halted to draw breath and, drawing level with him, Erikson said reassuringly, "It is not so bad as it looks, sir." He shaded his eyes with his hand, taking stock. "No, it is not," he added. "There is a path, do you see, sir?"

Glad of the respite, Phillip took out his Dollond. There was a path, he saw, where the Norwegian seaman had indicated— a narrow, twisting track made, he could only suppose, by mountain goats. "Can they get the ponies up that?" he asked incredulously. "It doesn't look much more than a foot wide."

Erikson smiled. He was in his element, sure-footed and confident and completely at home in these surroundings, Phillip noted with approval and was thankful that Graham had suggested him as the fourth member of their party. Like Cochrane and himself, Gunner's Mate Thompson, though he plodded resolutely on, was stumbling frequently now and becoming short of breath. He said nothing as he, too, halted to stare upwards, but the expression on his weather-beaten face was more than a little anxious.

"It will be more than a foot wide," Erikson said quietly. "Distances are deceptive in the mountains—that ravine is far- ther away than you would imagine. We shall be fortunate if we are able to reach the foot of it before nightfall."

His forecast proved correct. When darkness fell, the party was still some way from the ravine and the four naval members of it, who had dropped behind, were compelled to cover the last quarter of a mile in almost total blackness, guided by the small glow of the fire the Circassians had kindled when they halted. Dafir, Phillip saw, when they joined him at last, had chosen a deep cave as his camp site, protected from the wind by piled rocks close to the entrance—an obviously man-made barrier, which suggested that he had been there before. Inside the floor of the cave was dry and there was a plentiful supply of firewood, neatly stacked at its far end, from which the men replenished their fire. By its flickering light, the Bey's son indicated, by signs, that they should seat themselves and they did so thankfully, holding their chilled hands to the blaze with murmured exclamations of approval. A pot of water was already boiling on it and when Thompson, who was carrying the British party's rations, started to unpack his haversack, Dafir shook his head forcefully. One of his men, who had been squatting by the tethered baggage ponies, returned to the firelight with a haunch of meat which he deftly impaled on a spit, fashioned from a branch of green firewood, and suspended over the flames.

"Goat, one presumes," Cochrane observed, without relish but, as the meat sizzled and crackled on its crude spit, emitting a most appetizing odour, his expression changed. "You know, sir," he told Phillip gravely, "This mountain air gives one the very deuce of an appetite. I believe, after all, that goat may have a decided advantage over our stewed salt junk."

"I fancy it may," Phillip agreed, with equal gravity. He had eaten nothing since breakfast and, when the meat was cooked, he accepted a liberal portion, sliced off with the cook's long, curved dagger. Following the example of their hosts, the British party ate with their fingers, washing the meal down with strong and very sweet Turkish coffee and, when it was over,

Dafir posted a guard at the cave entrance, rolled himself in his sheepskin mantle and lay down. The rest of his men did the same and Cochrane looked enquiringly at Phillip.

"Watch and watch, sir?" he asked. "Or won't that be necessary?"

"I don't think it will be necessary, Mr Cochrane," Phillip answered. "These Circassians seem to know what they're about and we're in their hands. For our own sakes, in view of the climb facing us tomorrow morning, I fancy we had best get all the sleep we can." As Dafir had done, he drew his sheepskin coat closely about him and stretched out on the rocky ground, to fall asleep almost instantly.

The Circassians were early astir the following morning, taking a frugal breakfast of their coarse black bread with goats'-milk cheese and some sparing sips of ice-cold water from the stream with which to wash this down. The naval party had, perforce, to dispense with the steaming cocoa or coffee they normally drank, since the fire had been allowed to go out and, to all four of them—Phillip included—the stream water was a poor substitute, their dry rations unpalatable. They left the cave soon after daylight and, as Erikson had guessed he would, Dafir led them to a rough track which zig-zagged up the steep side of the ravine and then vanished into the grey, early morning mist shrouding the peak. It was very cold and the track slippery but, Phillip noticed with astonishment, although the opposite side of the ravine was thickly covered with snow, that on which they were making their ascent was virtually clear, save for a few odd patches.

"The prevailing wind, sir," Erikson explained, in his correct, careful English. "It prevents the snow from lying on this side. These men—and the young one in particular—are very good mountaineers. There are not many who would dare ride a horse on this path, but he is doing so—look at him, sir!"

Watching Dafir's progress, Phillip marvelled at the boy's consummate horsemanship. He did not appear to be hurrying but he never hesitated and quite soon was so far ahead of the rest of the party that the mist swallowed him up and it was possible to catch only an occasional glimpse of him when the track he was following doubled back, high above their own. The men leading the baggage ponies had, at times, to drag them, slithering unwillingly on the wet rock, but Dafir left his pony its head, letting the animal pick its own way and the sturdy little beast seldom faltered. As they climbed higher, the stream which had provided their unwelcome breakfast beverage became a rushing torrent, fed by a waterfall that cascaded down from a cleft in the rock a dizzy fifty or sixty feet above and to the right of the track. From where he was, Phillip could see no way round this obstacle but, as Dafir appeared suddenly in a break in the cloud on the far side of the leaping water, he pushed on doggedly, supposing that there must be a bridge or some other means of crossing higher up. There was, and he drew in his breath in shocked disbelief when he came in sight of it and realized that it consisted of four huge rocks set, like giant stepping stones, immediately above the waterfall.

"My God!" Cochrane drew level with him and he, too, was incredulous. "He surely didn't ride over *that,* did he, sir?"

"He seems to have done. I didn't see him dismount." Phillip moved forward slowly, bracing himself for what he knew would be an ordeal. For a man on foot, the crossing was perilous enough, in all conscience—the rocks were streaming with moisture and the gaps between them varied from a foot or so to well over a yard—but to have ridden over them, as Dafir apparently had, required an iron nerve and faultless judgement. The Circassians were grinning delightedly, indicating by signs what they thought of their young leader's feat and, as he followed them across, a few moments later and glanced at the sheer drop into the raging water beneath him, Phillip could not suppress a shudder. Heights seldom bothered him; his training, since his days as a naval cadet, had seen to that but . . . safely over the chasm, he turned back to meet Erikson's gaze.

"That boy, sir," the Norwegian said dryly. "I think it is good that we have him on our side."

Even Thompson, who had until now been a trifle mistrustful of their strange new allies, echoed his words with unusual fervour, as they paused to watch the baggage ponies being manoeuvred across. "They're good men, sir—darned good men, the whole bunch of 'em. Like Erikson says, I'd rather have them on our side than against us, and that's the gospel truth." He shifted the rifle he was carrying from one shoulder to the other and, despite the misty chill, mopped his brow with a big hand. "How much farther do you reckon we've still to go, sir?"

Phillip fumbled for his pocket watch. Up here, in the clouds where the sun did not penetrate, it was difficult even to guess at the time and he was astonished to see that the hands of his watch pointed only to ten-fifteen. The muscles of his legs were painfully stiff and his whole body ached—he had imagined that they had been toiling up the narrow goat track for six or seven hours at least, instead of which . . . he, too, passed a hand wearily across his brow.

"I should imagine we've come about three quarters of the way," he answered. "Another three or four hours ought to see us at the Pasha's camp, but I'm guessing—I could be wrong."

Anthony Cochrane, who had been massaging his cramped leg muscles, straightened himself reluctantly as the last of the baggage ponies was pushed and dragged over the giant stepping stones and the Circassians prepared to resume their march. "I trust you're right, sir," he said feelingly. "I don't mind telling you, I'm just about all in. And to think"—he sighed—"I was quite annoyed, when we set off, because they hadn't provided horses for us. All I can say now is thank heaven they didn't!"

Phillip laughed shortly and forced himself to continue the seemingly endless climb. About an hour later, still in cloud, they gained the crest of the ridge they had been ascending and he saw, to his surprise, that Dafir had halted. When the first of his men reached him, he slipped gracefully out of the saddle and flung his reins to the nearest of the baggage pony holders. The Circassians at once set to work to remove part of the ponies' loads, including the case of ammunition, which they broke open, distributing its contents between half a dozen of their number.

Phillip reached them, breathless and spent, intending to protest at their summary seizure of his ammunition but Dafir, guessing his purpose, caught his arm and led him forward a few paces. Holding him firmly by the arm, he gestured downwards and Phillip had to bite back a gasp of dismay. Below them was a precipitous wall of rock, far steeper than the one by which they had ascended, its foot indiscernible for the damp, swirling mist into which it disappeared. He did not need the stone Dafir cast down, almost derisively, to prove to him that the drop was a long one and virtually sheer.

"Erikson . . ." the Norwegian, still looking by far the fittest of the small party from the *Huntress*, came in response to his call, to peer downwards with narrowed, alert blue eyes. "What do you think of it?" Phillip asked.

"Well, sir, they are wise not to attempt to take the ponies," Erikson answered, his tone a trifle dry. "And in my country, we should use ropes for such a descent but . . . this is their country. Perhaps we should leave it to them, sir, and see how they propose to tackle it."

It was evident that this was good advice. The Circassians were quietly and efficiently making their preparations and Erikson went to join them. He had established a means of communication with them, consisting mainly of gestures and grunts, but it was proving quite effective and he returned to Phillip's side with the news that ropes were to be used.

"There's quite a clear way down, sir," he said. "Once you know where to look for the hand and footholds, and there are rocks and bushes suitable for belays. I think," he added, thoughtfully, "that this is a short cut . . . there must be an easier way, if the Pasha has brought mounted troops to a camp in these mountains. Indeed, sir, from what I've seen of that lad Dafir, I should not be at all surprised to find that we've been taking a different route from the Pasha's soldiers, ever since we left Ghelenjik. But we *have* covered a fair distance, sir, and at a fair pace, too, so I don't think we need complain on that score."

"You speak for yourself, Able-Seaman Erikson!" Anthony Cochrane groaned, as he flung himself gasping to the ground. "I have a score of reasons for complaint—not least because my legs seem to have turned to jelly and I can scarcely breathe!"

"It is the height, sir," Erikson assured him. "These men are accustomed to the rarified air but you are not." He squatted down and began to rub Cochrane's legs, kneading the stiff muscles with strong, skilful fingers. "You will recover very quickly once we descend to two or three thousand feet."

"Not if I have to go down *that* way," Cochrane retorted, glancing downwards as one of the Circassians, a rope loosely knotted about his waist and a pick-headed hammer thrust into his belt, stepped nonchalantly over the edge of the precipice. The rope, belayed round a rock, was slowly paid out by two of his companions, the sound of his hammer, as he plied it vigorously, reaching the ears of those waiting at the cliff top. Erikson smiled. "This, sir," he stated with conviction, "will be the easiest part of the whole journey. These men know what they are doing and they've been this way before, I'm quite certain."

Once again his forecast proved correct—initially at any rate. The Circassians lowered themselves and their four British allies to a mantelshelf ledge on the rock face, from whence— skilfully drawing the rope after them and making a fresh belay—they repeated the process. Predictably, Dafir waited till last and came down with only a hand on the rope, although he had insisted that even Erikson should secure himself to it for the first difficult phase of the descent. This became a good deal easier as the distance from the foot of the ravine decreased and they had no longer to watch for patches of ice or pockets of wind-blown snow in their path. For the last seventy or eighty feet the rope was dispensed with, the trees and bushes growing from crannies in the rock affording ample handholds. Visibility improved, as the grey mist of the mountain was left behind and, emerging into bright sunlight, three or four of the Circassians raced ahead, laughing and skylarking like so many small boys unexpectedly released from school.

It was then, without warning, that Dafir the sure-footed slipped on a loose stone and, after slithering helplessly for several yards, cannoned into Phillip, who was spread-eagled on the rock face just below him. He had, fortunately, a firm toehold for both feet and his right arm was hooked round the trunk of a tough young pine tree growing above his head but, even so, the impact almost unbalanced him. Dafir grabbed his

shoulder, clinging to him with all the strength in his wiry
young body and managed somehow to arrest his descent.
Phillip, reacting more from instinct than from reason, freed
his left arm and locked it about the boy's waist, driving both
knees as hard as he could against the unyielding rock. The
Bey's son was lightly built but his dead weight nearly wrenched
the arm from its socket, and they hung there for a long
moment in imminent danger of crashing down together, the
pine sapling bent over at so acute an angle it was little short
of a miracle that it was not uprooted.

Dafir did not utter a sound, although his face was deathly
pale and, just for an instant, Phillip glimpsed naked fear in his
eyes. Then one of his threshing feet found the hold it was seeking, he twisted his body round, clawing at the rock face with
both hands and contrived to regain his balance, thereby reduc-
ing the threat to his rescuer's stability. The whole incident was
over in a matter of seconds but as Dafir, cursing loudly and
angrily in his own language, dragged himself clear, Phillip was
conscious of a sharp stab of pain and knew that the old wound
in his right thigh had opened up again. The boy, unaware that
he was hurt, scampered down the rest of the way without a
backward glance and it was the alert Erikson who came to
his aid.

"That was a close thing, sir," he said anxiously. "I thought
he was going to bring you down. Take it easy for a minute or
two, until you get your breath back, and then I'll give you a
hand. You're not hurt, are you, sir?"

Phillip shook his head. "I wrenched my leg, I think, but it's
nothing," he evaded, grateful nevertheless, for Erikson's
steadying hand as he finally completed the descent, to find
Cochrane waiting for him.

"Are you all right, sir?" his second-in-command enquired,

studying his face with some concern. "I didn't see what happened but Thompson told me that Dafir nearly knocked you to kingdom-come. Silly young idiot, trying to make a descent like that without a rope! He's been asking for trouble, though, hasn't he, ever since we started? Trying to impress us, I suppose."

"He's very young," Phillip defended. He felt oddly light-headed and when Cochrane, still concerned, suggested that he should sit down, he did not argue.

"This is a pleasant spot for a breather, sir, and the Circassians don't seem to be ready to move on yet. I wonder how much farther it is to the Pasha's camp?"

Phillip lowered himself gingerly on to a patch of mossy grass and looked about him. They were now, he saw, in a narrow valley, hemmed in by mountains but completely free of snow and, although he could see no sign of human habitation, the presence of a large herd of goats, placidly grazing nearby, suggested that the valley could not be entirely deserted. It was, as Cochrane had observed, a pleasant spot and he, as much as any of them, welcomed the chance to rest and recoup his strength before having to move on. Dafir and his men, having coiled their rope and redistributed their various loads, were also sitting down—waiting, he could only suppose for some sort of signal, since none of them appeared in need of rest—and he did not feel disposed to hurry them. Instead, he lay back, his head pillowed on his linked hands, letting his weary muscles relax their tension and luxuriating in the warm sunshine. His leg did not hurt quite so much now, the pain having died to a dull ache . . . perhaps, after all, he had only jarred it. He sighed, recalling Graham's warning and deliberately made no attempt to ascertain whether or not the wound had reopened.

Beside him, Cochrane followed his example and stretched out at full length on his front, chin cupped between his hands.

"This is great, sir, isn't it?" he said happily. Able to breathe without effort now, he swiftly recovered his spirits, chatting away about their journey and the feats of their strange new companions. "If they fight as well as they shin up and down these infernal mountains, I can't see the Muscovs holding Anapa or Soujak for much longer, can you, sir?"

Phillip listened to him with half an ear, resisting an almost overwhelming desire to sleep. His feeling of light-headedness gradually passed and when Dafir waved to indicate that it was time to move on, he got to his feet willingly enough, shaking his head to Cochrane's offer of assistance. The brief respite had enabled him to recover some, at least, of his normal energy and the others, he saw, were looking much more cheerful than they had a few hours ago on the wind-swept mountain top. Even the taciturn Thompson was now attempting to trade jokes with some of the older Circassians and grinning to himself, when they failed to understand what he was trying to say to them but laughed uproariously just the same.

"They're a rum bunch of so-and-so's," he confided to Erikson. "Not a word of English between the lot of 'em and yet they're laughing their ruddy heads off! Still, as foreigners go, they're not bad blokes, are they, really?"

"I am also a foreigner," Erikson pointed out, with pretended humility. "Had you forgotten that, Gunner's Mate?"

"Come off it, lad!" the big gunner's mate besought him, "You've been educated and you speak English a sight better than I do . . . and besides, you're one of us, ain't you? Here"— he slipped the sling of the extra rifle his shipmate had been carrying for him from his shoulder—"I'll take that for a spell.

Yours, too, if you like, now we're back on terra firma—because we may have quite a way to go yet. I don't see no sign of a camp, do you?"

"And frankly, nor do I, sir," Anthony Cochrane remarked, lowering his voice and matching his step to Phillip's.

"They won't be in tents, Mr Cochrane," Phillip reminded him.

"No, I suppose not—stupid of me, I was just thinking they would. What then—caves or just out in the open?"

"It could be either, I imagine. As far as I can gather from the reports I've read, these people have been fighting their own brand of war against the Russians for a long while. They cannot fight pitched battles against trained and disciplined troops, supported by artillery, of course, but they raid and plunder, ambush supply trains—as Serfir Pasha is apparently planning to do now—and then escape to the mountains to avoid retribution."

"Pretty effective tactics, aren't they, sir?" Cochrane suggested.

Phillip shrugged. "Effective but not decisive, Mr Cochrane. The trouble seems to be their mistrust of the Turks as allies—with reason, the Admiral says—and the fact that old tribal feuds are remembered for years, so that one tribe won't unite with another against the common enemy. It takes a leader of the calibre of Schamyl, who is their paramount chief, to bring them together, although apparently Serfir Pasha is one who is universally respected, and also Emin Bey, who is one of Schamyl's lieutenants. I've sent the *Huntress* to Soukoum Kaleh to fetch him."

"With the object of trying to bring them together, sir?"

"That and to arrange a meeting with the Turkish commander at Batoum, Mustapha Pasha, who is now in a position to offer them quite considerable aid. In the Admiral's view, he is one of the better Turkish generals and . . ." Phillip broke off as the sharp crack of a rifle shot came from somewhere to their left. Instinctively his hand went to his own Minié, only to return to his side when he saw Dafir discharge a shot into the air and then run eagerly forward, shouting at the pitch of his lungs. From the concealment of a rocky defile about a quarter of a mile ahead of them, a score of leather-jacketed Circassian horsemen emerged and, setting spurs to their wild-looking mounts, galloped to meet the running boy. His own men ran after their young leader and were soon the centre of a chattering throng, evidently exchanging news and greeting old friends and, judging by the gestures in the direction of Phillip's small party, explaining the reason for their presence. The Minié rifles and cartridges Dafir's men carried attracted considerable attention and were minutely examined before the whole group, as if suddenly realizing that they had been wanting in courtesy, came trotting over to offer the new arrivals a belated welcome.

A handsome, grey-bearded man, who appeared to be in command of the scouting party, delivered a short speech, in response to which Phillip could only bow and nod his head solemnly, unable to understand a word. But it sounded friendly and, when the grey-bearded commander pointed to his horse, he nodded again and let the old man assist him into the saddle.

"Serfir Pasha?" he asked and the bearded lips parted in a beaming smile, as the man waved his rifle in the direction from which he had come, and then vaulted into the saddle behind him.

The others remounted, each with an extra man or one of the bundles of provisions on his saddle-bow but Dafir, after a low-voiced consultation with Phillip's escort, was given a horse of his own. Accompanied by two of the grey-beard's horsemen, he set off at a furious gallop, evidently determined to be the first to bring news of their coming to the Pasha's camp.

"He's in a tearing hurry, as usual," Cochrane observed dryly. "Ought we to have let him go, d'you think, sir?"

"Well, we obviously can't stop him now, Mr Cochrane." Phillip's tone was resigned. "I'm beginning to wish I hadn't let Aslam persuade me to leave him behind—it's damned awkward being unable to communicate with these people."

He hoped that Najib Bey's information concerning the linguistic powers of the Polish officer was also right or, if it was not, that he would find someone in the camp who would be capable of understanding his schoolboy French.

It took fifteen minutes' hard riding to reach the camp and, when they did so, Phillip was conscious of a keen sense of disappointment, for the place was all but deserted. He dismounted and took stock. As he had expected, there were no tents, only a few scattered wooden barns and huts, grouped about an old, stone-built farmhouse which, he could only presume had until recently been in use as Serfir Pasha's headquarters. A dozen or so Circassian riflemen were lounging about outside, apparently guarding the place and, if there were any women, he could see no sign of them, although it was possible that they were inside the building—Mohammedans, he remembered, kept their women in the harem, closely guarded. The ashes of what had obviously been bivouac fires were scattered here and there, a few of them still glowing and he deduced, from this evidence, that the camp had been occupied until a few hours before and by a much smaller force than he had expected—perhaps five or six hundred, at most. Turning to Cochrane, who was beside him, he saw his own disappointment mirrored in the younger man's face.

"The birds seem to have flown, don't they, sir? But where . . . and why?"

Phillip sighed. "I imagine they must have gone to set their ambush for the Russian supply train and that we've got here too late. Where's Dafir got to—can you see him anywhere?"

"I'll look around, sir," Cochrane volunteered. Accompanied by Thompson, he made for the farmhouse. Erikson, displaying his usual initiative, was doing his best to communicate in sign language with the grey-bearded leader of the cavalry patrol which had been their escort and Phillip crossed the littered ground to join him.

"Can you get anything useful out of them?" he asked.

"Well, sir"—Erikson shrugged despondently—"only that they're offering us food. I've asked for Serfir Pasha but all they do is wag their heads and grin and old Grey Beard here keeps putting his rifle to his shoulder and going through the motions of aiming and firing. But that may be because he wants me to show him how the Miniés perform; sir, I don't know. He's certainly taking a great interest in them."

"Then give him a demonstration," Phillip answered. "We may want him to take us to Serfir Pasha if we can't find any one in authority here . . . and it doesn't look as if we shall."

"Aye, aye, sir." The fair-haired seaman picked up one of the Minié rifles and, with murmurs of approval, the members of the escort surrounded him, one of them, at his behest, setting up a pile of stones as a target. "Here, shove this on top!" Erikson shouted after him and threw a nicotine-stained clay pipe in his direction. To roars of good humoured laughter, the man caught it and placed it upright on the pile of stones, wedging it firmly by the stem, as Erikson moved away, carefully pacing out the range. Attracted by the laughter and general excitement, some of the guards from the farmhouse came strolling across to attach themselves to his audience and, leaving them to their demonstration, Phillip strode restlessly on.

Cochrane and Thompson had left the farmhouse, he saw, and were extending their search further afield but he did not join them. He felt anxious and ill at ease, filled with a sense of anticlimax. They had come so far and with so much effort that he did not feel inclined to remain idly kicking his heels in the deserted camp until the Pasha returned from his foray. It might be days before he *did* return, since he might well change his plans according to the success or failure of his attempt to ambush the supply train. Phillip sighed. Anapa was a little under fifty miles from Ghelenjik along the coast, he knew from his charts, and Soujak Kaleh about sixteen—a wide area to cover, when the encircling mountain ranges were included, and he had very little time to spare. He took out his watch and his anxiety was allayed a little when he saw that it was not quite twelve-thirty. If he did go in search of Serfir Pasha, obviously he would have to do so in daylight and come up with him before dark but . . . that gave him a bit of latitude. The still warm ashes of the cooking fires were proof that the Pasha could not have left more than an hour or so before and a small mounted party, setting off in pursuit, should be able to overtake a force of several hundred, not all of whom could be on horseback. They . . .

"Sir—Commander Hazard!" Cochrane hailed him from the door of a hut about fifty yards away and, catching a note of urgency in his voice, Phillip hurried over to where he was standing. "What is it, Mr Cochrane?" he asked. "Have you found Dafir?"

"No, sir, the young devil seems to have deserted us. But"—
Cochrane pointed to the hut behind him—"I've found a
wounded officer in there, who speaks English. He says he's
Polish, sir, and a cavalry officer in the Turkish service, so I
thought you'd want a word with him."

"Indeed I do!" Phillip exclaimed, unable to hide his relief.
"Perhaps he'll be able to tell us what's going on and where we
can find Serfir Pasha. Is he badly wounded?"

Cochrane shook his head. "I don't think so, sir. He has his
right arm in a sling but he seems in quite good fettle and most
anxious to talk. Oh, by the way, sir—they're laying on a meal
for us in the farmhouse, as far as I could make out from the
guards. It smelt rather good, so do you think we—"

"Yes, of course," Phillip agreed. "Eat while you've got the
chance, Mr Cochrane. Collect Thompson—and Erikson, when
he's finished giving his demonstration with the Minié rifle. I'll
join you as soon as I've spoken to this Polish officer. Did he
tell you his name?"

"He said it was Gorak, sir—Jan Gorak, and that he holds the
rank of Colonel. Er—forgive my asking, but are we going after
the Pasha, sir, if this fellow's able to tell you where he is?"

"I'm afraid we shall have to," Phillip answered. "With or
without Dafir . . . but keep your eyes peeled, in case he shows
up, won't you?"

"Aye, aye, sir," Cochrane acknowledged and added with a
grin, "I hope we're in time for the scrap—that is, the ambush.
I'll do what I can to organize some horses, shall I? I don't know
about you, sir, but I don't fancy riding double in a cavalry
charge."

"We are not here to take part in ambushes, Mr Cochrane,"
Phillip reproved him. "Or cavalry charges, may I remind you!
We have been sent to bring Serfir Pasha back to Ghelenjik—

that and nothing more. But organize us a horse apiece, if you can, by all means. If we have to go far, it will be more comfortable."

"Aye, aye, sir." Cochrane took himself off, quite unperturbed by the reproof and Phillip smiled to himself as he knocked on the door of the hut. Young Anthony Cochrane had matured in many respects during the last year, he thought, and had certainly changed out of all recognition from the unhappy youngster whom the late Captain North had so sadistically bullied. He had confidence in himself now and . . .

"Enter," a deep, faintly accented voice bade him and he did so, ducking his head to pass under the low doorway into the hut. "So you are Captain Hazard, are you? I am happy to welcome you, sir."

"Commander Hazard, sir, of Her Britannic Majesty's ship *Huntress,*" Phillip corrected. It was dark inside the hut and, for a second or two, he could not adjust his vision to it, after the bright sunlight outside. "And you, sir, are Colonel Gorak, I believe?"

"Kazim Bey to my Turkish masters, Commander—but Jan Gorak to you. Please be seated, will you not?"

Phillip sat down. The Polish Colonel, he saw now, was a small, white-haired man with an oddly youthful and somewhat lugubrious face, adorned by an imposing cavalry moustache and a pair of neatly trimmed white whiskers. He was evidently in the act of dressing, for the buttons of his dark blue coatee were still unfastened and, impeded by the sling in which he wore his right arm, he appeared to be having some difficulty in donning his long riding boots, but when Phillip made to assist him, he shook his head.

"No, no—I must learn to manage this myself. There . . ." breathless but triumphant, he struggled into the boots. "It can be done, if one sets one's mind to it." His English was fluent and idiomatic, his accent a curious blend of Slav and Irish which puzzled Phillip until, sensing his bewilderment, the little man smilingly explained that, although his father had been Polish, his mother had hailed originally from Cork. "My father," he added, with conscious pride, "was one of the great Napoleon Bonaparte's cavalry commanders, who served with him in Russia and fell at Waterloo. We are soldiers of fortune, you see. I myself took service in the Austrian Army as a boy of seventeen, where I made the acquaintance of the man I have followed ever since—Richard Debaufre Guyon. He is an Englishman, of Irish descent, and his father was an officer in your Royal Navy. In the Turkish Army he is known as Kourshid Pasha and he holds the rank of Lieutenant-General . . . perhaps you have heard of him?"

"Indeed I have, sir," Phillip assured him. "My Admiral has spoken of him many times and in the highest terms. It is he who has won all the victories in Asia Minor, is it not? He and the Circassian chief, Schamyl."

The little Polish Colonel beamed his gratification at this tribute. "He has won victories for the Turks—I might almost say in spite of the Turks, for the native Pashas constantly intrigue against him, ignore his advice and even countermand his orders, although he is Chief of Staff and was elected to preside over the Military Council at Kars. They are jealous of him, you see. It is a great pity—he could achieve anything, if only they would give him the support and loyalty to which he is entitled. He is a brilliant strategist and the bravest man it has ever been my good fortune to meet. I served with him in Hungary in the Kossuth rebellion of eighteen-forty-eight and I was with him at Komorn, when he broke through the Austrian lines at the head of a single troop of Hussars . . ." Colonel

Gorak sighed reminiscently, his dark eyes suddenly bright. "And I fled with him to Turkey, where Kossuth and Bem had also taken refuge. When he offered his sword to the Sultan, I did the same. Such was his reputation that the Porte did not insist that he embrace the Mohammedan faith, when he expressed his reluctance to do so. He was the first Christian ever to be given the rank of General in the Turkish Army without renouncing his faith. Indeed, he . . . but I bore you, with my memories of past glories, Commander Hazard."

"You do not, sir," Phillip answered truthfully.

"Nevertheless, we must speak of the present. You have not, I feel sure, journeyed here without very good reason. May I enquire why you have come?"

Phillip explained his mission and the little Polish Colonel nodded vigorous approval, as he spoke of the Admiral's plan for a second attempt to send a naval squadron into the Sea of Azoff.

"Excellent!" he said warmly. "That is the best possible strategy to employ. Once the major supply routes to the Army of the Tchernaya and Sebastopol are cut, Prince Gortchakoft will be compelled to withdraw his forces from the city. As to Circassian co-operation . . . I am confident that this will be given very willingly, provided the Turks really intend to supply the help they have promised. Certainly they will meet with Zarif Mustapha Pasha, for whom they have considerable respect . . . he is a fine soldier who, unlike many of his colleagues, has never flinched from his duty. You say he will come to Ghelenjik?"

"Yes, within the next eight days, Colonel Gorak," Phillip confirmed. "That is why I must see Serfir Pasha without delay. My orders are to persuade him to come back with me and—"

"He will approve your Admiral's plan," the little Colonel

said with conviction. "It is one after his own heart. These Circassians are a brave people, Commander—and they have fought against Russian oppression for over thirty years . . ." there was a soft tap on the door of the hut and he broke off. "Ah, they bring us food at last," he announced with satisfaction. In response to his invitation, a boy of about twelve came in, bearing two earthenware containers, suspended from a yoke from his thin, bowed shoulders. "You will no doubt be hungry after your arduous journey, Commander Hazard but, if you are not, here is one who will help to restore your appetite. This is Selina, the joy of my heart."

Hearing the patter of sandalled feet on the wooden floor of the hut, Phillip glanced up indifferently. The Colonel would have a native wife, he supposed, as so many of the exiled Europeans in the Turkish service had. "Indeed, sir," he began, "I . . ." but the words died on his lips as he saw a girl coming towards him, a young girl of such extraordinary beauty that the sight of her took his breath away.

She was graceful and slender, aged at most seventeen or eighteen, and she wore no all-concealing *yashmak* or shapeless robe to hide her beauty from male eyes. Her oval face, with its pale skin and exquisitely shaped features, caught and held his startled gaze and, when she drew up a table and placed it in front of him, he found himself looking into a pair of wide, dark eyes which—save for the amber flecks in them—might have belonged to a fawn or some other small, untamed creature of the wild. There was, however, no vestige of fear in their shining depths, only a shy curiosity that turned to pleasure as she looked at him, clearly liking what she saw and making no coquettish attempt to pretend otherwise.

"Selina, my dear child, permit me to present Commander Hazard of the British Navy," Colonel Gorak said formally. He spoke in French—evidently the language in which they normally conversed—but Phillip scarcely heard him. He rose, the girl's hand touched his in silent acknowledgement of the introduction and then, with a smile, she motioned him to resume his seat. He did so but continued to watch her as if mesmerized, as she moved about the dimly lit room. The long years of harsh, uncompromising naval discipline to which he had been subjected, had accustomed him to keep his personal feelings under stern control and to make no open display of emotion but, in spite of this, he came near to betraying his feelings now. He was aware of the quickening of his pulses and of the hot blood rushing, in a revealing flood, to his cheeks and was shocked by his own primitive reaction. He was no gauche boy, he reminded himself angrily. Dear heaven—he had known many beautiful women, had known and loved Mademoiselle Sophie, for whom he . . . the Colonel said something to him and, although he had no idea what it was, it broke the spell and he was recalled abruptly to his surroundings. Recovering his composure, he turned back to the man he had come to see, with a murmured apology.

"Forgive me, sir . . . you were saying?"

"It was of no importance," Colonel Gorak assured him. But his tone was cold, Phillip noticed uneasily, and he was frowning, as if his visitor's momentary lapse had not entirely escaped him. "I trust you can stomach the flesh of the humble goat, Commander—it is all we have to offer. The wine is rough but, I think, quite palatable." He inclined his white head and the girl he had called Selina took two steaming bowls from the little serving boy and set them down on the rough-hewn wooden table, each with a horn spoon and a knife beside it. She poured wine for them both and then dropped to her knees, carefully slicing the Colonel's meat, so that he might eat it with one hand. He smiled down at her fondly, caressing the demurely bent dark head with his good hand. "Selina is my most precious possession," he stated gravely. "She consoles me in my exile and I should not know what to do without her. I observe that she pleases you—she is beautiful, is she not?"

"She is very beautiful indeed, sir," Phillip managed, his voice deliberately flat. This girl, he thought, suddenly sickened, this young and lovely child and this old, white-haired man for whom, on his own admission, she was a consolation for the country he had lost . . . he picked up his knife but could not bring himself to touch the food so lavishly filling the bowl in front of him. The girl flushed, evidently understanding what he had said and he exclaimed, surprised, "She speaks English, sir? I did not realize—"

"Oh, yes. Not quite so well as she speaks French and, of course, Osmanli . . . but reasonably well. We are not all savages, Commander Hazard, even if we are exiles from European civilization," the Colonel answered with dignity.

"No, sir, of course not." Phillip took a gulp of his wine, again cursing his own lack of tact. "I did not mean to imply . . . that is, I realize that she is very young and—"

"Selina is eighteen years old," Colonel Gorak told him. "Since I took her from a convent school in Erzeroum two years ago, she has learnt to ride a horse as well as any man, to climb and find her way among these mountains and to dress wounds with great skill . . . all necessary accomplishments, in our present circumstances. This war has made nomads of us, as well as exiles, you see."

"Yes, I see. But . . ." Phillip was appalled. Two years of this existence, for a gently born, convent educated girl . . . he bit back the question he wanted to ask lest he again offended his host, but the Colonel, guessing his thoughts, gave him a wry smile. "Is she safe, you mean? She is safer here with me than she would be in any town, over-run in turn by Turks and Russians, I give you my word. I would kill any man who sought to dishonour her, Commander Hazard. Besides"—he held up his heavily bandaged right arm—"but for her care, I should have lost my sword-arm. That is so, is it not, Selina?"

The girl's flush deepened. She murmured something in a language Phillip did not understand and, to his secret relief, softly withdrew, taking the small serving boy with her.

"Were you wounded recently, sir?" he enquired, feeling the need to change the topic of conversation.

The Colonel nodded. "A Cossack sabre all but severed this arm at Akhaltzick—I was there with General Guyon in the winter of eighteen-fifty-three. That was a battle, my young friend!" He laughed and, in high good humour again, attacked his food with gusto. "I should like to tell you of it but you have not come here to listen to me boasting of old campaigns or singing the praises of General Guyon, have you?"

"Alas, no, sir. As I told you, I have been sent here to request the presence of Serfir Pasha at Ghelenjik and if you could advise me where I may find him, then I—"

"We see action, with Serfir and his Circassians," the Colonel said, as if Phillip had not spoken. "This wound of mine, concerning which you kindly enquired, was from a Russian musket ball, two—no, almost three weeks ago. Just when I had begun to recover the full use of my arm, as ill luck would have it!" He took a long draught of his wine. "By comparison with the campaigns of Schamyl and General Guyon these are, of course, mere skirmishes but . . . we harass the enemy and give him no peace. Not perhaps on the scale your Admiral envisages, although we have our successes." He described the type of fighting in vivid detail and Phillip listened, picking at his goat's meat in an effort to hide his growing impatience and waiting for an opportunity to broach the question of how he and his party could best make contact with Serfir Pasha. Time, he was aware, was slipping by, and Cochrane would be wondering at the delay . . . he stole a surreptitious glance at his watch. He would need Colonel Gorak's help, if he were to find the Pasha, but Colonel Gorak, in his present mood, was not to be hurried . . .

The opportunity he wanted came finally when his host, after refilling both their earthenware drinking cups, started to speak of the ambush of the Russian supply train on its way to Soujak which, it seemed, he had helped to plan. "I should have been there, had it not been for this accursed arm," he said regretfully. "It is the biggest operation Serfir has undertaken, and I do not think he will abandon it, whatever inducements you may offer him. So why do you not wait here until he returns? You will be more comfortable and, I assure you, very welcome. You—"

"My orders are to make contact with His Excellency at the first possible opportunity, Colonel," Phillip put in quickly. "How long do you anticipate that he will be away?"

The Polish Colonel shrugged. "Two or three days, perhaps. No longer—unless our spies have misinformed us as to when the supply train is due to leave Taman."

"Spies, sir?" Phillip questioned.

"Of course . . . we have spies everywhere, in Kertch, in Yenikale, in Taganrog—even in Anapa itself. They are usually reliable. Occasionally they give us the wrong information but, if they do, it is because they have been bribed. It is possible that our information concerning the supply train is false but—"

"Do you mean that there may be no supply train?"

"Oh, there will be a supply train—Soujak is short of food

and fresh water. But it may not come at the time or by the route we have been told that it will take."

"Then, sir, if the information is *not* correct," Phillip persisted, "what do you expect Serfir Pasha to do? Will he return here, do you suppose?"

The Colonel hesitated and then shook his head. "No, he will most probably wait—or set another ambush, if he can ascertain which way the supply train is coming."

"Which might take him more than three days?"

"Perhaps. There is no way of knowing. His force is highly mobile, you understand, and—"

"And being mobile, such a force might well be hard to find, once it moves from its present position?" Phillip reasoned. Receiving a nod of assent, he went on, "You know its present position, do you not, Colonel?"

"I know where Serfir will make camp tonight, yes. But . . ." the little Colonel seemed about to argue. "It would be exceedingly unwise for you to venture in pursuit of him. You are a *Giaour*. Serfir's men might mistake you for a Russian and—"

"I must take that risk." His mind made up, Phillip got to his feet. "I must deliver my Admiral's message, Colonel, and I should be grateful for any help you can give me."

Colonel Gorak sighed. "What help, my impetuous young friend? You'll want horses, of course—but for how many?"

"Four, sir. That is, I have an officer and two seamen with me, in addition to a dozen of Najib Bey's men. I also have a case of Minié rifles and ammunition. Sir . . ." Phillip eyed his host expectantly. "If you can provide me with a guide and, perhaps, an interpreter, I could leave at once—although the interpreter may not be necessary because—"

"Because *you* speak Osmanli?"

"No, sir, only French. But Najib told me that Serfir had a daughter with him—a Christian girl, I imagine—who speaks French and some English."

"Yes, she is here at *this* camp. But she has no English and her French is poor—you could not use her as an interpreter. In any case, she is of the Moslem faith, she would not be permitted to accompany you." Colonel Gorak was frowning. "Did you not bring a guide, Commander? Did Najib not provide you with one?"

"His son Dafir acted as our guide, sir," Phillip answered. "Unfortunately he left us when we met your cavalry patrol and we haven't seen him since. He took a horse and dashed off on his own—I have no idea where he has got to. My men are searching for him but—"

"Dafir the Fearless One?" The Colonel's frown vanished and he threw back his head with a guffaw of laughter. "That young gentleman is even more impetuous than you are, my dear boy! He will, by this time, be well on his way to join Serfir, in the hope of playing an active part in the ambush. It is a pity, in the circumstances, that he did not wait for you . . . he could have saved me a good deal of discomfort."

"*You* sir? But—"

The old man clambered slowly and awkwardly to his feet. "I shall have to take you to Serfir myself, since you refuse to be sensible and wait here until he returns. There is no one else who can play the dual role of guide and interpreter . . . except Selina. She is not of the Moslem faith but, nevertheless, I could not permit her to accompany you alone." He waved aside Phillip's protests. "I can sit a horse, so do not concern yourself for me. I shall survive the journey, although I do not expect to enjoy it, and Serfir will be delighted if I help to bring him those Minié rifles! Right, then, it's decided. My coat is there—be so good as to assist me into it. Yes, the sheepskin one . . . thank you."

Phillip helped him don the heavy garment. "It is extremely good of you, sir. But are you sure that you are fit? You—"

"You have an English saying, do you not, about never looking a—what is it? Gift horse in the mouth?" The little Colonel thrust his bandaged arm under the sheepskin coat and smiled as Phillip fastened it for him. "Go and summon your sailors, Commander Hazard, whilst I choose horses and an escort. We must leave at once if we are to reach our destination before dark."

He stumped out of the hut and Phillip hurried after him.

CHAPTER FOUR

A *party of* twelve left Serfir Pasha's base camp half an hour later, all mounted and with the rifles and ammunition loaded on to two baggage ponies.

To Phillip's surprise, the girl Selina accompanied them, so muffled in a thick sheepskin cloak and with a cap of the same material pulled down over her eyes that, at first, he did not recognize her. The slight feeling of apprehension her presence engendered in him swiftly changed to one of admiration, as he watched her riding at the head of the column beside the Colonel for, as he had proudly proclaimed, she handled her horse as well as any man. And, indeed, a good deal better than himself, Phillip reflected ruefully, when his shaggy mount stumbled over a loose stone and he only saved himself from an ignominious fall by grabbing wildly at the animal's mane.

Anthony Cochrane, drawing level with him, grinned at his discomfiture and, gesturing to the small, dignified figure at the Colonel's side, observed thoughtfully, "Dafir will need to look to his laurels if he tries to compete with that lad, don't you think, sir?"

"That lad, Mr Cochrane," Phillip told him, mindful of the grin, "is a young and very beautiful woman, I would have you know."

"A woman?" Cochrane gasped incredulously. "And with us, carrying a rifle? I can't believe it, sir. Why—"

"It's the truth. Her name is Selina, she was educated at a convent school in Erzeroum, speaks English, French, and Osmanli and probably Polish as well, and is of the Christian faith. She is also, according to her husband, a capable nurse and she has campaigned with him for the past two years. She—"

"Her husband, sir?" Cochrane put in, sounding shocked. "You don't mean the Colonel, do you—Colonel Gorak? For God's sake, he's old enough to be her father! I've heard the Turks like their women young but he's a European, isn't he? He told me he was Polish."

"Yes, he is." Phillip hesitated, wondering whether, after all, he had jumped to the wrong conclusion. The Colonel had not specifically stated that the girl was his wife; he had described her as "the joy of his heart" and his "most precious possession" but such descriptions could apply equally to a daughter or a wife and . . . Cochrane was right, he *was* old enough to be the father of a girl of eighteen.

"Well, possibly he is her father, Mr Cochrane," he conceded and felt an odd tightness about his throat at the thought. It continued to haunt him, hour after hour, as they rode on, for all his efforts to banish it from his mind. He recalled his conversation with young Roberts and the uncompromising warning he had issued to his ship's company and his resolution hardened. He had no right to think of any woman, he reminded himself, least of all one encountered fleetingly in such circumstances as these. He had his duty to do, he had Admiral Lyons's orders to carry out and, as soon as he had completed his mission, he must return to his ship—as Lieutenant Roberts had also had to return—and to whatever fresh task might be awaiting him.

It grew colder as they climbed higher, following a track little wider than the one by which Dafir had led them the previous day but Phillip was too preoccupied with his own thoughts to worry unduly on this account. He let his horse have its head and pick its own way and the animal did not stumble again. The Colonel set a brisk pace, sitting hunched in his saddle and seldom looking back to ascertain how those who followed him were faring. His face was drained of colour, Phillip noticed when, during one of their infrequent halts, he caught a glimpse of it. Fearing that the gallant old man might have overtaxed his strength or be suffering pain from his wound, he ventured an enquiry, to which the only reply was a curt headshake and the immediate resumption of their journey. He did not ask again and maintained his silence even though, a little later, the Colonel dropped back, looking whiter than ever, and relinquished the lead to Selina. She slowed their pace a fraction—no doubt out of consideration for the Colonel—but, in spite of this, it was a tense, nerve-straining journey, the last two hours, as the light was fading, taking its toll of them all.

Erikson, who, on his own wry admission, had never ridden a horse before, was grey with fatigue; Cochrane confessed to suffering from vertigo and renewed shortness of breath and Phillip himself, although happier on horseback than on foot, was beginning once more to experience sharp twinges of pain from his old leg wound. Even the big, stoical Thompson, whilst he made no complaint, looked worn out and spoke very little, sitting his plodding pony like a statue. Concerned for his own party and still more so for Colonel Gorak, Phillip called out to Selina to suggest a brief rest, but she shook her head and gestured to the now rapidly darkening sky.

"Soon we shall descend, Commander Hazard," she called back, over her shoulder, her English a trifle hesitant but with hardly a trace of accent. "We must make the descent while

there is still some light. If we do not, then we must remain
here during the night and it will be cold, because we are very
high up, you understand."

Reaching a point where the track widened, however, she
drew rein and waited for him to catch up with her, and he realized then that she was leading the Colonel's horse, as well as
riding her own. The old man sat very erect in his saddle and
seemed scarcely to be breathing, his eyes closed and his face
deathly pale. Phillip looked at him anxiously.

"For his sake, ought we not to stop?"

"He told me to go on. Whatever happened to him, he said
I was to go on."

"Yes, but he is ill," Phillip objected. "Is there nothing we
can do for him?"

"He was ill when we set off," Selina answered. "I told him
that he should not attempt this journey, that he had not the
strength, but he would not listen to me. It is on your account
that he left his sick-bed, Commander Hazard—because of what
you said to him. Could you not see how frail and weak he was?"
Her dark eyes reproached him and Phillip met her gaze unhappily, aware that he deserved her censure.

"I am sorry," he began. "I did not realize. I thought it was
just his arm and because my mission is urgent, I—"

"It is done now." There was a note of resignation in her
voice.

"Do not blame yourself, Commander Hazard." The Colonel
roused himself, fumbling for a flask in his saddle-bow and
Selina slipped swiftly to the ground and, unstrapping the flask,
held it to his lips. He drank thirstily and then waved the girl
away, addressing her impatiently in French. "I shall do what
I have promised. Go on, Selina, I pray you."

She bowed her head obediently. "Very well, Papa, if that is
what you wish."

Phillip heard her reply but its significance did not dawn on him until they resumed their journey, once more in single file. He had been wrong, he thought, and was warmed by the knowledge that the girl whose beauty had made so deep an impression on him was, after all, the old Colonel's daughter and not his wife. But he said nothing; Cochrane was sunk in gloom, interested in little save his own acute discomfort and, as they rode on into the gathering darkness, Phillip's brief elation faded. It did not matter, he told himself, it could make no difference to him whether Selina were wife or daughter. In a day or so, he would be on his way back to Ghelenjik and the chances of his ever seeing her again were remote.

An icy, north-east wind met them when they reached the head of the pass through which they had been travelling and they changed direction, in order to begin the descent into a rocky valley of which they could see little or nothing in the fading light. Phillip felt the cold seeping into his very bones despite the heavy sheepskin draped about him but Selina, seemingly unaffected by either wind or height, led them unhesitatingly on. One of the Circassians, on her instructions, dismounted and, giving his reins to one of his fellows, climbed up behind the Colonel, who had now slumped over his horse's shaggy neck and appeared to be barely conscious.

There was no sign of a camp in the valley below, no flickering bivouac fires and Phillip began to wonder uneasily, as his horse slithered on the steep slope, how much farther they had still to go. He did not ask but, as if she had sensed his uneasiness, Selina pulled up to wait for him and, when he drew level with her, she pointed to where, far below them, he could just discern what looked like a road, snaking its way westwards in the direction of the coast.

"That is the route by which the Russian supply trains usually come," she told him. "Serfir Pasha will have made camp above the road, on both sides . . ." her arm went out, indicating first a patch of thick woodland, a mile or so to their right, and then what Phillip could only suppose was a fold in the ground or a narrow ravine, running at right angles to it. "The men sleep on the bare ground, each one with his rifle beside him and his horse tethered nearby, and they do not light fires. The Russians have become cautious, you understand, for they have been attacked many times. Lately they have taken to sending Cossack patrols to scout the route—days before the supply train is due. Our men remain hidden and do not molest them for, if the patrols did not return to report the road clear, the supplies would not be sent."

"Then Serfir Pasha may have to wait a long time?" Phillip suggested. To his relief, the girl shook her head.

"No," she answered, kneeing her horse forward. "He has his own scouts, as well as men paid to spy on the Muscov garrisons from inside. He does not take his main force into position for an ambush until it is reasonably certain that the train will come through within two or three days. It is cold in these mountains, even in summer, Commander Hazard—too cold for men who must sleep on the bare ground without fires. Often they must wait above the snow-line, so that the patrols do not suspect their presence." She talked on, telling him of Circassian raids on isolated garrisons, and of running battles with large bodies of Russian troops sent to subdue the rebellious mountaineers, whose villages they occupied and held to ransom in an attempt to weaken their resistance.

Her understanding of the military tactics involved astonished Phillip but, he supposed, recalling Colonel Gorak's conversation with him earlier, the old man—having no one else to whom he could talk—probably gave her chapter and verse of every action in which he had been engaged.

"You speak with authority, mademoiselle," he said. "No doubt the Colonel, your father, recounts the details of all his campaigns to you?"

Selina Gorak turned to look at him, her lips parted in an odd little smile, at once amused and pitying, as if what he had said reflected little credit on his intelligence. "No," she returned quietly. "I speak from—how do you say it in English? From personal knowledge, from experience, Commander Hazard."

"But do you mean . . ." Phillip was stunned, staring incredulously into her lovely face which, beneath the high-crowned fur cap, still seemed to him the epitome of youthful purity and innocence. "You surely cannot mean that *you* have taken part in these raids and ambushes?"

She bowed her head. "Yes, in many of them. Since my father came to Circassia he has kept me with him all the time."

"But . . . he takes you with him on these guerilla operations?" Phillip could still scarcely believe it. "Why does he not leave you where you would be safe, mademoiselle?"

Selina looked up. In the dim light, he could not see much of her face, could not read the expression on it but her voice was harsh with pain as she said, "*Safe,* Commander Hazard! In an unguarded village, with only women and children and a few old men . . . do you have any idea what the Cossacks do, when they occupy such a village?"

"No, I . . . I don't. You—"

It was as if she had not heard him. "They are given leave to pillage and plunder, to commit rape and murder, and, when they have done, they destroy the evidence of what they have done by setting fire to every building that may still be standing. My mother died in Bayazid, not quite two years ago, in . . . in such circumstances. My father was with the army of General

Guyon, which entered the town after Bubatoff's troops had left it, on their way to Erzeroum, where I was at school until, thanks be to God, he took me away. I did not go into the town where my mother died, for which also I am thankful—I was at Kars, the main Turkish camp, where I was what you are pleased to call safe. But my father took me from there as soon as he could and since then he has not permitted me to leave his side."

"I see," Phillip responded lamely.

"Do you?" she asked, her tone now very gentle. "I think perhaps you may see—and understand—if you stay with us for a little while, Commander Hazard. This is a cruel and bitter war and the Turks, when they capture a Christian town or village, behave no better, I assure you, than the Russians. They . . ." the man who was riding with her father called out in sudden alarm and Selina jerked her horse round instantly and went to him. Phillip heard their voices but, unable to understand what they were saying, reined in his own animal and waited anxiously. It was not so cold now; they must have come down quite a considerable distance, he realized although not, it seemed, quite far enough, for the daylight was all but gone. From where he sat on his weary horse, he could just make out the group which had gathered about the Colonel— Cochrane among them—but little else, and he was not surprised when Cochrane came to tell him that Selina had decided to call a halt.

"The poor old Colonel is in a bad way, sir," his second-in-command added. "It's obvious that he can't go on. And by the way, sir, the girl *is* his daughter—I heard her call him 'Papa.'"

"Yes," Phillip answered shortly. "So did I. Where are we going to doss down for the night, do you know?"

"The girl—Selina—said something about a cave. She's gone

to look for it now, I believe. I must confess, sir, I shan't be sorry to get some sleep."

"How are you feeling, Mr Cochrane?" Cochrane's face was a white blur in the darkness and Phillip eyed him with concern, hearing the exhaustion of his voice.

"A lot better than I was, sir," Cochrane admitted. "It's the height that affects me—I find I can't get my breath."

"How about Thompson and Erikson?"

"Done up sir, both of them. They'll be glad of a few hours' sleep, too, I fancy."

"Commander Hazard . . ." Selina was beside them, gliding up like a shadow. "I have found a shelter where we may rest for the night. Lead your horses, if you please, and follow me . . . but be careful, it is a steep descent."

A slow, cautious walk, leading their horses, brought them to a narrow cleft in the rocks—hardly to be termed a cave but it stretched so far back and at its extremity, afforded such good cover that Selina decided that a small fire might safely be lighted. While the others searched for brushwood, Phillip helped to carry her father inside and the old man began to recover a little when the fire burned up and its welcome heat dispelled the damp chill of their rocky shelter. Selina, solicitous as always, knelt at his side, giving him sips from his flask and then, having carefully checked the bandage on his injured arm, piled two sheepskin cloaks on to his recumbent body and begged him to try to sleep.

To Phillip she said, as the Colonel closed his eyes, "He is not really an old man, you know, but he has been severely wounded so many times that now his strength is going, although he will not admit to it."

"I am sorry to have put so great a strain on him, mademoiselle," Phillip apologized. "But it was his decision to accompany us—I give you my word, I did not ask him to."

She smiled. "I know. As my father himself said—do not blame yourself. He will recover, when he has slept and eaten." She gestured to where two of their Circassian escort were busily engaged with a spit of meat over the fire. "Our meal, such as it is, will not take long to prepare. In the meantime, I have sent two of our men to Serfir Pasha's camp, to inform him that you are here. If he wishes to speak with you tonight, I will take you to him . . . but we shall have to make our way on foot. In darkness, it is too dangerous to go on horseback and, in any case, the horses are worn out."

"As you must also be, surely, mademoiselle?" Phillip suggested, but she shook her head, her dark hair, released from the confines of her cap, falling in a shining cascade about her shoulders. In the warm glow from the firelight, her beauty caused him to catch his breath in wonder. She eyed him gravely and then answered his question. "I am used to long marches in the mountains. But you are not, or your sailors either . . . why do you not all snatch some sleep, close to the fire? I will waken you when the food is prepared."

Phillip took her advice gratefully. It seemed, however, that he had barely closed his eyes when she shook him back to wakefulness and he sat up, rubbing the sleep from his eyes, to see Dafir standing beside her, grinning sheepishly down at him.

"The wanderer has returned," Selina said in English, her tone disapproving. "It appears that he has taken the news of your coming to Serfir Pasha already, Commander Hazard, and the Pasha is anxious to speak with you as soon as possible. He asks also that you will bring your rifles and the bullets for them, so that they may be used for the ambush . . . Dafir has been boasting of their superiority over our weapons, I imagine." She studied his face searchingly. "Do you feel able to continue the journey? You have not slept for long and—"

Phillip forced himself to get to his feet. "I'm ready to start whenever you wish, mademoiselle." He should, he knew, be feeling elated at the prospect of a swift and successful end to his mission but instead he was conscious of a keen sense of regret. By this time tomorrow, he thought, he might be on his way back to Ghelenjik, and Selina . . . the girl, as if he had spoken his thoughts aloud, laid a hand gently on his arm.

"We will eat first," she told him. "Dafir has brought men to carry the rifles and I will go with you, to interpret what you wish to say to the Pasha. My father must rest here until morning."

They ate their frugal meal almost in silence. The Colonel, who had evidently eaten before them, had dropped into a deep sleep and Selina was careful not to rouse him.

"Leave your sailors here with him," she advised. "It is not very far to Serfir Pasha's camp—we can return, when you have spoken with him."

Cochrane glanced questioningly at Phillip. "I'm game to come with you, sir," he offered. "If you want me."

"No," Phillip decided. "Stay where you are, Mr Cochrane, and do what you can for Colonel Gorak. I'll take Erikson to demonstrate the rifles . . . if you're fit, Erikson, my lad?"

The Norwegian was instantly alert. "I'm fit, sir. And willing . . . so long as we're not going on horseback! I'm better on my feet, sir, believe me."

They set off, ten minutes later, with Dafir in the lead. A short climb, with an icy wind in their faces, brought them to the edge of a steep, tree-grown ravine, along the sheltered side of which Dafir guided them with uncanny skill, flitting from one clump of trees to the next like a ghost and occasionally pausing to listen. The moon, which had risen while they were in the cave, came from behind a cloud after they had been walking for about twenty or thirty minutes, to bathe the surrounding countryside in pale, silvery light and make the going a great deal easier. Phillip had been feeling stiff when they started off but his short sleep and the meal he had eaten had put fresh life into him and he experienced no difficulty in keeping pace with the others. Gaining in confidence, he opened his mouth to speak to Selina, who was just in front of him, when she turned, a finger to her lips, and then motioned him to squat down beside her. The rest of the party did the same and Selina pointed, her mouth silently forming the single word: "Cossacks!"

Phillip peered down in the direction she had indicated, seeing nothing save a dark bank of shadow below the tree-line until, suddenly, the shadow moved, resolving itself into several separate shadows and he heard the metallic chink of a steel bit. A horse whinnied and a voice growled out what sounded like an order, in a language he did not understand. The whinnying ceased, to be succeeded by the soft but unmistakable thud of hooves, which gradually became fainter and finally faded altogether. Dafir rose and continued on his way and Selina whispered, her mouth close to Phillip's ear, "They have gone. Our men have orders to let them pass through our lines unmolested, as I told you. They watch but do not challenge them." She touched his arm. "Come—it is not far now."

Fifty yards along the track, a man stepped out to bar their path, flintlock rifle at the ready. Dafir exchanged whispers with him and he stood aside, waving them on and, as they filed past him, Phillip saw that two other riflemen were positioned on either side of the first, half-hidden among the trees. They encountered two other such outposts, where the same procedure was followed, emerging eventually into a clearing, denuded of trees but scattered with huge boulders ranged in apparently haphazard fashion, which constituted so perfect a defensive position that it might have been man-made.

"We are here," Selina told him and smiled, as Phillip looked about him blankly, unable to see any sign of the men and horses he had expected to find at the Circassian headquarters. Again, as if she had read his thoughts, she pointed to a tall pile of boulders to the left of the clearing, behind which the rock-wall rose, seemingly unbroken, to a height of sixty or seventy feet. "These rocks hide a network of caves and caverns," she explained, urging him towards the heaped boulders. "They are many hundreds of years old and were the hiding place and refuge of wolf packs and mountain bears. Now *we* use them for the same purpose and the wild animals must seek shelter elsewhere. There are many such caves all over the mountains which the Russians never search, because they believe them fit only for animals, but our people have worked cleverly to make them safe and habitable, as you will see. It was an idea of Serfir's, which he learnt from Schamyl." A man in the shapeless garb of a goatherd was standing with his back to an opening in the rock; Dafir spoke to him and he rolled one of the carefully balanced boulders effortlessly to one side, to reveal an aperture large enough to admit a horse and rider. It closed behind them, and Dafir led them along a dank, narrow passageway, the walls of which were encrusted with moss and lichen. It appeared to come to a dead end, but a second sentry put his shoulder to the rock wall and this, too, rolled back to admit them to a vast cavern, capable of accommodating sixty or seventy men in comfort and three times that number, if they were packed in tightly. The interior was warm and dry, illuminated by rushlights at intervals along the walls and, looking about him in amazement, Phillip saw that it was a hive of activity, as well organized as any battle headquarters he had ever entered. A few men slept, rolled in their cloaks, but the others were engaged in cleaning and priming rifles, checking and packing ammunition, and filling saddle-bags and pouches, and there was a busy to-ing and fro-ing at the far end of the cavern, where upwards of a score of horses were tied up.

"That is the Pasha," Selina said, indicating a small, dark-faced man of indeterminate age seated cross-legged in the centre of a group of about half a dozen others, to whom he was talking quietly. At first sight he was unimpressive but when Dafir drew his attention to the arrival of the visitors and he rose to receive them, he had a natural dignity and ease of manner which set him apart from his fellows and their instant obedience to any command he gave them stamped him a leader. In marked contrast to the Turkish officers of his rank, Phillip noticed that he made no attempt to stand on ceremony, and his dress was similar to that of his men, save that he wore a Cossack *cherkerska* with leather cartridge-holders across the chest, in place of the sheepskin or goats' hair mantles which most of them draped about their persons. His weapons, too, were of the highest quality, the scimitar and the pistols at his waist beautifully inlaid with gold and silver and, in addition to these, he carried a long, curved dagger, with a jewelled hilt which was obviously worth a small fortune.

He listened, without comment, to Phillip's message, which Selina translated for him. Then, after a moment's thoughtful consideration, he proceeded to fire a succession of rapid questions concerning Admiral Lyons's plans for a second expedition to Kertch, his intentions when an Allied naval squadron should succeed in gaining entry to the Sea of Azoff and precisely how much aid Mustapha Pasha was prepared to offer the Circassian tribes. Phillip answered these questions to the best of his ability, Serfir's swift and thorough grasp of the scope of the Admiral's proposals, seen in relation to the overall situation, evoking his admiration. Here was no ordinary chieftain of a brigand tribe, he thought, elated, but an experienced military commander, with courage and a shrewd brain, who could be relied upon to carry out whatever promises he might make— one, indeed, who would not give his word until he had satisfied himself that he would be able to keep it. He continued to question the proposed Turkish aid, his tone openly sceptical, and Selina translated his doubts on this score adding, in explanation, that Turkish help had, in the past, frequently fallen short of Circassian expectations.

"Serfir Pasha wonders if you are aware," the girl went on, "that we have repeatedly requested Zarif Mustapha Pasha to visit us and judge our needs at first hand, but our requests have been ignored. He asks if you can guarantee that Mustapha Pasha will come in person to Ghelenjik?"

"Tell him my Admiral is confident that he will come," Phillip answered. "Arrangements have been made for his transport by Turkish steamer from Batoum, and two of our British ships-of-war—in addition to my own—will also be at Ghelenjik on or before the eighteenth of this month. If his Excellency will return there with me, in order to confer with Mustapha Pasha and the other Circassian chiefs, I am sure that he will be able to obtain satisfactory guarantees of Turkish co-operation."

Selina translated his reply and Phillip saw the Pasha's dark face relax a little. He asked several more cautious questions, still reluctant to commit himself, and then Selina said, "Serfir Pasha wishes me to tell you, Commander Hazard, that he would gladly co-operate with your Admiral and the English Navy. He estimates that a force of between twenty and thirty thousand Circassians could be raised for the purpose of attacking the Russian held posts at Anapa, Soujak, and in the Kouban. They could, he believes, be collected within three weeks, perhaps less, and he says that Circassian officers, forced into Russian service in the Kouban, would rise with them and assist their efforts to drive out the oppressors. If this rising of the Circassian people takes place at the same times as your Admiral's attack on Kertch and the entry of a naval squadron into the Sea of Azoff, Serfir Pasha is confident that it will be successful. He—" she broke off, in obedience to Serfir's raised hand, and he spoke to her in low, earnest tones. Phillip waited, endeavouring to guess, from the expression on his face, what he was saying. It was evidently something of importance, for his lieutenants were listening with rapt attention and, when he had done, two or three of them added their voices to his, addressing Selina, who nodded her understanding.

"Well, mademoiselle?" Phillip prompted. "What does the Pasha say?"

Selina turned, meeting his gaze gravely. "He asks if, when you return to Ghelenjik, you will forward a request to your Admiral to send ships to bombard Anapa and Soujak? He says that our forces have no artillery and, if they are to attack fortified places, they must have the support of guns or they will be throwing their lives away to no purpose. He will ask the Turks for field guns, with trained gunners to man them, but he would feel more confident if he could be assured that some English ships were at hand to help him if need be."

Phillip smiled into her anxious eyes, recalling the Admiral's final instructions to him before he had left the *Royal Albert* in Kertch Bay. *"If you see fit and believe such a manoeuvre necessary to impress the Circassians,"* Sir Edmund Lyons had said, *"take some of the leaders with you and fire a few broadsides at the Anapa batteries . . ."*

"I will forward His Excellency's request," he promised. "In the firm belief that it will be acceded to and I will also—provided that he accompanies me to Ghelenjik within the next two or three days—take him aboard my own ship and endeavour to disable the gun batteries at Anapa."

Selina translated what he had said and a concerted roar of approval greeted her words. Serfir's dark eyes glowed with satisfaction as the girl, turning to Phillip again, intimated his agreement to this suggestion. "The Pasha will accompany you to Ghelenjik within the time you have specified, Commander Hazard. He says that according to the information he has received from his scouts, it seems likely that the Russian supply train will attempt to pass through the Hamri Valley sometime before noon tomorrow. If it should be delayed, it will probably only be for twenty-four hours, so he asks that you will wait here until the ambush he has planned has been successfully carried out."

Phillip inclined his head. "Tell him, if you please, mademoiselle, that I will wait. And tell him also that if I and my men can be of any assistance to him tomorrow, our services are his to command."

Selina repeated his answer and the Pasha clapped a friendly hand on his shoulder, speaking at some length in his own language. "He says I am to thank you," Selina explained, smiling herself now. "You are to consider yourself his honoured guest. He is grateful that you have come to him and he promises that he will arrange for you and your sailors to occupy a safe vantage point tomorrow, so that you may watch how the Circassians make war. When he, in his turn, is *your* guest on board your ship, he will ask you to extend a like courtesy to him."

"I shall be happy to do so."

"One thing more," Selina begged. "Serfir asks if you will leave him the rifles you have brought. He has some marksmen who would like to put them to the test tomorrow."

"They are a gift from my Admiral, mademoiselle. I trust that his men will find them useful." Phillip glanced enquiringly at Erikson, who snapped smartly to attention.

"I've given them the basic instructions, sir. They won't have any trouble with these rifles."

"Good. We'll retain our own, with fifty rounds apiece, and leave the rest for the Pasha's marksmen."

Serfir Pasha accompanied them to the cave entrance, where he bade them a ceremonious farewell.

"He will send us word when the supply train is sighted," Selina said. "And, if my father is no better by tomorrow morning, Serfir Pasha will have him brought here, so that he may rest in safety."

They returned, under the reluctant escort of Dafir, by the way they had come, to find the remaining members of their small party asleep in their refuge, with the exception of the sentry, who sat by the fire, his rifle across his knees.

"We would be as well to follow their example, Commander Hazard," Selina advised, evading Phillip's attempts to thank her. "One of our men will remain on guard and I shall attend to my father, so . . ." she smiled at him warmly and, weary though he was, Phillip felt his heart quicken its beat. In the faint glow of the dying fire, he watched her kneel down at her father's side and he continued to watch her, whilst making a pretence of sleep, until the fire finally flickered into extinction and his heavy lids closed . . .

CHAPTER FIVE

Phillip was roused by someone shaking him gently. He had been dreaming, a happy, golden dream from which he was reluctant to wake, because Selina had been in it and, for a moment, he stared dazedly about him, not recognizing his surroundings, the beautiful face that peered down at him seemingly part of his dream.

"Selina," he murmured, "Oh, Selina, I—"

"I let you sleep for as long as I could, Commander Hazard," Selina told him apologetically. She thrust a cup of wine into his hand, urging him to drink it. "The others are up already and Serfir Pasha has sent word that the supply train has been sighted. Unless we go to our position at once, we shall have to stay here until the ambush is over, for he permits no one to move, once the enemy enter the valley."

Phillip sat up, roused to full wakefulness by her words. He passed a hand over the two-day growth of stubble on his chin and decided regretfully that there was no time to remove it.

"There is only our drinking water," Selina said. "No one else has shaved."

"Right—then I shall be ready to leave in a couple of minutes." He stood up, stretching his cramped limbs and then asked, as memory returned, "How is the Colonel, your father, mademoiselle?"

"He is almost himself, thanks be to God. Although"—she sighed—"I am not sure that I should give thanks for this, since he insists on riding with us, when he would be wiser to rest. However, we shall be in no danger—Serfir has sent men to escort us and we are to watch the—the proceedings from this end of the valley." She excused herself and Phillip made a hasty toilet. Emerging from the darkness of the cave, he found the sun up and the rest of his party already mounted or about to do so, including Colonel Gorak, who greeted him cheerfully, brushing aside all enquiries as to his health with an impatient wave of the hand.

"Do not concern yourself on my account—I am perfectly all right, Commander. Mount, I beg you, and let us be on our way." He looked almost himself, as Selina had said and when Phillip swung himself on to his horse, it was the Colonel who gave the order for the small cavalcade to move off.

Anthony Cochrane reined in, to allow Phillip to catch up with him. "I hear, sir," he said, "that your conference with the Pasha last night was extremely successful . . . I trust that's so?"

"Yes, I think it was, Mr Cochrane. At any rate, he's agreed to come back to Ghelenjik with us . . ." Phillip gave him a brief account of what had passed between Serfir and himself and described the Pasha's mountain headquarters at some length.

"These Circassians seem to be pretty well organized, sir," his second-in-command observed.

"They are, indeed. Mind you, they have been engaged in this type of warfare against the Russians for nearly thirty years, according to the Colonel."

Cochrane nodded thoughtfully. "Yes, he told me that it cost the Russians twenty thousand men a year to maintain even nominal control of Circassia . . . they're remarkable people, aren't they, sir? I hope they win their independence. God knows they deserve to! And talking of remarkable people—the old Colonel's a tough old bird, isn't he? Last night, after you'd gone, I was pretty worried about him—he just lay like a log and I kept getting up to feel his heart, to make sure he was still alive. And now look at him, leading us into battle!"

"We are to be spectators of the battle," Phillip told him. "As honoured guests of Serfir Pasha. And," he added, with a wry smile, "we are to extend a like courtesy to His Excellency, when we take him aboard the *Huntress* and throw a few shells into the Anapa batteries."

"Are we, sir?" Cochrane's eyes lit with a furtive gleam of amusement. He pointed ahead. "Do you see who else is leading us? I can't see young Dafir being content with the role of spectator, somehow, can you, sir?"

But Dafir, it seemed, had his orders and too healthy a respect for the Pasha to risk disobeying them. He led them to the tree-grown edge of the valley and instructed them to dismount. Leaving the horses in concealment among the trees, guarded by two of the Circassians, he led them on to the top of a steep rise, beneath which there was a sheer drop of about seventy or eighty feet to the floor of the valley. It was an excellent vantage point, well screened by rocks, and overlooking a curve in the narrow, winding road through the pass, of which it afforded a clear view in both directions and it had the added advantage of being inaccessible by any route save the one by which they had come. Phillip stretched out at full length behind the shelter of a rock and, his Dollond to his eye, studied the scene below him with keen interest.

Immediately opposite where he lay and on the far side of the road, the ground rose in a series of craggy ridges, falling to a thick belt of trees and a patch of open ground to his right, bordering the road. As far as he could see, there was no movement along the whole length of the valley. He swept the opposite side of the defile with his glass without being able to pick out a single Circassian rifleman and then, swinging the glass round, he made a careful inspection of the belt of trees with precisely the same result. From behind him, Colonel Gorak observed with satisfaction, "Well, Commander—if you were in charge of that supply train, would you have any hesitation in ordering it through the pass?"

Phillip turned, lowering his glass. "No, sir, I don't suppose I should. However, since this is a natural place to expect an ambush, I'd probably send a mounted patrol ahead of me and, if I had any men to spare, possibly some skirmishers into that belt of trees over there before I approached this point."

"The Russians will send out a mounted patrol—they have had patrols out here for two or three days and will have received negative reports from them all." The Colonel smiled. "Serfir has seen to that!"

"Are they large trains, sir?"

"They vary in size. Sometimes they consist of fifteen or twenty wagons, sometimes of twice that number, and they are usually well protected, with cavalry in front and rear and a column of infantry marching with the wagons." The old man lowered himself stiffly to the ground and came to lie at Phillip's side, "This should be a fairly large train—supplies are urgently needed at Soujak and, because they are, I think the column will make an attempt to get through."

"And you think it will make the attempt today, sir?" Phillip asked.

"Serfir does, my young friend!" The Colonel pointed to the steep, craggy slope opposite their vantage point. "There is a man behind almost every rock and fold in the ground across there—a man who has lain there, with his rifle in readiness, since first light and who will wait without betraying his presence, for hour after hour with incredible patience, until the enemy train is sighted or he is recalled."

The men of whom Selina had told him, Phillip thought, those who lay on the bare ground and did not light fires . . . "What tactics do they employ for an ambush, sir?" he questioned curiously.

"The simplest," Colonel Gorak answered, his tone oddly apologetic. "They know nothing of strategy and have no idea of what is meant by a refused flank, for example—and they have no artillery. They are not easy to discipline, either, as we Europeans understand discipline—you could not induce Circassians to advance in line under gunfire or to form square, as your British soldiers do so admirably. Yet, in his own way, the Circassian fights with great courage, I can assure you. His natural instinct is, of course, to fight for plunder . . . to strike swiftly on horseback, seize whatever he can lay his hands on and then make off with his booty as fast as he knows how. If he suffers a reverse, he will take refuge in flight, not from cowardice but rather on the principle that he who fights and runs away will live to fight another day, as your English saying has it." He sighed. "Serfir has managed to instil the rudiments of discipline into his own band of picked men, as I trust you will see for yourself before long. But . . . they are still a trifle unpredictable, by European standards, and they tend to repeat, again and again, tactics they have found successful."

"And those are . . . what, sir?" Phillip prompted.

The Colonel raised himself on one elbow and pointed below them. "That curve in the road will slow down the wagons," he said. "The men posted on the hill opposite will roll down boulders, with the object of cutting the column in two. The riflemen, who are strung out all along the ridge, then open fire on the troops guarding the wagons, forcing them to take cover. They are remarkably good shots and, being well hidden, offer difficult targets for the Russian troops' return fire. The best marksmen concentrate on the cavalry escort, to prevent any of the Cossacks going to the aid of the column and, if there is any danger of that, they hurl a few more boulders down or some of them get on their horses and charge down to draw off the escort. When sufficient confusion has been created, separate bodies of Circassian horsemen sweep in from concealment, striking simultaneously at different parts of the train and cutting the wagons off from one another. Depending on the size of the train and the strength of the escort, of course—if it is a very large train, only one part of it may be attacked . . ." he went into military technicalities and added, with a faint smile, "Their tactics are those of expediency, you understand. If they meet with unexpectedly strong opposition, they abandon their attack and, without waiting to destroy munition wagons—as we should—they simply make off. However, Serfir's spies have reported that there will be a comparatively small escort with today's train. Baron Wrangel, who commands at Kertch, is evidently expecting that your Admiral will launch an attack on him in the near future and is consolidating his forces . . . although it seems foolish, on the face of it, to risk sending a supply train if it cannot be adequately protected, don't you think?"

"Indeed I do, sir," Phillip agreed. He hesitated, a frown drawing his brows together. "Can the reports from these spies be relied upon?"

The Colonel nodded. "Usually they can, yes. Serfir's spies

have been known to report what the Russians wanted them to report but, on the whole, they are very useful and the information they provide always contains an element of truth . . ." he talked on, waxing eloquent on the subject of spies and the Circassians' type of warfare, and Phillip listened, occasionally putting his glass to his eye in order to scan the apparently deserted valley. Thompson and Erikson, he saw, when he glanced round, were lying down on his left, watching the road, their Minié rifles beside them, and Cochrane was engaged in a low-voiced conversation with Selina and two of their Circassian escort. Dafir, as he had expected, had vanished— presumably in order to position himself nearer to where he anticipated the action would be.

Phillip's gaze went back to Selina, drawn there almost against his will and he thought, as he watched the swiftly changing expressions on her mobile face, that he had met few women who could look as beautiful as she did in such circumstances as these. She was laughing now, amused by something Cochrane had said to her, her laughter gay and untroubled, her head, in its tall fur cap, thrown back to reveal the long, shapely line of her throat. Her clothing was, to say the least of it, unglamorous yet somehow she contrived to look womanly in the heavy sheepskin coat, and as fresh and wholesome as if she had just emerged from a brisk swim in some mountain pool, whereas the rest of them . . . he rubbed his unshaven chin ruefully.

"She pleases you, my little Selina, does she not?" the Colonel suggested, breaking into his thoughts.

"She is . . ." Phillip caught his breath, realizing that he had been about to say more than was politic. "She is a revelation to me," he finally admitted quite truthfully. "You are fortunate to have a daughter of her beauty and intelligence, sir."

The old man looked pleased. "How did she carry out her duties as your interpreter last night?"

"Quite admirably, sir. No one could have done better, I assure you. Her English is perfect and—"

"It should be, my dear Hazard. Her mother was English, you know—she was a sister of General Guyon."

"I did not realize that, sir." Phillip was taken aback. "I had thought—"

"That she learnt her English in an American convent school? No, my friend, she learnt it at her mother's knee. And I . . . I was fortunate also in my wife who, alas, is dead." The Colonel did not go into the manner of that death but instead, with an abrupt change of tone, asked Phillip if he was married. He shook his head, reddening and Colonel Gorak went on, with a regretful note in his voice, "You are wise. It is better, in wartime, to have no ties and I confess I envy you. Do not misunderstand me . . . my own marriage was a very happy one and, whilst my wife was alive, I envied no man. But now, for Selina's sake, I wish I were not an exile and a mercenary in the service of an Oriental power engaged in a savage war. She is the most loyal and courageous of daughters—no man could ask more of his child than Selina has given me but . . . this is no life for her, Hazard, is it? Oh, she does not complain, she insists that she is happy and that she wishes only to be with me and yet . . . if anything should happen to me, she would be alone. That is my nightmare, for she has no one else—apart from her uncle, of course. But Guyon is more embroiled in this war even than I am."

Phillip was silent, at a loss to know what to say. Until this moment he had given little thought to Selina's unusual and precarious situation, had accepted her for what she was or appeared to be and—in what he was now compelled to admit was a cowardly attempt not to allow himself to become involved—he had endeavoured not to think of her at all. Now, however, in the light of her father's distress, his conscience began seriously to trouble him. He owed a debt of gratitude to Colonel Gorak and, indeed, to Selina herself, a debt that, if it were possible, he would gladly repay . . . but was it possible? What help could he offer! Unless . . . an idea occurred to him.

"Colonel, I might be able to arrange a passage to Constantinople for her," he began. "In one of our transports, if—"

"Thank you, Hazard," the Colonel put in. "But that is not the problem—the Turks would provide transport to the Bosphorus if I asked them to, only Selina cannot go alone, you understand. I should have to go with her and my duty is here. However"—he brightened—"if your Admiral's plans succeed— if he takes Kertch, and the Circassians, aided by Zarif Mustapha, drive the enemy from Anapa and Soujak, then my task here will be at an end, will it not? I could return to Constantinople for a time—for long enough, that is to say, to see Selina married and—"

"*Married*, sir?" Phillip exclaimed, startled. He glanced involuntarily at Selina's lovely, serene face, conscious of a bitter and quite unreasonable anger welling up inside him. "But surely—"

"You are surprised?" Colonel Gorak demanded stiffly. "Is not an honourable marriage, to a good husband, what every father desires for his daughter?"

"Yes, sir, of course it is. I only—"

"I do not understand why you should be surprised, Commander Hazard. You have said yourself that Selina is a beautiful, intelligent girl. She would make any man a wife to be proud of, and I have had many offers for her hand, I can assure you." The Colonel's tone was still stiff and, fearful that he might inadvertently have offended him, Phillip's swift surge of anger faded.

"I am not surprised, believe me, sir. Indeed, I—"

"There was one in particular that I should have been happy to accept," the old man said, ignoring the interruption. "It came from a young Irish officer, Captain Patrick O'Hay, of the East India Company's Engineers, who is serving under General Cannon. He greatly distinguished himself at the capture of Guirgevo last year."

"And why did you not accept Captain O'Hay's offer for your daughter's hand, sir?" Phillip asked.

"For the simple reason that Selina would not have him," the Colonel answered, with a wry smile. "She is a good, obedient child but her head is full of sentimental notions. Perhaps I should have insisted, only it was too soon after her mother's death. I had not the heart and I was lonely and selfish in my loneliness . . . I listened to her pleas and allowed her to come here with me, which was a grave error, I am afraid." He sighed and went on, talking more to himself than to Phillip, "She sees no one but these Circassians and she has made their cause her own, which is understandable, I suppose—although it has its dangers. I do not want my Christian child in a Mohammedan harem, Commander Hazard, so I have made it clear to her that she must choose a man of her own faith or allow me to choose one for her. But whilst she goes unveiled and accompanies me on these forays of theirs, there is always a terrible fear in my heart that, perhaps, she might let her eyes stray to one of them . . . as theirs stray constantly to her. Oh, they treat her with fitting respect, none would lay a hand on her but—"

"Sir . . ." Thompson's voice broke in. "I think they're coming, sir." He spoke with commendable calm but his hand shook a little as he pointed towards the road below them. Phillip had the Dollond to his eye in an instant. At first all he could see was a small dust cloud, rising above the surface of the road, but then it resolved itself into a column of horsemen, moving at a steady trot and he said, passing his glass to Colonel Gorak, "The cavalry patrol, sir."

"Yes," the Colonel confirmed. "And not a large one. It will of course, be permitted to pass here without a shot being fired."

Cochrane wormed his way to Phillip's left side, his own glass raised. "I'd say only about fifteen or twenty men, wouldn't you, sir?"

"Twenty-two, sir," the keen-eyed Thompson supplied. Both he and Erikson had their rifles to their shoulders and Phillip said crisply, "No opening fire without orders, either of you. The patrol is to be allowed through."

"Aye, aye, sir," Thompson acknowledged. "Just sighting, that's all, sir."

They waited in silence and Phillip could feel the tension mounting as the patrol came steadily nearer. The horsemen— Cossacks, in sombre grey greatcoats, mounted on shaggy, unclipped horses and carrying lances—rode in pairs, keeping to the road and making no attempt to send scouts to investigate the belt of trees which he himself had noted as a possible source of danger, when he had first taken up his position on the heights above it. Either they did not expect an ambush, he decided, or else they were confident of the ability of the supply train's escort to ward off any attack that might be made on it . . . if, in fact, the supply train was following them through the pass. Certainly they were riding with almost arrogant confidence, their lances slung, and watching them, Phillip was puzzled, conscious of an odd premonition that all was not well. His glass to his eye, he scanned the road anxiously and, about five minutes later, caught sight of a second and larger dust cloud.

Selina forestalled his announcement, her voice, quiet and without a tremor, coming from behind him. "It is the supply train, Papa. I can see it."

"Good," her father returned, shifting his position and holding out his hand. "If I may borrow your glass, Hazard . . . thank you." He studied the approaching dust cloud for several minutes and then handed back the Dollond.

"Yes, it's the supply train all right and, at a guess, I should say it's a large one."

"Sir . . ." Erikson pointed to his left. "The Cossack patrol—they've halted, do you see, just round the bend there? And . . . they're getting off their horses. Why would they do that, sir?"

He was right, Phillip saw, and once again felt instinctively that something was wrong. The Colonel, too, was watching with a frown as the grey-coated cavalrymen abandoned their horses and, leaving the animals under guard about a hundred yards beyond the curve in the road, climbed some way up the boulder-strewn hillside, each man carrying the carbine he had taken from his saddle. Spread out in a semicircle, they took cover and waited, facing the road. Their position was good for, although they had their backs to the Circassian riflemen on the ridge above them, they were protected by the rocky over-hanging ridge and could only be fired upon from that quarter if the Circassians left their concealment and came further down the slope. The Colonel touched his arm and Phillip, who had been estimating the range between themselves and the entrenched Cossacks, guessed what he was about to say and nodded.

"We could pick them off, sir, without too much risk of ricochets, so long as the Circassians hold their positions."

"They will," Colonel Gorak assured him. "But what I am asking myself is *why* that patrol has done what it has . . . they must have a reason."

Phillip, too, had been wondering precisely the same thing. "Perhaps, sir," he suggested, "the commander of the supply train is simply taking precautions against a possible attack? This is an obvious place to set an ambush and, presuming that he knows the road, he's being careful."

"Yes," the Polish Colonel conceded, "No doubt he is . . . as I confess I should be, were I in his place. Ah . . ." he added, with relief, "The Cossack officer is going to signal to the convoy that the road is clear."

Phillip, eyes narrowed, watched the commander of the scouting party ride back to the bend in the road. He had an orderly with him and the two sat their horses in motionless silence until they, too, were able to see the head of the approaching convoy, when the officer drew his sabre and, raising it high above his head, waved it vigorously. The sunlight glinted on the naked blade and, in the distance, the answer came from the supply train in a brief flash, as an officer at its head waved his own weapon. The train was moving slowly and would probably take another ten or fifteen minutes to reach the road-bend, Phillip thought. He turned to Cochrane and said in a low voice, "We're supposed to be non-combatants, Mr Cochrane, but if those Cossacks cause trouble, I think we'd be justified in taking a hand, don't you?" Cochrane nodded without hesitation. "Right, then . . . pass the word to Thompson and Erikson, if you please, to spread out and take up firing positions. I'll give the order to open fire, if it's necessary. Warn them to watch out for ricochets—the Circassians are on that hill there and we don't want to hit any of them. Keep your shots low and only fire when there's a target in your sights."

"Aye, aye, sir." Cochrane moved across to pass on these instructions to the two seamen. As they took up their new positions, Phillip heard a rustle close behind him and glanced over his shoulder to see that Selina had slipped into Cochrane's place at his side, her long, old-fashioned flintlock rifle gripped purposefully in her two small hands. He deplored the competent familiarity with which she handled the weapon and, when she smiled at him in reassurance, he shook his head, unable to overcome an instinctive revulsion to the thought of her taking any part in what would almost certainly be violent action.

"Not you, Selina," he said in a harsh whisper. "We are enough without you."

"But I am a good shot," she told him.

"That's beside the point. Fighting and war are not for women."

Her eyes met his in innocent and faintly hurt surprise. "In Circassia everyone must fight, Commander Hazard. Not only women but children also."

"All the same, I would rather you did not fight in this battle," Phillip answered firmly. "Put away your rifle." She obeyed him with a resigned shrug, obviously unable to comprehend the reason for his request, yet anxious, if she could, to please him. "Then I will—what is it called? I will spot for you, if you will lend me your telescope."

She sat back on her heels, obedient but by no means docile, a hand held out for the glass. "In a moment," Phillip promised. "I want to have another look at the train." As he focused the Dollond on the slowly moving line of wagons, he thought suddenly of his mother and sisters. What, he wondered wryly, would they think, if they could see him now, with a girl like Selina at his side—a girl whom he had been compelled to dissuade from using a rifle to maim and perhaps even to kill her enemies? His mother, entertaining her staid and impeccably mannered guests to tea in her Kensington drawing-room, would not have approved of his present companion and would be quite incapable of understanding a woman who, on her own admission, had been more than willing to play an active part in the destruction of a Russian supply train. For that matter, he himself found it none too easy to understand the attraction Selina Gorak had for him, yet . . . the Colonel's hand gripped his arm and he thrust the problem of Selina to the back of his mind, concentrating all his attention on the advancing Russians.

The wagons, he now saw, were drawn by four horses each, with the exception of the leading one, a cumbersome and obviously heavily laden vehicle, which had six straining animals attached to its shafts. There were thirty-one—no, he checked them again—thirty-two wagons in all, preceded by four mounted scouts, with grey-coated infantrymen plodding on either side of and between the wagons. The long column was well strung out, the last in line only just coming into sight as the leading wagon approached the curve in the road. The Cossack officer, who had been waiting there, again waved his sabre to indicate that the way was clear and trotted on, the scouts falling in behind him. Phillip trained his glass on the first wagon, curious as to what cargo it could be carrying to render it so much heavier than the rest. The horses were sweating, he noticed, their driver belabouring them with his whip, and the wheels sinking so deeply into the sun-baked surface of the road as to leave distinct tracks to mark its passing. There was something odd about those tracks, his mind registered although, despite a renewed study with the Dollond, he could not at first decide what it was. Then a possible reason for their oddity dawned on him and he was conscious of a sick sensation in the pit of his stomach. He could be mistaken, of course, but . . . he thrust his glass into the Colonel's hand and said urgently, "That first wagon, sir—it has an extra pair of wheels, as well as an extra pair of horses to draw it, and it's excessively heavy. Have a look, sir, would you? Because I wouldn't be surprised to find that it's concealing a field-gun— a nine- or even a twelve-pounder, judging by the way those horses are straining. And if it is . . ." he did not complete his sentence but, after a swift inspection, Colonel Gorak lowered the glass and completed it for him.

"If you are right, Hazard," he said grimly, "then Serfir's horsemen will be cut to pieces if they attempt an attack on this end of the train. And I fear"—he raised the Dollond again— "that you may well be right. Those extra wheels do *not* belong to the wagon. Dear God in Heaven! The Russians must have received warning . . . they're expecting an ambush and—"

"Is there any way of warning Serfir?" Phillip interrupted. "Can we make a signal? His horsemen are waiting under cover of the trees, I take it, so they won't have seen that wagon clearly."

The Colonel shook his head. "If we tried to make any sort of signal from here, they would almost certainly take it as encouragement. There's only one way to stop them charging— I shall have to go to Serfir myself." He gestured behind him, down the slope, to where they had left their horses, silencing Selina's offer to go in his place with a brusque, "He would not listen to you, chérie."

"We could pin down the gunners from here, sir," Phillip said. "There are five of us, with rifles"—unconsciously, he had included Selina—"we might be able to prevent them firing their gun and . . ." his voice was drowned in the thunder of crash- ing rocks and he turned, startled, to see that a mass of boulders and loose earth was cascading down from the hillside oppo-site his vantage point, with perfect timing and almost perfect accuracy. The mass, gathering momentum as it fell and uprooting any trees and bushes which lay in its path, hurtled down to spread itself in a cloud of choking dust across the road, engulfing both the fifth and sixth wagons and cutting off the rear portion of the supply train from its head. And from the field-gun, if his guess was right and that was what the first wagon was concealing, but . . . *was* that the only gun? If the Russians had been warned to expect an ambush, would there not be others—or at least one other—similarly hidden at the rear of the long column?

He grabbed the Dollond but let it fall again. Dust, rising from the man-made avalanche, obscured his view. All he could see were men, struggling free of it and running for cover and, as a crackle of musketry from the hillside told him that the battle had now begun in earnest, he shouted to Cochrane at the pitch of his lungs to sight on the first wagon. There was no need to tell him why, for as he shouted, the muzzle of the gun came thrusting from the back of the wagon, propelled by a score of grey-coated infantrymen, who tipped the wagon over on to its side the better to bring their weapon into action with-out loss of time. The horses, cut free of their traces trotted dazedly away and, from the wagons which had given them shelter, the gunners—distinguished from the rest by their green uniforms—grouped themselves round their gun, as the horses were led back to drag it into position.

"Fire!" Phillip shouted. "Aim for the gunners and fire at will!" He sighted his own Minié on one of the green uniforms and heard four other rifles bark almost in unison but the range was long and only one of the green-clad figures staggered away from the gun, clutching a shattered arm. To his chagrin, the

Russians got off a round of grape, which was aimed accurately at the trees to his left, and beside him, reloading her long, cumbersome flintlock, Selina said with a sob in her voice, "They know—they know where our men are waiting! We have been betrayed . . ." she thrust the stock of her rifle into place against her shoulder, took careful aim, and fired again. "Too low," she added regretfully, as the smoking field-gun sent a second shower of grape into its target and the gunners sponged and started to reload.

In the distance, Phillip thought he heard the boom of another gun, coming from his right and, as he sighted on one of the green uniformed artillerymen, his mind registered the fact that there must be two field-guns, at least, with the train . . . and there might well be more. He squeezed the trigger of his Minié and knew a savage but short-lived satisfaction when the man at whom he had aimed pitched forward across the gun barrel and lay still. Two of his comrades flung his body into the dust of the road, one grabbed the ramrod he had been about to use and rammed home a fresh charge. They were working fast and well, Phillip saw, and had completed the loading of their gun before he had reloaded his rifle. Dear God, he thought, if there were two or three more guns' crews as well trained as this one in the column, the Circassians would be annihilated if they attempted to employ their usual tactics. But Serfir must surely, by this time, have realized what he was up against, he must hear the guns, even if he could not see them and . . . he drew in his breath sharply. Had not the Colonel said that, when faced with unexpectedly strong opposition, the Circassians would not press home their attack but instead were more likely to abandon it and make off, to seek safety in their mountain hideouts?

He looked round for the Colonel and Selina said, as if she

had guessed his thoughts, "My father has gone to Serfir . . . he will ride as fast as any man could, you may be certain." She had not turned her head and the cough of her rifle added a strangely poignant emphasis to her words. "Ah!" she exclaimed, raising herself on her elbows to look down into the smoke and dust below them. "I have hit their officer at last. They will not work so well now."

She was right, Phillip realized, on the first count, at all events, and would probably be proved right on the second. He was reminded suddenly of young Henry Durbanville who, in somewhat similar circumstances to these, had held off a Russian attack with a pair of Minié rifles and an almost arrogant pride in his own skilful marksmanship. Selina had the same oddly dispassionate attitude that Durbanville had displayed: indeed she—"Look!" she cried, far from dispassionate now, her voice high-pitched with emotion. "Oh, look—they are coming, they are charging down from the hill! And Dafir is leading them . . . oh, the fool! Does he not see the gun?"

From the clump of trees to his left front, Phillip saw them coming, forty or fifty Circassians on their shaggy mountain ponies, with the unmistakable figure of Dafir at their head, his scimitar drawn and his long hair flying behind him . . . driven from their concealment, he could only suppose, by the rapid and accurate fire which the Russians had directed into it. They were coming at breakneck speed down the steep slope, at an angle and well spread out, and they had chosen their moment well, for the field-gun was still being sponged and had yet to be reloaded but . . . if any of them were to survive, the gunners must be prevented from getting off another round of grape at close range.

Phillip yelled to Cochrane and, leaping to his feet, fired down at the milling green figures, reloaded and fired again, at a speed of which he had never imagined himself capable. He hit the gunlayer with his first shot, heard Thompson's voice raised in a cheer and did not consciously notice the crunch of musket balls striking the parapet a few feet below him. It was impossible to tell in the noise and confusion who was firing or from whence the shots came but, one after another, the gunners fell and, as they did so, others ran forward to take their places. They got off one more round and Phillip watched, in horror, as more than a dozen of the galloping Circassians went down before a hail of grape. A horse squealed in mortal agony, the sound rising above the thunder of hooves and the crackle of discharging rifles but then, with Dafir still at their head, the horsemen were among the gunners, hacking them down and driving them back from their gun, some of them riding at the grey-coated infantrymen who came forward, with bayonets menacingly fixed, to dispute their possession of the gun. It became a desperate, hand-to-hand struggle, with neither side giving quarter and, unable to fire without the risk of hitting their own men, Phillip shouted to his small party to cease their efforts and laid his smoking Minié down to cool.

The Cossack scouts, led by their officer, turned and charged into the mêlée, in an attempt to take the Circassians from the rear but Dafir, as if some sixth sense had warned him of the danger, was ready for them, he and six or seven of his followers meeting them with a counter-charge. Only when the Cossack saddles were empty did they break off and, shackling the gun to some riderless horses which they had rounded up, they galloped off with their prize, firing their rifles into the air with exultant yells of triumph.

"By George, sir!" Cochrane exclaimed, his voice hoarse. "That was a sight for sore eyes, wasn't it?" He came to Phillip's side, leaning against the rock parapet to mop his heated, smoke-grimed face. A fusilade of shots from somewhere below peppered the rock and sent a shower of splinters uncomfortably close to their faces and they both ducked down hastily.

"It isn't over yet," Phillip warned. "There's at least one other field-gun at the rear of the convoy, I think. I'm pretty sure I heard it open up a short while ago—though I confess I can't see it. Can you?"

Cochrane, still breathing hard, shook his head. Joined by Thompson and Erikson, they peered down at the road. Shots were still being exchanged between the Circassian riflemen—posted on the hill opposite and to their right—and the supply train escort, most of whom had taken cover, either behind their own wagons or among the boulders which had cut the train in two. Neither side appeared to be firing with rapidity or, indeed, with much effect and most of the wagons were or seemed to be undamaged, as far as Phillip could make out. He moved across to his right, beyond the pile of earth and rocks in the centre of the road but, even with the aid of his Dollond, he could not see a second gun.

"I must have imagined it," he said to Cochrane, who had followed him. "Or else it was an echo from the gun Dafir has just captured so splendidly. Although I could have sworn . . ." he broke off, frowning, still not quite convinced in his own mind that he had imagined the deep, booming sound he had heard. If the Russians *had* received warning of the ambush, he asked himself, and if they had intended to turn the tables by setting a trap of their own for Serfir's guerillas, surely they would have added more than one light field-gun to the supply train? They had obviously gone to considerable pains in order to conceal the gun at the head of the train and had doubled the number of artillerymen required to serve it, so therefore . . . Phillip grasped Cochrane's arm. "I think we had better make quite sure there are no more guns, Mr Cochrane. Check your ammunition, if you please." He glanced at the two seamen. "How many rounds have you got left, Thompson?"

"Twenty-two, sir," Gunner's Mate Thompson answered promptly.

"Twenty-four, sir," Erikson said.

"And you, Mr Cochrane?"

"Only eighteen, I'm afraid, sir."

"And I have twenty . . . we shall have to choose our targets carefully." Phillip slung his Minié and prepared to move on.

"There's some spare ammunition with the horses, sir," Erikson volunteered. "The Circassians we left to guard them should have about fifty rounds of Minié ball apiece. Shall I get as many as they'll part with and come after you?"

"Yes, do that, Erikson, if you please," Phillip agreed. "Be as quick as you can—you'll find us farther along this ridge"—he pointed—"I want to check the rear wagons in that supply train."

"Aye, aye, sir." The Norwegian was off down the steep slope and Cochrane asked diffidently, "Where's the girl, sir—the Colonel's daughter—do you know?"

Phillip turned in shocked dismay. "Isn't she here?" Fool that he was, he reproached himself wrathfully, not to have noticed that Selina was no longer with them! Thrice-damned fool, not to have taken better care of her in her father's absence, instead of imagining guns that probably did not exist . . . "Did you see where she went?"

"I'm afraid not, sir," Cochrane began, "I—" Thompson put in quietly, "She slipped away just after the Circassians took that gun, sir. I caught a glimpse of her out of the tail of my eye, but I thought she was going down to get the horses, so I didn't try to stop her. I'll have a look . . ." he moved lower down the slope, slithering awkwardly in his haste and then called back reassuringly, "All right, I can see her, sir. She's coming back with Erikson and one of the Circassians." He returned breathless but smiling to where Phillip and Cochrane were waiting. "Must have realized we'd be running short of ammunition and gone to get some for us. She's a bright young lady and, my word, sir—she can use that rifle of hers! I've not seen better shooting for many a day, sir, and that's a fact."

Phillip felt relief flood over him as he recognized Selina coming towards him, tackling the steep, rock-strewn slope with the graceful ease of one to whom climbing was—or had become—second nature. She seemed scarcely to pause and, when she reached him a few minutes later, her cheeks attractively flushed from her exertions, he held out both hands to her in welcome, not caring what Cochrane and the others might read into the gesture. The Circassian who was with her, a tall, raffishly handsome young man in a grey astrakan cloak and cap, was a stranger and, as he dumped a leather bag of Minié cartridges at Phillip's feet, the girl said, smiling at her companion, "This is Serfir's son Yusef, Commander Hazard. He says that my father attempted to cross the road, in order to reach Serfir and warn him of the gun, but it was impossible. The Muscovs—the Russians, I mean—have a strong rearguard, which is spread out for half a mile or more along the road, and—"

"Where is Serfir, Selina?" Phillip asked.

She pointed. "He is on the other side of the valley with his horsemen, hidden among the trees. My father rode on, with the intention of trying to work his way round the rearguard, but Yusef has sent a rider to recall him. He says there is now no other gun."

"No other gun? But—"

Selina's lips parted in a smile of singular radiance as they rested on the young Circassian's bent head. "Oh, there *was* a second gun . . . and it might have lost us the day but fortunately, after it had fired only once, it blew up. Yusef thinks that it was damaged when our men rolled down the boulders."

Once again Phillip was conscious of a feeling of relief. As Selina had said, it was a fortunate accident—fortunate for Serfir's horsemen, at all events—and one the Russians could hardly have foreseen. With both guns out of action and the road ahead blocked, the supply train could now have little or no chance of reaching its destination. Indeed, unless the escort put up a very spirited resistance or took refuge in retreat, the whole long line of wagons could scarcely escape destruction when Serfir decided that the moment had come to unleash his mounted men in search of plunder. But . . . he listened. The escort was *not* putting up a spirited resistance. All the firing was spasmodic now and, clambering back to his vantage point on the cliff-top, he saw that most of it was coming from the Circassians. The Russian infantrymen, although under reasonably good cover, were not replying, either because they were short of ammunition or . . . Phillip took out his Dollond.

They had suffered a number of casualties, it was true, but not enough, surely, to cause them to give up the struggle? Puzzled, he swept the length of the supply train, wagon by wagon, with his glass. Judging by the number of opened cases scattered about, they were in no danger of running out of rifle ammunition—why, then, were they refusing to return the Circassians' fire? And why—with a large enough escort to cover their retreat—why were they making no attempt to bowse round the wagons and return by the way they had come? Because they weren't; the wagons all faced the barricade of boulders and earth which had split the column in two and, apart from those which had been buried or cut off, there appeared no reason why the rest could not be removed out of range . . . Phillip stifled an exclamation, as he turned his glass towards the rear of the train. As Selina had told him, the Russians had a strong rearguard, composed mainly of Cossacks, strung out for some distance along the road to his right, out of range of the Circassian riflemen on the hillside. The Cossacks had not dismounted, he saw; they were clustered about the last wagon in the train, as if determined to defend it against attack. This wagon had not entered the narrow defile from which the ambush attempt had been launched and it could very easily have been turned and driven to safety but, instead, it was now starting to move slowly towards the defile . . . unless his imagination was once more playing tricks on him. Phillip wiped the lens of his Dollond on the cloth of his sleeve and again raised it to his eye, every instinct he possessed crying out to him that his fear that this was a trap was about to be justified. There was a movement beside him and Selina's soft voice broke into his thoughts. "Something troubles you, does it not, Commander Hazard?"

"Yes," he answered. "Perhaps I am being unduly suspicious but I think that this train has been sent—not with supplies—but in a deliberate attempt to wipe out Serfir's guerillas . . ." he gave her his reasons in a few clipped words and saw her eyes widen in shocked surprise. "Will you tell the Pasha's son what I have told you?"

She did so, without hesitation. Yusef listened, his expression sceptical at first but, when Phillip lent him the Dollond and he was able to see for himself that the last wagon and the Cossack rearguard were, in fact, moving closer to the rest of the beleagured train, his expression changed and his voice held a note of apprehension as he gave Selina his answer. "Yusef says," Selina translated, "that he shares your suspicions. But he does not know what we can do. There is no time to send riders to warn his father and the horsemen up there will be getting restive. They will charge soon and nothing will hold them back—unless they see that the Russians have guns." She looked up at him, her eyes trusting and unafraid. "What should we do, Commander Hazard?"

Aware that they were all watching him—Yusef and Selina, Cochrane and the two seamen—Phillip hesitated, his brain racing. Something, he knew, had to be done and done at once but, recalling what the Colonel had said about any signal almost certainly being taken as encouragement, he dismissed the possibility of attempting direct communication. If Serfir's horsemen were already restive, then shouts, waves or even a rifle shot might send them to their death in a wild, undisciplined charge that could not be stopped but . . . what had Selina said, a moment ago? *They will charge soon and nothing will hold them back, unless they see that the Russians have guns . . ."* of course, that was it, that was all they could do. They must force the Russians to reveal those guns, if any guns existed. There were seven of them and, thanks to Selina and Erikson, they had plenty of Minié ammunition . . . his decision reached, Phillip told Selina in English what he intended to do and he was already moving along the ridge at a run, with Cochrane pounding after him, whilst she was translating what he had said to Yusef. The Pasha's son called out something and vanished momentarily from sight but, as Phillip got into position and raised his Minié to his shoulder, Selina said, flinging herself against the rock at his side, "Yusef has gone to get more men— the horse-minders, any he can find. He says we are too few."

Perhaps they were, Phillip thought, but at least they could try to create confusion in the enemy ranks, if nothing more.

"Rapid fire," he told Cochrane. "Into the top of that last wagon. If there's a gun there, we'll smoke the gunners out."

His tactics—those of expediency, like the Circassians', he reflected wryly—proved initially ineffective. The marksmanship of his small party was good, however, and, just as Yusef came dashing up the slope to join them, with another nine or ten of his countrymen at his heels, they gained a lucky and unexpected success when a reserve of powder blew up, shattering one side of the wooden wagon. It did no appreciable damage to the gun which, as he had suspected, was concealed beneath it but, to the accompaniment of excited cheers from the newly arrived Circassians, the piece was hauled out from beneath the wreckage and, surrounded by a milling throng of artillerymen and Cossacks, dragged clear and into the open.

Its crew, with commendable speed, commenced firing and Phillip himself could not refrain from letting out a derisive cheer when a shower of grape struck the cliff below him. The gunners, it seemed, had panicked and were firing—at extreme elevation and with scant chance of scoring a hit—on his own virtually impregnable position, instead of laying their gun on the main body of Circassians on the opposite side of the valley.

An officer, limping from a wound in his leg, endeavoured to rectify his men's error, striking at them with the flat of his drawn sword in an effort to hasten them and the gun was resited a moment or so before he fell to a spent rifle-ball, which ricocheted at an acute angle into his chest. The gun was in full view—Serfir's horsemen could scarcely fail to see it now— and, in a general panic he had not anticipated, Phillip observed that two other light field-guns were being hauled from their concealment. From the other wagons, men were pouring into the road—grey-coated infantrymen, Cossacks, and here and there more green uniformed gunners. The whole train, he realized, had been a veritable arsenal, with at least as many men hidden inside the wagons as there had been marching openly beside them.

Fire from the hillside opposite had slackened and, as the guns ranged on this target and on the belt of trees to his right, the firing from the hillside ceased altogether and Phillip was again reminded of something the Colonel had said. *"If they meet with unexpectedly strong opposition, the Circassians abandon their attack and without waiting to destroy munitions, as we should, they make off . . . on the principle that he who fights and runs away will live to fight another day."* Well, in the circumstances, this was not such a bad principle, he thought philosophically, as he watched a line of Russian infantrymen, with bayonets fixed and in skirmishing order, prepare to start up the rough, boulder-strewn hillside in what would almost certainly prove an abortive attempt to bring their elusive opponents to bay.

Serfir's men had not won a victory; they had neither plunder nor territorial gain to reward them for the long, cold hours they had waited for the supposed supply train to make its appearance but, on the credit side, they had not fallen into the trap the Russians had set for them and there had been no wholesale slaughter. Phillip smiled to himself. As a result of today, there must be a strong possibility that Serfir would welcome the opportunity offered by the Turks to engage in hostilities on a wider scale and thus be willing to return with him to Ghelenjik without too much delay, in order to talk with Mustapha Pasha and his fellow chiefs. Indeed, he . . . Yusef clapped a hand on his shoulder. He, too, was smiling and he said, in hesitant French, waving in the direction the Russian infantrymen were about to take, up the hillside, "They will find no one. Their guns fire only at trees. It is finished." He jerked his dark head towards the slope at their backs, indicating that it was time they made their own retreat and, as Phillip got up to follow him, he realized, with some surprise, that the light was beginning to fade. He glanced enquiringly at Selina. "Where are we going? Are we not to wait for your father?"

She shook her head. "Yusef thinks it best that we return to the cave where you met Serfir last night. My father must, after all, have managed to cross the road to join him, so we will wait for them both there, if you do not mind. They will have a long ride but they should be with us again in an hour or so."

"We are in your hands," Phillip told her. "But I must endeavour to persuade Serfir to leave with me tomorrow or the day after, Selina, because there's not much time. May I count on your help in persuading him?"

"Of course," she promised readily, giving him her shy, charming smile. "But after all that you have done today—and in the light of what the Russians attempted to do—I do not believe that Serfir will be hard to persuade. Also, you have a new ally—Yusef is already your friend. He will add his persuasion to yours, if it should be needed. Both he and his father, the Pasha, are eager to accompany you when you take your ship to shell Anapa, you know."

"Are they? I'm delighted to hear it." Phillip's flagging spirits lifted as he followed her down to where they had left the tethered horses.

CHAPTER SIX

The whole party, British and Circassian alike, were in cheerful mood when they began the ride back to Serfir Pasha's mountain headquarters.

Despite their weariness, a spirit of optimism prevailed. Even when they were joined by four more Circassian horse-minders, with a string of about a dozen spare horses, Phillip noticed that no one enquired the fate of those who had set out earlier that day, on the now riderless horses, in order to do battle with the enemy. Instead they laughed and joked with one another and, when Erikson expressed guarded pleasure at the prospect of riding instead of walking, it brought a guffaw from the normally taciturn Thompson.

"Horse-back riding's not so bad, once you get the hang of it, my lad," the gunner's mate assured him, with conscious superiority. "I was an apprentice in a racing stable in New-market before I joined the Queen's Navee"—he grinned—"But I grew a mite too tall and put on too much weight to make a jockey. Pity, in a way . . . not that I regret it, mind you, but I'd have liked to ride a Derby winner."

Erikson echoed his shipmate's grin. "And I was a school-teacher, believe it or not, Gunner's Mate," he said wryly. "An unambitious, well fed, neutral schoolmaster in a beautiful mountain village called Djupvenshetten!"

They both laughed and Thompson said, addressing Phillip, "Talking of being well fed, sir . . . d'you suppose they'll feed us, when we get back to that cave of theirs? I reckon I could even relish goats' meat now—although I'd give a month's pay for a real man-sized helping of plum-duff and that's the Gospel truth, sir."

"So would I," Cochrane agreed feelingly. He, too, turned to Phillip. "Is there any prospect of our starting back to the ship tomorrow, do you think, sir?"

"I hope so, Mr Cochrane—provided the Pasha is willing to accompany us, of course. We can't leave without him. But"— Phillip's smile was warm, as he looked from one to the other of them—"you've done well, my boys. I'll promise you one thing, when we're back aboard the *Huntress*—all three of you shall . . ." he was interrupted by the thunder of galloping hooves, coming from a tree-grown depression in the ground— hardly wide enough to be termed a valley—slightly ahead of them and to their left. By common consent, the whole party cantered across to see what was afoot and there was a startled cry from Selina.

"Look!" she bade Phillip unsteadily, when he drew rein beside her on the lip of the depression. "Oh, look—it is one of our horsemen, with the Cossacks after him! He must be wounded because he . . ." her voice broke on a sob. "Holy Mother of God, it is my father!" Yusef joined them and she turned to him, white faced and weeping, to repeat her assertion in a spate of incomprehensible words.

In the gathering dusk it was hard to be sure who the fugitive was but, as he came nearer and emerged from the shadow of the trees, Phillip saw that there was a tattered fragment of white cloth—which might once have been a sling—dangling from his right arm. He could not bring himself to confirm

Selina's shocked claim to recognition, although there was little doubt in his own mind that she was right and that it could only be her father. The Colonel was leaning forward, clinging to his horse's shaggy mane and, as the gallant little animal bounded forward, his hunched body swayed from side to side, as if he were making desperate efforts to keep himself in the saddle.

Less than twenty-five yards separated him from a yelling band of some forty or fifty Cossacks, who pounded after him, strung out in an extended line, the leaders with lances lowered in anticipation of a swift end to their chase. It was obvious that they could have ended it at any moment they chose, but instead, they were playing with their hapless quarry, driving him this way and that, now allowing him to gain a few yards and then, with derisive shouts, cutting off his escape and forcing him to return by the way he had come. They sounded for all the world like a pack of baying hounds with their kill in view and Phillip's blood ran cold as he listened, his brain racing as he sought for some way—any way—in which to distract them from their hunt, at least for long enough to enable the brave old Colonel to elude them.

He was aware that he could count on no acts of outstanding bravery or sacrifice from the dozen or so Circassian horse-minders whom Yusef, the Pasha's son, had recruited. They were not all of the calibre of Dafir and had not the Colonel himself said that they would never attack, if the odds were against them? The odds were heavily against them now, so that a charge was out of the question . . . although Yusef looked capable of leading one. In any case, they were too few for such a measure to be effective but they could all shoot and, from the slope below them, the range would not be extreme and there was plenty of cover.

Phillip turned to Cochrane, waiting alertly beside him. "See that ridge down there, beyond the clump of trees to our right, Mr Cochrane? Get every man you can dismounted—leave a couple with the horses—and spread them out along the ridge. Open fire on those Cossacks as soon as they come within range and aim for the leaders' horses. But for God's sake go easy with the ammunition—we've none to spare, so every shot has to count. Here"—he thrust three or four rounds into his pocket and gave Cochrane his cartridge pouch—"you'd better take this. I'll reclaim it when I join you. When you're in position, yell your heads off, all three of you . . . cheer, anything you like, and get the Circassians to do the same. Make it sound as if there are a hell of a lot more of us than there are, understand? Right then, off you go . . . and good luck to you." Cochrane was already off his horse and eagerly unslinging his rifle. "One thing more," Phillip warned, before letting him go. "If anything should happen to me, it'll be your responsibility to take Serfir to Ghelenjik. That and nothing else, Mr Cochrane."

Cochrane gave him a crisp "Aye, aye, sir," and with the two seamen at his heels, set about assembling his small force. He wasted no time and Thompson and Erikson dealt none too gently with any who displayed reluctance to obey his shouted but unintelligible commands, and, seeking to make his task easier, Phillip called to Selina to translate for him. She did so, in a flat voice devoid of all feeling and he sensed, rather than saw, that she was edging her horse towards the top of the slope.

"Stay where you are!" he bade her harshly and was shocked when she turned her head and he glimpsed the stark misery in her tense white face. "I need you here," he added more gently. "To tell Yusef what to do and to take those spare horses to—"

"Horses!" She flung the word at him with blazing scorn. "Yusef knows what to do, better than you do. And my father needs me . . . can't you see that? The Cossacks are making sport with him, hunting him like an animal and you imagine you can stop them with rifles! I am going to him . . ." without waiting for his reply, she started down the slope, her horse slithering over the loose stones and rubble with which it was strewn.

"No!" Phillip exclaimed, appalled. "Come back, Selina! In God's name, come back!" She ignored his plea and he had no choice but to follow her, the Minié he had just unslung still clutched in his hand. Small chance he would have of using it with any accuracy on horseback, he thought ruefully, but he could not abandon the weapon, so he looped its leather sling over his shoulder again and started to coax his unwilling horse down the steep hillside after Selina. The animal slipped on the treacherous surface, almost throwing him over its head but he managed somehow to drag himself back into the saddle. Selina was already so far ahead of him that he began to despair of his ability to catch up with her but he pressed on, obstinately determined to bring her back if he could or, if he could not, then to keep her in sight, at least until reasonably certain that she was out of danger.

There was the sharp crack of a rifle, coming from behind him, then a second and a third, from which he guessed that Yusef's horse-minders must be firing from the top of the hill. The fools! They were wasting ammunition—the Cossacks were out of range on the far side of the valley and making such a row themselves that they probably would not hear the shots. He hoped fervently that Cochrane would be able to control those of Yusef's men whom he had taken to the ridge with him—make them hold their fire and start cheering and kicking up a shindy at the right moment. It was a pity he hadn't had time to tell Yusef to let the spare horses loose and send them galloping down through the trees, when Cochrane opened fire, in an attempt to confuse the Cossacks. Everything depended on confusing and taking them by surprise . . . hitting them hard when they were least expecting to come under attack and then holding them, in order to give the Colonel his chance to escape. Always supposing, of course, that they did not bring their hunt to its fiendish and bloody conclusion without returning to this side of the valley, within range of Cochrane's waiting riflemen. They were making enough noise to suggest that, perhaps, they had ended it and . . . a prey to sudden fear, Phillip reined in, to risk an apprehensive glance across the shadowed valley.

But it was not yet over. The Cossacks were coming back, he saw, still driving their quarry in front of them to the sound of shrill yelps and catcalls . . . so there was still a chance, if the poor old Colonel and his rapidly tiring horse could keep going for a little longer. He kicked his own horse into a reckless canter and, within earshot of Selina at last, again called out to her to come back or to pull up and wait for him. Either she did not hear or had chosen once more to ignore him, for she rode on at a furious pace, her gaze fixed on the lonely, fleeing figure below them. Heedless of her own safety, she urged her horse on, her long, dark hair streaming out behind her and her light weight and superior horsemanship setting Phillip a hopeless task, as the gap between them widened.

"Selina!" he shouted despairingly. "You can't help him alone . . ." and then he saw her small, erect body stiffen, as the Colonel's horse met some obstacle in its path and stumbled. It recovered almost miraculously and struggled up, its flanks heaving, urged on by mocking yells from the pursuing Cossacks. One of them, a black-bearded giant, spurred ahead of the rest, to prod the labouring animal with the tip of his lance, gleefully swinging round in a half-circle in order to pluck the Colonel's fur cap from his head by the same means. The man's whoop of triumph, as he turned to rejoin his comrades with his trophy held arrogantly aloft was suddenly more than Phillip could stomach. Feeling a savage anger catch at his throat, he jerked his own mount to a standstill, unslung the Minié and, raising it to his shoulder, sent a wild shot echoing towards the line of galloping riders.

He had taken very hasty aim, had fired more to give vent to his outraged feelings than in the hope that his shot would be effective and bit back an incredulous gasp when he saw the huge Cossack clutch his chest, then slide slowly from his saddle into the path of the shouting, jostling horsemen. There was no time for them to turn aside and the giant's shriek of terror ended abruptly as the thundering hooves pounded his body to a bloody pulp. The horses passed without checking speed, leaving behind them a shapeless mass which bore little resemblance to a human form and Phillip permitted himself a grim little smile, as he saw the Colonel's fur hat—crushed but still recognizable—go rolling across the rocky ground in their wake.

A moment later a fusilade of shots came from the ridge above him and to his right and he roused himself from his shocked contemplation of the hat with the realization that Cochrane, with perfect timing, had opened fire on the enemy. The first volley emptied three more Cossack saddles and the remainder, taken by surprise at the unexpected outcome of their bloodthirsty game, instantly abandoned it, as he had prayed they would. They reined in, hesitated, and then wheeled to mass into two tightly packed ranks, ready to receive what they obviously took to be an attack of considerable strength on their flank, their eyes warily searching the sloping side of the narrow valley for a glimpse of their assailants.

Even in the fading light, it would not take them long to discover that they were being challenged by a mere handful, Phillip knew, and when they did . . . he shivered involuntarily. For the moment, however, the challenge had brought them to a halt and won a brief respite for the Colonel—if only the valiant old soldier was not too badly wounded to take advantage of it and make good his escape. His horse had come to a standstill about two hundred yards from the Cossacks, but Selina was moving down the slope towards him, skilfully weaving her way through a clump of trees, now vanishing into a patch of shadow, now briefly coming into view again, where the trees thinned. She was having to make a detour to avoid coming into Cochrane's line of fire but she was going very fast and should come up with her father before long. Satisfied that she was in no immediate danger, Phillip turned his attention to what was happening in his own vicinity.

The Circassians were doing all in their power to create the impression that they were about to attack in force, the wild battle cries they uttered waking blood-curdling echoes from the surrounding hills and mingling effectively with the deep-throated British cheers of his own men. The sound would undoubtedly have struck terror into the hearts of less experienced troops but the Cossacks, although still wary, were evidently not deceived by it. They held their ground, pistols and carbines out as they started to return the fire directed against them with a straggling volley, aimed at any targets they could see. They did not dismount but remained sitting their horses, ready to make a rapid withdrawal should this be necessary or, if it should not, then to charge and try to come to grips with their as yet unseen foe.

About a dozen of them—chosen marksmen, presumably—cantered off to right and left of the main body and, reins looped over their arms, led their horses into the cover of the trees and bushes with which the foot of the valley was lined. Realizing that their presence might well make his own position untenable, Phillip moved into the shelter of a rocky outcrop, dismounted and tied his horse to a stunted bush growing out of a cranny in its broken, uneven surface. He reloaded his Minié, experiencing a moment of uneasiness when he felt for his pouch and then recalled that he had given all his spare ammunition to Cochrane. However, his young second-in-command was making better use of it than he could have done, and he had three rounds left, in addition to the one he had just rammed into the barrel of his rifle, which would have to suffice until he could join Cochrane and his party on the ridge.

Judging by the rapidity of the fire they were keeping up, their ammunition would not last much longer than his own meagre supply, but they had done better than he had dared to hope . . . and all credit to Cochrane for that. The boy had kept even the Circassians under admirable control; he had positioned them well and now, by pinning down the entire Cossack patrol and forcing them to remain on the defensive, he was effectively discouraging any attempt on their part to pursue and recapture the Colonel. All the same . . . Phillip's brows met in an anxious frown. The Cossacks were hitting back and Cochrane was heavily outnumbered. So small a force could not be expected to hold an exposed position indefinitely; some casualties were inevitable and—unless Serfir heard the firing and sent them help—they would be compelled to withdraw when their ammunition ran out. The Circassians might do so before this happened, leaving Cochrane and the two seamen on their own, and he would be powerless to stop them . . . he looked up at the darkening sky. Once he was certain that Selina and her father were safely out of the valley, he would signal

Cochrane to fall back to the top of the hill, he decided and, the Minié to his shoulder, he raised his head cautiously above the protective screen of rock. Selina should have had ample time to . . . one of the Cossack marksmen took a shot at him and the ball ricocheted inches from his head, sending a shower of rock splinters to sting his face and neck. But the man had shown himself as he took aim and Phillip squeezed the trigger of his rifle before diving back into cover, and had the satisfaction of hearing his attacker fall heavily into the undergrowth in which he had been concealed.

A furious burst of firing followed, aimed for the most part at the unyielding rock of his providentially chosen refuge. The Cossacks weren't short of ammunition, he reflected a trifle sourly, if they could afford to waste it blazing away at rocks in this senseless manner. But at least he was drawing some of their fire from the defenders on the ridge behind him, which was all to the good, although he wished that his sight of the far end of the valley had not, perforce, been so brief and inconclusive. It had looked deserted, except for a path of shadow by the edge of the trees, not far from where he had last seen Colonel Gorak, with Selina riding confidently towards him. A shadowy form, rather than a shadow, perhaps, whose resemblance to a lone and motionless horseman might well have been a figment of his imagination. But he could not be sure that he had imagined it . . . and he would, he was uneasily aware, have to make sure before he dared give Cochrane the signal to withdraw, because if the Colonel *was* still in the valley, then all their efforts to save him would have been wasted. As wantonly as those thrice-damned Cossacks were wasting their ammunition . . . Phillip rammed a fresh charge into the Minié and swore under his breath.

At all costs he must make another, more careful inspection

of the valley, before the light faded—with the Dollond this time, he told himself, so that there would be no margin for error. He hesitated, in two minds whether to attempt to fall back on Cochrane's position—from which he would have an unimpeded view—or to stay where he was and try again from the other side of the rock. He would have to abandon his horse if he joined Cochrane, since it would be madness to ride uphill to the ridge—it was too steep and he would make too much noise. His best chance would be on foot and, even then, one of the hidden marksmen might put a ball into his back before he had climbed more than a few yards. Better then, to stay here, where he was under reasonably good cover, he decided—at least until he had taken a second look across the far end of the valley. The Cossacks had not yet managed to dislodge him and, for as long as he could continue to use the Minié, they would no doubt keep their distance. With only one shot and two spare cartridges left, his rifle would not serve him for much longer, of course, but the Cossacks were not to know how little ammunition he had left. If he could hold them off until darkness fell and the party on the ridge could . . . there was a movement just in front of him and he made out the pale outline of a face in the gloom, a black-browed, bearded face, surmounted by a tall bearskin *papenka*. He fired, a split second before the Cossack recovered from his astonishment at finding him there and, at that range, he could not miss.

The face disintegrated and Phillip stared at what was left of it, the palms of his hands clammy as blood and brains spattered his own face and the front of his cloak. Dear God, he thought in horror, how close he had let the man come! He had heard no sound, apart from the crackle of musketry and the occasional shouts and cries from the ridge above him, yet the unfortunate fellow he had just killed had come within an ace

of killing him. And there were probably more of them, waiting to try the same trick—unless his shot and the fate of their
comrade had temporarily scared them off.

He wiped his brow and cheeks with the back of his hand
and waited tensely, straining his ears, then heaved the body
out of his way, hating the touch of the still warm flesh against
his own. The man's carbine fell with a clatter at his feet; he
picked it up and, almost as an afterthought, felt under the
coarsely woven *cherkerska* for the ammunition pouch and
pistol the dead Cossack had carried. The pouch, he noticed
without surprise, was almost empty; so, too, were the cartridge-
holders on the front of the *cherkerska,* but both pistol and
carbine were loaded and might prove useful, if any of the
others did make an attempt to rush him. He listened again,
half expecting them to do so, but could hear nothing to indicate an impending attack, although they were still blazing
away in his general direction. Relieved, he slid the pistol into
his belt and, preferring to trust to his own weapon for as long
as he could, propped the heavy carbine against the rock beside
him and started to reload the Minié.

He was ready for them, he thought . . . and this might be
the best chance he would have to make his inspection of the
valley. He eased the Dollond from his breast pocket, so that it
would be ready to hand, and began to edge his way along the
outcrop of rock, every sense alert. An uncanny silence had
fallen; the firing from the ridge had virtually ceased and only
a few spasmodic shots were coming from the Cossacks.
Puzzled and anxious to ascertain the cause, he reached the
vantage point he had chosen and saw, to his dismay, that the
Cossack main body had broken ranks. With the exception of a
few horse-minders, they had dismounted and were advancing
towards the slope on foot. Carbines at the ready, they spread

out in skirmishing order as they approached the trees, with the evident intention of launching a final assault before darkness enabled their enemy to escape them.

Phillip watched for a moment, cursing them impotently and then, making a swift dash from cover, waved his rifle high above his head as a warning to Cochrane to delay his withdrawal no longer. The ridge was a dim outline in the gloom and he had to shout twice before the flutter of something white answered him. He waved his rifle again in the direction of the crest of the hill and this time received a prompt acknowledgement, both from the ridge and from a mounted man—whom he took to be one of Yusef's Circassians—posted on the hilltop. Satisfied that his signal had been seen and was already being obeyed, he ducked hastily back into the shelter of the rock, as half a dozen musket balls whined overhead from uncomfortably close range. But the Cossack sharpshooters had, for once, been caught napping, he thought with elation, or else they had been too busy watching the approach of their comrades from the foot of the slope to notice him. His elation faded almost immediately, however, when they gave him their undivided attention, keeping up so heavy a fire on his position that it was impossible to use the Dollond from behind the breast-high rock. After several abortive attempts to do so, he decided regretfully that he would have to make his own withdrawal or risk being over-run by the advancing skirmishers.

He had left it a trifle late, he knew and, for this reason, wondered whether he might be wise to trust to his horse for as long as he could, making a detour through the trees to his left, out of the skirmishers' line of advance. If he had the misfortune to encounter any of those who had been sniping at him so persistently, at least on horseback he would have the legs of them and, if he did nothing else, he told himself grimly, he would try to give them a run for their money. His horse, apparently unconcerned by the shooting, was still stoically cropping the bush to which he had tethered it but, as he bent to untie the reins, the animal lifted its head and backed away from him, whinnying in sudden, inexplicable fear.

"Whoa, boy—quiet now," Phillip urged soothingly. "We're getting out of here, we're . . ." and then he spun round, as startled as his horse had been a moment before, when a cascade of earth and loose stones came rattling down the steep hillside somewhere behind him. The Minié was half-way to his shoulder but he lowered it again, with a stifled exclamation, realizing that the small landslide had been caused by a man on horseback, who was coming towards him from the top of the hill.

The solitary rider had begun his descent from just above the ridge, on which—a bulky silhouette against the skyline—another man, who might have been Thompson, was holding his rifle aloft. It was too dark to see the rider's face and Phillip's first thought was that Cochrane, displaying a foolhardy disregard for the orders he had been given, had come to aid his retreat, instead of attending to the evacuation of the men entrusted to his command. Although it was not like Anthony Cochrane to disobey an order . . . surely his second-in-command could not have misunderstood his signal or read it—and his shouts—as a call for help? Devil take the boy, he thought wrathfully. If he had misread the signal, there was no reason for him to risk his neck in this irresponsible manner—had he gone out of his mind? It was sheer lunacy to tear headlong down a slope so steep and so littered with obstacles that, even in daylight, it would have taxed the skill of the most expert horseman . . . and Cochrane's horsemanship, like his own, was far from expert. Why, in heaven's name, had he not kept under cover, taken the hill at a sensible pace? Although the light had almost gone, the Cossacks could hardly fail to hear his thunderous descent, even if they had not yet seen him . . . and by this time, the lower part of the slope would be swarming with dismounted riflemen, only waiting to fire until they could get their sights on him.

Feeling the muscles of his stomach harden into a tight, painful knot, Phillip resisted the impulse to yell out to his young second-in-command to make for the trees, as he himself had earlier planned to do. It was too late for that, much too late—Cochrane, God help him, was coming too fast to change direction now. If, by a miracle, no unseen boulder brought his horse down, there might be a chance that his speed would carry him past the waiting enemy, but it was a very slim chance and there was little he could do to help the boy. Even if he ran or rode to meet him, even if he showed himself as proof that he was in no need of rescue, it would be of scant avail—he could not draw the fire of upwards of forty Cossack carbines.

For all that he stepped out from behind the rock, aware that now it was he who was behaving irresponsibly, yet unable to stand by and watch Anthony Cochrane plunge to his death without making some attempt, however futile, to prevent it. Against the darkening skyline he could still make out the vague shapes of what appeared to be a group of men and horses but no help was, it seemed, likely to come from them and he turned his gaze back to the rider coming so precipitately towards him. It was the first clear glimpse he had had and he realized suddenly, that, whoever he was, the solitary horseman could not possibly be Cochrane. Very few Englishmen could have ridden as this man was riding . . . least of all Anthony Cochrane, who had been at sea since his thirteenth birthday.

This man was a Circassian, born and bred to the saddle, Phillip thought thankfully, and undoubtedly his skill would give him a better chance of survival than Cochrane would have had. He was a superb horseman, the movements of his body so finely balanced against those of the small, unclipped grey Tartar horse beneath him that each seemed an inseparable part of the other. He came boldly, scorning any attempt at concealment but, by reason of his speed and the twists and turns of the track he was following, he presented so difficult a target that, after a few ill-aimed shots had failed to touch him, the Cossacks held their fire. Once again an eerie silence enclosed the whole valley, pregnant with menace and Phillip watched in horrified fascination, the battle that had been raging and even the danger of his own position momentarily forgotten, as the thud of the grey's galloping hooves pounded remorselessly in his ears. It was the only sound he heard, as horse and rider came rapidly nearer—then he recognized the high-domed astrakan cap and wolfish features of Serfir's son, Yusef, and horror was succeeded by bewilderment.

Yusef was an experienced mountain fighter, imbued with all the hard-headed caution and cunning of his race—to have survived years of this type of savage guerilla warfare, he must obviously be well versed in the hit-and-run tactics that Colonel Gorak had described. Why, then, was he inviting disaster in this lone charge from the top of the hill, when he must have observed the movements of the enemy's main body and be aware that he was heading straight for a veritable hornets' nest of armed and vengeful Cossacks? Surely no Circassian—unless he were out of his mind—would take the risks Yusef was taking for the sake of a recently acquired British ally, to whom he owed nothing? For Colonel Gorak, perhaps, or for Selina . . . dear God, yes, for Selina's sake he might well risk life and limb!

But that suggested . . . Yusef suddenly changed direction. Standing high in his stirrups, he emitted a piercing banshee yell—intended, Phillip could only suppose, as a signal to those he had left behind on the hilltop—and discharged his rifle into the air. Then he let the weapon fall and, with a swift, sinuous twist of hips and shoulders, swung himself out of his saddle to continue on his way with scarcely a check, his body half-under and now protected by the shaggy body of his horse.

It was a spectacular feat of horsemanship on that treacherous, uneven slope and, as Yusef bore right-handed and headed in the direction of the trees below the ridge, Phillip came out of his brief trance with the realization that the hornets' nest was starting to erupt. To his right, a Cossack carbine spat fire, then another and another. Aiming the Minié at the nearest spurt of flame, he pressed the trigger and jumped back into the cover he had left, groping blindly along the surface of the rock for the captured carbine, which he had placed there only . . . sweet heaven, *could* it only have been a few minutes before? He shook his head dazedly, feeling as if half a lifetime had gone by since he had first taken up his position behind this rock.

His groping fingers closed about the barrel of the weapon he was seeking but his horse, startled by his sudden reappearance, took fright and reared up, sending the carbine spinning from his grasp and knocking him hard against the moss-grown wall of his refuge. Phillip grabbed the bridle, cursing under his breath as he dragged himself to his feet. Having pacified the excited animal, he broke out the last of his Minié cartridges, conscious of the futility of his action as he rammed the charge home, for now the valley was echoing to the continuous discharge of musketry and the raised and menacing voices of an enemy eager to close in for the kill.

Yusef hadn't a bat in hell's chance of breaking through them, he thought angrily, despite his spectacular and utterly inexplicable manoeuvres—and he was coming back, being driven back by a hail of bullets from the line of skirmishers, whose fire was concentrated on him almost exclusively. A few shots appeared to be aimed at some target he could not see, over to his left, but it was Yusef who was running the gauntlet of their fire with suicidal determination, he who . . . a Cossack rose from a clump of bushes, carbine to his shoulder. Like his comrade before him, he had crept up stealthily and come very near to the base of the rock, obviously not expecting it to be defended. Phillip fired an instant before the man could bring his weapon to bear on Yusef's sweating horse and the high-pitched whistle of the Minié bullet, streaking towards its target, was succeeded by a muffled scream.

But this could not go on, he knew and, the now useless Minié still gripped in both hands, he waited, sick with despair, for the inevitable end . . . the end, it seemed certain, for Yusef and probably for them both, unless he could make his escape before the enemy skirmishers overran his position. It went against the grain to abandon Yusef to his fate but he had a mission to perform, Phillip reminded himself, eyes and ears straining into the misty darkness for the first warning of what was to come. Serfir must be escorted to Ghelenjik for the all-important conference with the Turks and, little though he relished the prospect of having to bring news of the death or capture of his son to the Circassian chief, it was his clear duty to do so . . . and, in spite of this, to hold Serfir to his promise. Such a responsibility could not properly be delegated to Cochrane and there was nothing he could do to change the course of events if he remained on this bleak hillside, armed only with a pistol. He could not help Yusef, and the Cossacks, he was only too well aware, would show him no mercy if they found him there, virtually defenceless . . . but he had been lucky, he thought, with a sudden upsurge of hope. The skirmishers had come no nearer and that would give him a little leeway.

Escape was possible, provided his luck held—his horse was standing quite quietly now and if he made a break for it on horseback, he might get away before they suspected his intention. Even on foot, he would stand a fair chance of gaining the ridge before they saw him and . . . some instinct, stronger than reason, made him hesitate and his new-born hope abruptly faded. Above the exultant yells of the Cossacks he heard the sound for which, subconsciously, he had been listening—the unmistakable sound of a heavy body crashing down, not very far away, on the slope behind him. It struck chill into his heart and he sensed, before he turned to look in the direction of the sound, what he would see . . . a shot or some unexpected obstacle had, at last, brought Yusef's horse to its knees. The animal bellowed in pain and, a grey blur in the fading light, rolled over, its legs threshing wildly. He waited and then realized to his dismay that the Pasha's son was pinned beneath it unable, for all his frantic efforts, to free himself.

But at least he was alive . . . without pausing to consider the consequences, Phillip made a dash for the stricken rider, covering the thirty or so yards of rock-strewn ground which separated them bent almost double. The Cossacks did not see him until he was more than half-way across and then they blazed away at him with more speed than accuracy. The poor light was not conducive to good shooting and, although musket balls whined over his head like a swarm of angry bees, he reached his objective unscathed, to fling himself face downwards behind the fallen horse. It needed only a glance to tell him that the grey was done for, although it was still valiantly struggling to get to its feet. He waited for a moment to recover his breath, hoping that, for Yusef's sake, the unfortunate creature might somehow manage to do so but blood was pouring from a wound deep in its chest and he could see that its off foreleg was broken. He felt for the pistol in his belt, intending to put an end to its struggles when, to his relief, the grey twitched suddenly and lay still. Yusef said something to him, in a language which sounded like French but be scarcely heard him, as he heaved and tugged at the dead weight of the animal's quarters, his hands sticky with blood.

"Leave me . . ." the Circassian repeated, quite clearly and distinctly, in French. "Look to yourself. They are coming, they . . ." Phillip got his shoulder against the saddle and, using his Minié as a lever, managed at last to raise the horse's limp hind-quarters high enough to take advantage of the camber of the slope on which it lay.

"Now!" he gasped urgently, feeling the dead weight yield, and heaved with all the strength he could summon. "Now, Yusef!"

The shaggy body slithered downwards for a foot or two and Yusef was able to free his trapped limbs, as the stock of the Minié cracked under the strain and the buckling barrel broke away from it. Yusef rolled clear just in time and, still lying on his back, passed anxiously questing fingers down the length of his right leg, cursing loudly and fluently in his own language as he did so. Phillip abandoned the Minié and gestured to the rocky outcrop behind which he had sheltered for so long. The Cossacks' fire had slackened a little but one or two shots were coming alarmingly close.

"Can you walk?" he asked in English, unable to think of even these simple words in French just then, but Yusef understood the gesture, if not the question, and a gleam lit his dark eyes when he noticed the tethered horse. He inclined his head in assent and, moving with a lithe agility Phillip had not expected of him after his fall, led the way back to the shelter of the rock, gliding across the rough ground like a shadow and making skilful use of every bush and boulder he encountered. He limped a little but that was all and, following him less skilfully, Phillip came under so concentrated a fire that he was compelled to crawl the last twenty yards on his stomach, with musket balls peppering the ground all round him.

When he finally reached the rock, spent and breathless, Yusef was waiting for him, the horse already untethered and its rein looped over his arm.

"You permit me?" he enquired. His French was hesitant but his tone quite the reverse and Phillip stared at him in bewilderment.

"You mean . . ." it was an effort to force his tired brain to translate the words. "You want my horse?"

"I regret the necessity," Yusef told him. "But yes." He pointed to the sky, from which the last furtive glow of daylight was fading. "The accursed Cossacks will go very soon—they will not stay to face us in darkness. You will be safe if you remain here . . . you are armed?" Phillip indicated his pistol and saw the Circassian frown. "Do not show yourself," he advised and swung himself into the saddle. "They will suppose you dead . . . and leave you alone. I shall keep them occupied, do not fear."

"But where are you going?" Phillip demanded, suddenly roused. "And what, in the name of God, are you trying to do?" For a moment, he thought that Yusef intended to make off without giving him an answer, for he gathered up his reins and swung round but, instead, the wolfish features twisted into a beaming smile which, for all its expansiveness, was oddly cruel.

"I? Oh, I am going to lead the misbegotten Cossacks another little dance," he returned arrogantly. "The sons of whores will break their necks before they shoot me down a second time!"

"But *why?*" Phillip caught at his bridle, forcibly holding him back.

Yusef eyed him with astonishment. "Have you not seen Colonel Gorak?"

"He's not still in the valley?"

"But of course he is and his daughter also. I am not leading the dogs of Cossacks a dance merely for my own amusement—I am trying to give my men time to reach them and to escort them both to a safe place. The Colonel is badly wounded and . . ." Yusef broke off, evidently hearing some sound whose significance was lost on Phillip and his expression hardened. "May Allah send them to eternal perdition! They are *not* going, the curs! I am sorry that I must leave you," he added, almost as an afterthought. "I am in your debt, my friend, and this is not the way I would wish to repay you. But for your own protection, it is all that I can do. Rest assured that I will come back for you when I am able . . ." he took his own pistol from his sash and, before Phillip had any inkling of what he was about to do, the butt descended with stunning force on the side of his head.

His last memory, before a suffocating blackness closed him in, was of someone—he had no idea who—dragging him painfully along the ground by his heels. He tried to struggle but his consciousness deserted him and he sank, protesting feebly, into the blackness that was all about him . . .

"Sir . . . sir, are you all right?" Phillip recognized Cochrane's voice, harsh with concern. He opened his eyes to see the dim white blur of a face close to his own—Cochrane's face, presumably, since the voice was his. There were other faces, too, but he could not make them out clearly enough to be certain whose they were. It was very dark and there were stars in the night sky above him, whirling this way and that . . . he was lying on his back, he realized. Flat on his back on a rock and he vaguely wondered why. But Cochrane was here, Cochrane would tell him . . . he struggled to sit up and an arm went round him.

"Lean on me, sir," Thompson's voice invited and, in spite of the acute vertigo he was experiencing, Phillip managed to do so. After a while, the stars ceased their extraordinary gyrations and he was able to sit up unaided and, a little later, to identify the faces of the men grouped about him. Yusef was there, Cochrane, of course, several Circassians and Thompson . . . but he could see no sign of Erikson and neither Selina nor her father were there. He must have asked a question, although he had no recollection of having done so, because Cochrane answered him with the assurance that he need not worry.

"The Cossacks have withdrawn, sir, all of them. And Erikson's with Colonel Gorak and the girl . . . they're being taken back to the cave. We'll probably catch up with them before they get there, because the Colonel's badly wounded and they're having to carry him on a litter. But we've got horses and, as soon as you're fit to ride, we can go after them."

Horses, Phillip thought, trying to take it in. He drew a rasping breath and a hand came out to touch his right temple, gently and speculatively. Yusef said, his tone apologetic, "I struck you harder than I intended, my friend, but in truth, I could think of no other way to save you. The accursed sons of bitches were almost on top of us and I had to make them believe that I had left you for dead, for I could not otherwise have deprived you of your horse. Not, that is to say, with a clear conscience."

Of course, it was Yusef who had hit him with the butt of his pistol, Phillip thought. Memory slowly returned and he grinned at the young Circassian ruefully. "I should not like to be your enemy," he confessed. "If this head of mine is an example of how you treat your friends!" He had spoken in English; Cochrane translated for him and Yusef gave vent to a delighted guffaw of laughter.

"But all is well that ends well, is it not?" he suggested. Then, gesturing to the sky, he asked whether Phillip felt sufficiently recovered to mount a horse. "I have brought your mare back to you, monsieur, without a scratch on her. But we should not delay any longer here than we must so, if you are ready, let us get out of this place."

With Thompson's unobtrusive assistance, Phillip limped stiffly down the slope to the waiting horses. He felt unbearably weary and every bone in his body was aching as well as his head, but he managed to sit his horse and the frosty night air helped to revive him. As they rode, Cochrane gave him a report of his operations on the ridge and added, with conscious pride, that his total casualties had been three men—all Circassians—slightly wounded. "The Circassians fought well and I fancy we could have held them till nightfall, sir, if we hadn't run our ammunition so low. I was thankful that I had those extra rounds of yours, sir—they were a godsend."

"You did well, Mr Cochrane," Phillip told him, with sincerity. "Damned well . . . and that goes for you all. But tell me—what happened to Colonel Gorak? I couldn't see him from where I was but I thought that Selina would get to him without any trouble. Didn't she?"

Cochrane shook his head. "Not for quite a while, sir. Her horse fell and broke its neck and she couldn't just dash straight across to the Colonel, you see, she had to work her way round through the trees to him. And he just stood there, making no attempt to get away on his own . . . I don't think he was fully aware of what was going on or the danger he was in and his horse was pretty done up, too, of course." Then the shadowy form he had glimpsed *had* been the Colonel, Phillip thought, remembering, as his young second-in-command continued his account. "I confess I didn't notice him at first, sir. But Yusef did, after you signalled us to retire from the ridge. It was he who organized the rescue party—Erikson went with them, sir, he volunteered to take a fresh horse down for Selina, so I let him go. He's better than the rest of us at mountaineering, so I thought—"

"You did the right thing, Mr Cochrane," Phillip assured him.

"Thompson and I stayed at the top of the hill," Cochrane went on. "We were rather worried about you. Yusef promised he would signal us if you needed help, and he told me that he would keep the—er—the accursed Cossacks occupied."

"He didn't tell you how he was going to do it, I imagine?"

"No, he did not, sir," Anthony Cochrane agreed with feeling. "You saw rather more of that than we did, of course. But the way he went down that hill . . . I felt quite sick, just watching him!"

"Frankly, Mr Cochrane, so did I," Phillip admitted. "How was the rescue organized?"

"Yusef divided the men into two parties, sir. One party went down on foot, working their way behind the Cossacks, and the others—including Erikson—took the horses. They didn't ride, they drove them down in front of them, when Yusef gave them the signal. I think, sir, he intended them to distract the Cossacks, too, in case anything happened to him." Cochrane smiled. "He's quite a man, that Yusef, isn't he, sir? And he must think a good deal of the Colonel, to have taken the risks he did to bring him out."

Of the Colonel . . . or of his daughter, Phillip wondered, shifting his weight awkwardly, in an attempt to ease the nagging pain in his right leg. His old wound was playing up, as it was wont to, when he had been under physical stress but he shook his head to Cochrane's anxious enquiry.

"There's nothing wrong with me that food and sleep won't cure, Mr Cochrane. And, reverting to your earlier observation—Yusef is indeed quite a man."

"Yes, sir. I—er—I rather fancy he thinks the same about you, sir," Cochrane said. "He told me that you . . ." he was interrupted by a shout from Yusef himself and Thompson, who was just ahead of them, said with relief, "It's the rest of them, with the Colonel and Miss Selina, sir. I'm glad to see that she's all right, sir, though I'm afraid the Colonel's in a pretty bad way."

Selina was, as Thompson had observed, apparently unharmed. She was on horseback, riding beside the litter—fashioned from rough tree branches—on which her father was being carried. Her face, Phillip saw, as he drew level, was deathly pale but she replied to his greeting composedly. He could see little of the Colonel, who was wrapped in sheepskin cloaks but he was obviously unconscious and Selina shook her head to his unvoiced question.

"I have done all I can for him," she stated flatly. "All that is in my power. But he has so many wounds and he has lost so much blood, I fear that he . . ." her voice trailed off into silence. She did not weep, as most other women would have done; instead her teeth closed fiercely over her lower lip in a valiant struggle for control and Phillip, sick with pity, laid his hand gently on her shoulder.

"I'm sorry, Selina, truly I am. We all are, we—"

She weakened for a moment then and there were tears in her eyes when she thanked him and added, half in explanation, half in apology for her momentary weakness, "He . . . he is all I have, you see. My father is the only person in the world who . . ."

Phillip's throat tightened. The Colonel, he recalled unhappily, had said much the same to him, only a few hours ago. *"If anything should happen to me, Selina will be alone. That is my nightmare . . ."* and now the nightmare had become tragic reality. He racked his brain for some words of consolation to offer but could think of none. Selina turned in her saddle to look at him and then, her head erect, she rode to the head of the small procession and they resumed their journey, silent now as the moon came from behind a cloud, bathing the scene in bright, silvery light.

CHAPTER SEVEN

It *took* the better part of an hour to reach the cave and Colonel Gorak was still unconscious when the litter-bearers laid down their burden and carefully moved him on to the pile of skins Selina had prepared as a couch for him. She stayed at his side, refusing food and all offers of assistance and Yusef drew Phillip aside and said quietly, "Come—eat with us, monsieur, you and your sailors. It is best to leave the girl with her father. That is her wish and"—he shrugged despondently—"I do not think that he can last very long."

Despite the fact that they had been for a long time without food, none of the party from the *Huntress* could do justice to the lavish helpings of goats' meat which their Circassian hosts offered them. Phillip was grateful for the thick, sweet coffee, however; he was completely worn out, his right leg causing him agonizing pain and his head feeling as though ten thousand demons were at work inside it. He longed to sleep but his conscience, roused on Selina's account, gave him no peace. He sat apart from the others, his arms about his knees, gazing morosely into the fire and wrestling with the seemingly insoluble problem which, he knew, her father's death would pose. He had his duty, he reminded himself. His orders were to return to Ghelenjik, with Serfir, the day after next, at the latest . . . the meeting with Mustapha Pasha and the other

Circassian chiefs was of vital importance, he knew, and must not be delayed, whether the poor old Colonel lived or died. And yet . . . he frowned, stifling a tired sigh. Had it not been for him, the Colonel would still be safe and sound, nursing his injured arm at the base camp . . . it had been in order to assist him in the successful completion of his mission that the old man had left his sick bed and risked his life. How could he bring himself to leave Selina here, when the time came to accompany Serfir to the rendezvous with Mustapha Pasha, if her father's wounds proved to be mortal? The alternative was to take her with him, of course but . . . he and his ship could not remain at Ghelenjik indefinitely. The *Huntress* would have to rejoin the Fleet—within a few days, if Admiral Lyons had his way and a second expedition to take Kertch was launched, so that . . . his head fell on to his knees and he slept, the questions that plagued him still unanswered.

Serfir and his officers returned to the cave sometime afterwards. Phillip roused himself for long enough to see that the Circassian leader looked tired but less disappointed than he had expected and, lulled by the sound of their voices as they, in turn, broke their fast, he again drifted into an uneasy sleep, haunted by nightmarish dreams, from which he wakened in a cold sweat of fear, to find Erikson shaking him by the shoulder.

"What is it?" he demanded, reaching automatically for his rifle. "Are we being attacked?"

The seaman shook his blond head reassuringly. "No, sir, it's all quiet. It's the Colonel, sir—he's conscious and he's asking for you."

"Conscious?" Phillip echoed incredulously. He sat up, his head swimming and Erikson's hand rested for a moment on his forehead. "Are you all right, sir?" the young Norwegian asked with concern. "Your head's burning hot, sir, and—"

"I'm all right, thanks," Phillip said, aware that this statement was far from the truth. He attempted to get to his feet and would have fallen but for Erikson's supporting arm. The seaman was too well disciplined to dispute his assertion; instead he offered his arm in silence and Phillip was glad enough to lean on it as he limped across the dimly lit cave to where Selina knelt beside her father. She looked up at his approach, a tremulous smile on her lips and then rose to yield her place to him, with a whispered apology for having had to waken him.

"I am so sorry—you need your sleep, I know but . . . Papa is insisting that he must speak to you and I did not think that you would mind. You . . ." her eyes widened in concern, as Erikson's had done a moment before. "You are sick, Commander Hazard, you—"

"I'm all right," Phillip managed thickly. He dropped stiffly to his knees, fighting off the waves of nausea that swept over him. "Colonel Gorak . . . you wanted to talk to me, sir? It's Hazard."

The Colonel had aged almost out of recognition, he saw, shocked by the change a few short hours had wrought in him. His face was ashen and the skin had the look of old parchment, criss-crossed by a myriad of tiny lines and stretched so taut that it seemed almost transparent. His eyes had sunk deep into their sockets and were glazed and lacklustre, peering sightlessly in the direction from which his visitor's voice had come. "Hazard . . . it is you?" The bloodless lips parted in a thin parody of a smile. "My young friend, I . . . I have a favour to ask of you. That is why I . . . had to disturb your rest."

"What can I do for you, sir?" Phillip asked, guessing his answer. He hesitated, fighting a losing battle with his conscience and then went on with new-found determination, "I will do any-thing you ask of me."

The thin, bony fingers tightened about his. They felt cold, as if the life had already gone from them and he leaned closer in an effort to catch the whispered words, although he had lit-tle doubt what they would be. "Will you take care of Selina for me? It is . . . a great deal to ask of you but . . . you are British and there . . . is no one else whom I can trust, you see. That was why I . . . why I had to get away from the Cossacks. I had to find you, to . . . beg that you would . . . look after her. She cannot stay here without . . . a protector."

"I'll look after her," Phillip promised, his throat tight. "To the very best of my ability, sir."

"A . . . Christian marriage, Hazard," the Colonel urged, his voice now clear and firm. "I do not want my Christian child in a Moslem harem, you understand."

"I understand, Colonel Gorak. I'll do everything in my power, sir, to see that your wishes for Selina are carried out. That is, of course, if it should be necessary. You—"

"It will be necessary, my dear young friend." The old man spoke with finality. "I wish that it were not so but . . ." his voice faded once more to a faint whisper. "We do not . . . choose the moment when . . . we come to the . . . to the end of the road, alas." He closed his eyes and lapsed into so long a silence that Phillip bent over him anxiously, feeling for the pulse at his wrist. The movement roused him and he said, his tone dry, "No, not yet. I am a soldier, you know, and my instinct is . . . to fight, not to . . . surrender. Strangely, I feel no pain. That is odd, is it not? I had expected that there would be pain."

"I am thankful that you feel none, sir." Phillip sat back on his heels. He felt curiously light-headed, uncertain whether he was awake or dreaming and the Colonel's parchment-yellow face swam and then seemed to dissolve in front of his eyes, adding to his sense of unreality.

"Selina is . . . a good and dutiful child, Hazard," he heard the tired old voice say. "And she . . . she pleases you, does she not? You find her . . . beautiful?"

"Yes, indeed, sir," Phillip managed to respond, his sense of unreality growing. This could not be happening, he told himself—he must have dropped asleep again, must still be dreaming the confused, nightmarish dreams which earlier had haunted and given him no peace.

"I would give my child to you, Hazard," the Colonel told him faintly. His voice was a thin whisper of sound in the dimly lit cave of sleeping, exhausted men. "I would give her to you . . . more gladly than to any other man living, for I know that with you she would be safe. Take her, my dear young friend, so that I may go in peace. She will make you a good wife . . . a good and dutiful wife, as her . . . as her mother was . . . to me."

The words hung between them, unanswered and unanswerable and then, to Phillip's shamed relief, he was saved from the need to commit himself to a reply by Selina's light touch on his shoulder. She gestured to the small, still figure on the couch of piled-up skins, whose eyes, he saw, were now closed. "He cannot hear you, Commander Hazard," she whispered. "He is no longer conscious."

He stumbled to his feet, wondering uneasily how much of his conversation with her father she had overheard and then, as the significance of her words slowly sank in, he asked anxiously, "You don't mean that he's—"

"Dead?" Selina finished for him, when he shied from the word. "No, he is not yet dead, poor Papa." She spoke without bitterness and sinking to her knees beside the couch, quietly resumed her vigil, her face a white blur in the flickering firelight, apparently devoid of expression. Phillip turned away, at once moved and further shamed by the sight of her digni-fied resignation. He wanted to go to her, to kneel at her side and share her vigil but his leaden limbs would not take him the few paces that lay between them. He staggered unsteadily, the roof of the cave seeming to disintegrate above his head and the alert Erikson put an arm round him and helped him back to his place beside Cochrane and Thompson near the fire.

"You're bleeding, sir," the seaman told him. "You must have been hit without realizing it. I'll have a look, shall I?" Without waiting for permission, he rolled up Phillip's right trouser leg. "Your boot's full of blood, sir."

"It's an old wound," Phillip said indifferently. "Nothing to worry about . . . what are you doing, man? You—"

"You've lost a lot of blood, sir," Erikson informed him, work-ing deftly with his clasp-knife.

"I tell you, it's an old wound," Phillip snapped irritably. "It probably opened when we were coming down that cliff face, on our way here, and Dafir fell on top of me. For the Lord's sake, Erikson, it only needs a fresh bandage . . . don't ruin my boot, as well as my trousers . . ." Ignoring his protests, Erikson busily hacked at the trouser-leg and then started to ease the boot off, exclaiming as he did so.

"This is no old wound, sir," he said and began to cut away the bandage. "I can see the old wound all right but"—he probed painfully, with rough, untutored hands. "You have a musket ball in the thigh—a ricochet or a spent ball, I'd say, sir, which may be why you didn't feel it when it hit you."

"I can feel it now, my lad!" Phillip gritted his teeth. "Lay off, will you?"

"I'm sorry if I hurt you, sir—but I've found where the ball is and it's pretty deep." Erikson ceased his painful probing and looked up enquiringly. "Shall I pass the word for Miss Selina to remove it for you? Because it'll have to come out, sir, and she—"

"No!" Phillip flung at him wrathfully. "Leave Miss Selina in peace, can't you?" He controlled his irritation and, craning his neck in order to inspect the wound for himself, was astonished to see how much bleeding the spent ball had caused. The bandage he always wore on his right leg to protect the still imperfectly healed injury from jolts and knocks had absorbed most of the blood but, as a result, it was now saturated and useless. Erikson finished cutting it away and eyed him expectantly. "The ball ought to come out, sir," he said at last, his tone apologetic.

"Then take it out for me, if you please," Phillip requested.

"Me, sir? But"—the big Norwegian paled—"I've never done anything like this before, sir, never. I don't know how."

"You have your knife, man . . . heat the blade in the fire to cleanse it and then use the point."

The seaman drew in his breath sharply but he obeyed, thrusting the knife blade deep into the glowing embers of the fire. "Perhaps Mr Cochrane—" he began.

Phillip glanced at Cochrane. Like the other occupants of the cave, his second-in-command was sleeping soundly, oblivious to what was happening and deaf to the voices a few feet from him. He looked very young in the firelight, young and vulnerable and, at that moment, very peaceful. It seemed inconsiderate to waken him, particularly since he probably had no more experience of removing musket balls from the human flesh in which they were embedded than Erikson had. There was Thompson, of course, but . . . Phillip shook his head. "Learn to take responsibility, Erikson," he said with well simulated sternness, aware that Gunner's Mate Thompson would relish this task no more than Erikson did. "You surely don't wish to remain an AB throughout your service in the Royal Navy, do you? You are an educated man but if you are to merit promotion, you'll have to accustom yourself to accept responsibility, you know."

"Aye, aye, sir," Erikson acknowledged. He took his knife from the fire and stood staring down at the cooling blade in an agony of indecision. "I have never sought promotion, Commander Hazard," he pointed out, his tone injured and faintly resentful. "I joined your English Navy because I have a hatred for the Russians and—"

"You're wasting time," Phillip put in curtly. He could feel a cold sweat breaking out on his brow and the palms of his hands were clammy. For no reason that he could have explained, he was determined that Selina should not be called upon to take the ball out for him but, if Erikson continued to argue, she would undoubtedly hear him and might well come over to ascertain what was amiss, and if she did . . . "For God's sake, man!" he said impatiently. "If you can't do as I ask, then waken the gunner's mate. At least he can be relied on to obey orders when I give them."

"I can do it, if you order me to, sir," Erikson assured him. His blue eyes held an angry glint as he knelt, gripping the clasp-knife resolutely in his right hand.

Phillip tensed as the knife blade bit deep into the muscles of his thigh, sending a ripple of pain running through him and it took every vestige of self-control he possessed to stifle the cry which rose to his lips. Somehow, he managed to do so and, jamming his clenched fist against his mouth, he lay face downwards on the rocky floor of the cave without emitting a sound but the sweat pouring off him, so that he seemed to be immersed in a pool of ice-cold water.

Erikson made an unhandy surgeon. Fearful of damaging

the surrounding tissue by making his cuts too swiftly, he hesitated and then, encouraged by his patient's silence, started to gouge carefully and methodically in the direction which the musket ball had taken, using the point of his knife somewhat in the manner of a corkscrew. His progress was slow and, by the time he reached the object of his search, Phillip was almost at the end of his endurance and it required a tremendous effort of will not to scream his agony aloud.

"I've found it, sir!" Erikson announced triumphantly. "I've found it . . ." forgetful of his earlier caution, he thrust the knifepoint hard against the sphere of metal in a clumsy and unsuccessful endeavour to lever it out. But the bullet was evidently deeply embedded and, after three more abortive attempts to dislodge it, he too, was sweating profusely. "I'll give it one more try," he muttered, more to himself than to Phillip. "If it doesn't come this time, I . . ." the knife went in again but still the lump of flattened metal eluded him and he swore, loudly and despairingly. "I can't, sir . . . before God, I can't! I'm no surgeon and I can't see what I'm doing."

Phillip let a smothered groan escape him as he heard the knife clatter to the ground and Erikson moved away, retching his heart out. Then, coming from what seemed a great distance, another voice said something he could not catch and gentle hands replaced the rough, awkward ones of the unfortunate Erikson. There was a metallic click and the pain ceased, to be succeeded by a dull ache which, by comparison, was not unpleasant.

"The ball is removed," Selina's voice stated reassuringly. "I will dress the wound for you and you must try to sleep. Now . . . this will hurt a little but it is necessary, to make sure that the wound is clean."

Phillip felt a sharp, stinging pain, as liquid was splashed about his injured leg but this sensation quickly passed and

thankfully he let himself relax and slowly sink into unconsciousness as the gentle hands moved soothingly about his
weary, tortured body and Selina softly bade him sleep . . .

He wakened to find Cochrane bending over him, looking
worried but his young second-in-command's expression turned
to one of relief when he sat up and greeted him quite cheerfully.

"My God, sir, you gave me a scare," Cochrane confessed,
when his enquiries as to his commander's health had been
reassuringly answered. "Poor Erikson is still in quite a state,
too—he was as sick as a dog for most of the night, I gather.
And to think I slept through it all and didn't hear a thing!" He
shook his tousled red head in frank bewilderment. "The Pasha
was asking after you and—"

"Oh, Lord, where is he?" Recalled to his duty, Phillip looked
at him apprehensively. "We've got to get him to Ghelenjik in
the next two days, Mr Cochrane, and—"

"Don't worry, sir, he's ready and willing," Cochrane put in
eagerly. "He hasn't gone far away—just to the ravine, to see if
there's any plunder the Russians have left and to help Dafir
bring in his gun. They'll be back by nightfall, I understand. I
let Thompson go along with them, sir—partly to inspect the
gun and see if it could be adapted to the Circassians' use and
partly because I thought you'd want him to keep an eye on
Serfir." Phillip nodded his approval and he grinned. "Do you
feel like eating anything, sir? I'm afraid it's still goat but . . .
Selina said I was to persuade you to eat, if I could."

"I need no persuasion, Mr Cochrane."

"Right, sir, I'll see what I can rustle up for you." Cochrane's
grin widened. "I take it you won't be averse to some coffee
either?"

"Not at all averse. In fact I . . . what time is it?" Phillip looked
round but, in the dim light of the cave, it was impossible to

tell night from day. There were a few men squatting about the fire but he himself, he realized, had been moved to the far end of the cave and now lay on a couch of skins as the Colonel had lain when . . . he caught at Cochrane's sleeve, as memory flooded back. "What about Colonel Gorak?" he asked apprehensively.

Cochrane's smile faded abruptly. "He's still hanging on, sir, but he's not conscious and Selina says he's not in pain. She's with him now and I think she's fallen asleep. I didn't disturb her, although she said I was to tell her when you woke up. She's exhausted, sir, and just about at the end of her tether. And it's"—he took out his pocket watch—"four-fifteen in the afternoon, sir."

"And the date?"

Cochrane frowned. "I fancy it's the eleventh or twelfth of May, sir."

He went off in search of food and Phillip lay back on his softly yielding couch. He must have slept for over twelve hours, he realized, which doubtless accounted for the fact that he felt almost himself again. And that was just as well, since half his allotted limit of ten days had now expired and he would have to leave for Ghelenjik with Serfir first thing next morning . . . pray heaven he could still walk! He flung off the skin rug which covered him and gingerly inspected his right thigh. It was heavily bandaged but the bandage was clean and free from any ominous stains and, although it felt stiff, he had little difficulty in flexing it. It would probably take his weight if he stood up, he decided, and subjected it to a cautious test, elated to discover that the leg gave him no pain, apart from its accustomed ache. When Cochrane returned, accompanied by a Circassian, bearing two steaming bowls and a brass jug of coffee, Phillip limped across to meet them.

"Selina didn't think you'd be able to use that leg for a

couple of days, sir," Cochrane said doubtfully. "Ought you to try? I mean, sir, you—"

"I shall have to be able to use both my legs by tomorrow, Mr Cochrane. We cannot delay our departure any longer, you know."

"No, sir, I realize that." Cochrane set down his burden and Phillip motioned him to seat himself on the couch. The contents of the bowl smelt appetizing and so, too, did the coffee and they both fell-to with a will. It was good to be hungry again, Phillip thought, wryly recalling his nausea of the previous evening, when faced by a similar meal to the one he was now enjoying.

"Where's Erikson?" he enquired, setting down his bowl at last with a satisfied sigh.

"He was helping Selina with her father, the last time I saw him, sir." Cochrane half rose. "Yes, he's there still but I think he's asleep—shall I get him, sir?"

Phillip shook his head. "No, don't bother—I'll have a word with him later. I owe him an apology for what I ordered him to do last night."

"I don't think he expects one, sir."

"Don't you? Why not?"

Cochrane's eyes were on his coffee cup. "Well, sir, he told me he was very grateful to you. I couldn't quite follow his— well, his reasoning, but he said you'd shown him how to accept responsibility and he seemed pretty pleased that he'd been able to . . . though why he should be when, according to Selina, he damned nearly killed you I don't pretend to understand." Phillip grunted and the younger man went on, still avoiding his gaze, "Another thing puzzles me, sir. I know it's none of my business but—" he broke off, his freshly shaven cheeks a trifle pink. "I beg your pardon, sir—I shouldn't ask."

"Ask away, Mr Cochrane," Phillip invited. "But before you do—I need a shave very badly and I observe that you've managed to have one. Could you procure me the means, do you suppose, so that I can follow your example?"

"Yes, of course, sir. I'll only be a moment." He was as good as his word and, when he returned with a bowl of warm water and a razor, Phillip thankfully set to work to remove the four-day growth of unsightly stubble from his cheeks. "Well?" he encouraged. "What did you want to ask me, Mr Cochrane? I'm listening."

"It's about Selina Gorak, sir," Cochrane told him, his expression now carefully blank. "I was wondering . . . if the Colonel dies, we can't just abandon her here, can we?"

Phillip sighed. The question of Selina's future was one he would gladly have evaded—he had not, as yet, been able to give the matter the thought it required—but, faced by Cochrane's perfectly reasonable enquiry, he knew that he would have to reach a decision and reach it very soon. "The Colonel," he said slowly, "asked me to be responsible for her, Mr Cochrane—he asked me last night, in the conviction that he was dying. I promised that I would do all in my power to see that his wishes concerning her were carried out—I could hardly refuse, in the circumstances, although heaven knows, my power is very limited." He scraped glumly at his chin with the latherless razor and then set it down, looking up to meet his young second-in-command's anxious gaze. "Colonel Gorak told me that he did not wish Selina to be left here alone, in the event of his wounds proving mortal, so . . . it looks as if we shall have to take her to Ghelenjik with us."

Cochrane looked relieved. "I'm glad about that, sir," he admitted.

"Are you, Mr Cochrane?" Phillip's tone was wry.

He sighed and levered himself up from his couch. "Let's walk a little in the fresh air, shall we? I fancy it would be as well if I were to exercise this leg of mine, in preparation for tomorrow's journey. If we are to return by the route Dafir chose to get us here, then I cannot afford to run the risk of falling by the wayside."

Cochrane offered his arm. "If you're not fit to undertake the journey, sir," he said diffidently, "you may rely on me to take your place. Perhaps if you had a couple of days more in which to recover you'd find it less of a strain."

"Thank you, Mr Cochrane." Phillip eyed him with real affection as he accepted the proffered arm.

They walked together towards the entrance to the cave, pausing for a moment in silence before the Colonel's couch. He was still deeply unconscious, Phillip observed pityingly, and he signed to Cochrane to move on. Selina was sleeping the sleep of the utterly exhausted, her head resting on her hands and her face hidden from his gaze and neither she nor Erikson, who was stretched out close beside her, even stirred at the sound of his limping footsteps.

It was evident, even to a cursory glance, that the sands of Colonel Gorak's life were running low and Cochrane said, as they emerged into the fading afternoon sunlight, "He cannot be moved, can he, sir? And if we sent a surgeon from Ghelenjik, he would not be able to get here in time." It was more a statement than a question and Phillip regretfully confirmed it. "Yet he still holds on," Cochrane mused. "Poor old man! It seems very sad, somehow, that he should die here, away from his own people, does it not? But at least he'll go out in a blaze of glory, so far as Serfir's Circassians are concerned."

Which, no doubt, was what Jan Gorak would have wanted, Phillip thought although, for Selina's sake, perhaps . . . he bit back a sigh as Cochrane went on, "It seems, sir, that he *did* get across the ravine to warn Serfir about the guns the Russians had concealed in that supply train, or so Yusef told me. Yusef's French isn't too easy to understand, but from what I could gather, the Colonel ran into the Cossack rearguard, when he was on his way to rejoin us."

"That's what he was trying to do, was it? I wondered how they came to get on his trail." Phillip frowned. "It was a pity Serfir didn't stop him."

"Yes, sir," Cochrane agreed. "He'd have been all right if he had stayed with Serfir's cavalry, because they all moved out of the line of fire and they suffered very few casualties, as a result of the Colonel's warning."

Phillip smiled, without amusement. "'An exile and a mercenary in the service of an Oriental power' . . . that was how he described himself to me, you know. But he's of the stuff from which heroes are made—let us hope the Oriental power he served will remember him and his like, when the war is over."

"The Circassians will remember him, sir."

"And so shall I, Mr Cochrane." Phillip took out his watch. "We've about another hour of daylight. Let us make a leisurely ascent of that hill to our left, shall we, and see if there's any sign of Serfir's return?"

Serfir did not, however, make his appearance until long after darkness had fallen and those in the cave had already partaken of their evening meal. He and his officers flung themselves wearily down beside the fire but they looked not ill-pleased with their day's work and Thompson reported to Phillip that, in terms of plunder, they had salvaged one damaged and one workable field-gun, a quantity of rifles and ammunition, and about a score of horses from the wreckage of the Russian train.

"And the Russians went back the way they'd come, sir,"

the gunner's mate added, with satisfaction. "They took their dead and wounded with them, so there was no way of judging what casualties they suffered—but they weren't light and they didn't wait to blow up all the ammunition they abandoned. We buried twenty-three Circassians, sir."

Not a victory, Phillip thought as he dismissed Thompson for his well-earned meal, but still not the ghastly shambles it might have been and it was to be hoped that Serfir would be content. He waited, with what patience he could muster, for the Circassian leader to finish his meal, glancing occasionally across to where Selina—who had wakened from her exhausted sleep a short while ago—was attending to her father. Erikson was with her, fetching and carrying for her, and he did not disturb them, aware that his reluctance to do so stemmed from his own conscience-stricken failure to reach a definite decision concerning her. He continued to wrestle with his conscience, returning monosyllabic answers to Cochrane's cheerful chatter over a shared jug of strong, sweet, black coffee which, at least, served the purpose of keeping him awake.

Yusef presented himself, twenty minutes or so later, with a message from his father. "He says," the tall, young Circassian told him, in his slow, carefully enunciated French, "that he will be ready to accompany you to Ghelenjik tomorrow, in order that he may hold council with Mustapha Pasha and the other chiefs . . . if you are sufficiently recovered to make the journey."

"Tell His Excellency that I am," Phillip answered, without hesitation. "And that we can leave at any hour he wishes to-morrow."

Yusef, his message delivered, became less formal. He gestured to Phillip's leg. "My father feels concern for you."

"He need not, I assure you. I have been exercising outside,

with Mr Cochrane, for over an hour. I am quite fit and—"

"Nevertheless, monsieur, it is a long journey and my father intends to make it on horseback, with a body of his cavalry— a sufficiently large body to attack any Muscov patrols which may be encountered on the road. He will follow the coast road, which passes behind the fort at Soujak, thus—" he squatted on his heels and, with the hilt of his dagger, drew a crude map on the powdering of earth on the cave floor. "You see? He will descend to the foothills and join the road at this point, three miles north-west of Soujak. It is possible that patrols may be met with and, if they should be . . ." his gesture was explicit and Phillip stared at him in dismay. This was a complication he had not anticipated and he knew that he must do all in his power to dissuade Serfir from any diversion calculated to delay him. He caught at Yusef's arm.

"It is of vital importance that His Excellency your father should confer with Mustapha Pasha as soon as possible, Yusef," he urged. "I beg you to persuade him of this." He did his best to explain, finding his French inadequate and Yusef's under- standing far from certain.

"I think, Commander Hazard," Selina's voice suggested qui- etly, "that if you would permit me to speak to Serfir Pasha on your behalf, I could make clear to him how urgently his pres- ence is required in Ghelenjik."

Phillip turned, startled and more than a little embarrassed, to find her at his elbow. "I . . . I'd be immensely grateful if you would," he said, recovering himself quickly.

"Why did you not send for me to do so?" she asked, her eyes reproaching him. "That is what I am here for, is it not?"

"I . . . I'm sorry." He reddened. "I thought that you would not wish to leave your father. That was my only reason, Selina. You see, I—"

"And was that also the reason why you did not call upon me to extract the bullet from your leg, Commander Hazard? You preferred to torture yourself and to distress poor Einar Erikson by ordering him to remove it, when he has never performed such a service in his life and I have done so many times?" She spoke in the same quiet, controlled voice but Phillip glimpsed a hint of tears in her eyes and once again his conscience troubled him. *Had* that been his reason, he asked himself and, in all honesty, was forced to admit that it had not. He started to stammer a lame excuse but Selina waved it aside. "My father is not conscious—he does not know whether or not I am with him. His spirit has already gone from here—it is now only his poor, broken body which remains. I shall be within call for as long as it is necessary but this does not debar me from serving you in any way I can."

"No, I . . . of course not." Aware that he had hurt her, Phillip made to take her hand but she evaded him. "I will tell Serfir all that you have said to Yusef and bring you his answer," she informed him with dignity. "And then—since you must return to Ghelenjik tomorrow with your wound far from healed—perhaps you will allow me to dress it for you. I should not like you to lose your leg, Commander Hazard, but you must know that you run the risk of losing it, if infection sets in. The Circassian women have a certain skill with herbs and I have learnt from them, so—"

"Thank you," Phillip acknowledged, cursing himself for his tactlessness. "I should be very much obliged."

"Obliged?" Selina echoed. "You need feel under no obligation to me, Commander Hazard. In serving you, I am merely carrying out my father's wishes." She gave him a cool little inclination of the head and, turning to Yusef, addressed him briefly in his own language. The young Circassian glanced at

Phillip with unconcealed suspicion but finally shrugged and went with Selina to the far end of the cave, where Serfir and his officers still lingered over the remains of their meal. Cochrane, who had listened in some bewilderment to their exchange, looked at his commander as Selina walked away, opened his mouth to ask a question but—warned by Phillip's expression—wisely left it unasked.

"I think, sir," he said diplomatically, "that I'll turn in—if there's nothing you want me to do."

"Nothing, thank you, Mr Cochrane," Phillip returned with restraint. "I trust you'll sleep well because I imagine—and hope—that we shall make an early start from here in the morning."

"Aye, aye, sir. Good night." Cochrane took himself off and, left alone, Phillip sat watching the faces of those grouped round the fire, his gaze resting longest on that of Selina, who was talking earnestly to Serfir. In the reddish glow of the firelight, she looked more than beautiful and as he watched the changing expressions on her mobile face, he was again acutely aware of the attraction she had for him. *"Selina is a good and dutiful child,"* the Colonel had said last night, he remembered, with a pang. *"And . . . she pleases you, does she not? You find her beautiful?"* He had been in a strange state last night, half-way between sleeping and waking and running a temperature, too, probably, thanks to the musket ball in his thigh but . . . he expelled his breath in a long-drawn sigh. He had not given the poor old Colonel an answer, he reminded himself; he had neither accepted nor rejected the offer the old man had made him. Admittedly it had been an offer born of desperation, flatteringly couched and yet he could have no doubts as to its sincerity and he owed the Colonel an answer. *"Take her, my young friend, so that I may go in peace,"* he had pleaded and, a little earlier, he had also pleaded for a Christian marriage for the daughter he loved.

The familiar vision of Mademoiselle Sophie's face came suddenly, as it had so often come during the past year, to float tantalizingly before his eyes and he felt an aching tightness grip his throat, as it grew, blotting out the group seated round the fire. This time, though, it was not just Mademoiselle Sophie's face he saw but her whole body—small, slight, in the black robes of widowhood and awkwardly distended by the child she had been carrying when he had seen her in the Cathedral at Odessa. Andrei Narishkin's child, he thought, the son who had been born to the sound of Odessa's pealing church bells, as he had ridden down to the Imperial Mole under the escort of his erstwhile jailers two months ago, on his way to the *Wrangler*'s boat.

"I know my duty," she had told him, when she had first broken the news of her betrothal to Narishkin, just before the declaration of war had reached the Fleet—how long ago that now seemed! And—Phillip caught his breath—imagining that he heard her say it again. *"I know my duty, Phillip . . . do you not know yours?"* Well—did he not know it, he asked himself resignedly. Did he not owe a duty—and an answer—to the man who was dying on a couch of piled-up skins a few yards from him?

He rose and strode resolutely across to where the Colonel lay. Erikson, who had been sitting beside the couch, jumped up at once, eyeing him curiously as he bent over the wounded man. "He's not conscious, sir," the young Norwegian ventured. "He can't hear you, he's too far gone."

Phillip ignored his warning and, indeed, was scarcely aware of the seaman's presence. "Colonel Gorak . . ." he spoke softly and insistently. "Colonel, it's Hazard, sir . . ." he reached for the thin hand which lay, limp and drained of blood, on the skin rug. As it had before, the Colonel's hand felt cold to his touch and he chafed it between his own two palms, in an instinctive attempt to restore its warmth. "Sir . . . Colonel Gorak, can you hear me?"

The Colonel's eyes flickered. He did not open them but his lips moved and Phillip leaned closer, straining his ears in order to catch the faintly whispered words. "A . . . Christian marriage . . . Hazard," he made out and thankfully gave his answer.

"I understand, sir," he said. "You need have no fear on Selina's account. I pledge you my word that I will carry out your wishes if I have it in my power and . . ." but it was no use going on. The wounded man had lapsed deeper into unconsciousness and Phillip could not be sure whether he had heard or understood the promise he had endeavoured to make. He straightened up, to see Selina coming towards him, flushed and hostile.

"What are you doing?" she demanded. "Can you not leave him in peace?"

"There was a—a matter unresolved between us, Selina. I was trying to tell him that I would accept a responsibility he placed upon me last night." Even to his own ears, his explanation sounded unconvincing and Selina treated it with the scorn it merited.

"If the matter concerns me," she said bitterly, thrusting past him to kneel beside the Colonel's couch, "Your assurance comes too late, Commander Hazard. Whatever my father may have said to you last night, *I* do not expect you to assume any responsibility for me." She rose and turned to face him and her voice was cold as she added, "Please leave us now. I will come to dress your leg as soon as I can. And, in case you should be anxious, Serfir has agreed to change the route he will take tomorrow, as you requested."

Phillip accepted his dismissal, thanked her quietly and returned to his own couch. She came to him, ten minutes later, accompanied by Erikson, who set down a bowl of warm water and some bandages and, under her instruction, removed the soiled dressing from his thigh. Selina examined the wound with impersonal care. "It's clean," she informed him. "And is beginning to heal but I am bound to tell you that you will be running a grave risk, if you insist on making the journey to Ghelenjik tomorrow."

"I have to take that risk, Selina. I—"

"It is for you to decide, Commander Hazard." Her tone was still cold and she studiously avoided his gaze. "But you would be well advised to postpone your departure for another twenty-four hours."

"I dare not. If I were to do so, Serfir might well embark on another ambush or—"

"Very well," she conceded indifferently. "Then I will apply some healing herbs and a very firm dressing. It may cause you some discomfort but it will protect the wound. Einar, if you please—would you hold that bowl for me?"

Erikson obediently lifted the bowl. He, too, avoided Phillip's eye and, when he spoke, it was to Selina. Between them, however, they made an excellent job of his dressing and Erikson responded to his thanks with a faintly cynical, "It was you, sir, who introduced me to the role of surgeon's mate. I am pleased that you think I perform it better than I did." He stood up, carefully balancing the bowl in his two big hands. "Will that be all, sir?"

"Yes, thank you, Erikson. Be prepared to leave in the morning—you and Gunner's Mate Thompson—with Mr Cochrane and myself. Perhaps you'd be good enough to pass the word to Thompson."

"Aye, aye, sir." Erikson acknowledged. "Just one thing sir . . ." his blue eyes met Phillip's with the light of defiance in them. "And Miss Selina, sir? Will she be coming with us?"

"I trust so," Phillip answered. "It is my intention to invite her to accompany us." He glanced at Selina, who was kneeling, with downcast head, making the final adjustments to his bandage, apparently deaf to their exchange. "I'll have a word with her. Right, Erikson—carry on. Perhaps you'd be good enough to keep an eye on the Colonel after you've spoken to Thompson."

"Aye, aye, sir." Erikson hesitated. He seemed as if he were about to say more but the habit of discipline reasserted itself and he turned on his heel and went obediently to join Thompson.

"Selina," Phillip said. "Can you spare me a few minutes? I want to talk to you." She rose then, her cheeks a trifle flushed and asked guardedly, "What do you wish to say to me, Commander Hazard?"

"Please—won't you sit down?" Phillip gestured to the end of the couch, swinging his legs to the ground in order to make room for her. "My name is Phillip, you know. I wish you'd use it." She made no response to his second invitation but seated herself, with obvious reluctance, on the couch beside him. He sighed. "There are matters we must discuss and settle, if we can, because—"

"The matter of your responsibility for me?" Selina put in, an edge to her voice. "I thought we had settled that question. Whatever my father asked of you, I absolve you of responsibility. And as to whether I accompany you to Ghelenjik tomorrow, that must depend on my father. If he is still . . . that is, if he still has need of me and if you cannot postpone your departure—even for your own sake—then I must remain here."

"I wish I could postpone my departure," Phillip said apologetically. "But in the circumstances I dare not."

"I understand your reasons," she assured him, her tone more conciliatory. "And *you* must understand why I cannot leave my father so long as he is alive. Even if he does not know me, I must stay with him." Tears shone in her eyes but she wiped them away with the back of her hand, in an oddly childish gesture that was somehow a measure of the grief she was trying so valiantly to hide. "No man can live for long with such wounds as my poor father has suffered. For his sake, I pray that God will put an end to—to his suffering soon."

He knew that what she said was true and did not argue. Instead he said gently, "We shall be at Ghelenjik for several days—perhaps for a week or more, I don't know—and there will be two other British ships, in addition to my own. If you are unable to come with us tomorrow, I want you to follow us, Selina. I can leave one of my men to look after you. He'll escort you to Ghelenjik when—when the time comes."

He had half-expected that she would refuse his request but she inclined her head in agreement. "Yes, I will go to Ghelenjik," she answered. "But there is no need to leave anyone behind to look after me, Commander Hazard. I shall be quite safe here."

No doubt she would be safe enough, Phillip thought, but she would also be alone when her prayer was answered and her father found release from his sufferings . . . she would need someone of her own faith and kind to help her then. He said so, as kindly as he could and saw the bright gleam of tears again in her eyes.

"Very well," she consented. "Will you leave Einar, please—

Einar Erikson? He is a mountain man, he gets on well with these people. They like and trust him and so do I . . . and he has been very good to my father. Also I do not think he will mind staying for a little longer—he told me he felt at home here."

Erikson was the obvious choice, of course, and Phillip nodded his assent. "I'll tell him."

"Do not worry, I will tell him. But, Commander Hazard"— Selina's dark eyes met his gravely, still with a hint of tears in their depths—"you must please understand that I—"

"Phillip," he reminded her. "Could we not dispense with formality, Selina?"

She ignored the interruption, intent on what she had to say to him. "I have told you that you are absolved of responsibility for me."

"Yes, you told me. But I—"

"But you are trying to assume it."

"I gave my word to your father. I can't break that promise simply because you—because I may have hurt your feelings without intending to."

"You did not hurt me," she returned, with contradictory bitterness. "My poor Papa should never have tried to place so great a burden on you. I sensed your reluctance to accede to his request last night but he, poor soul, was too far gone to understand."

"I was reluctant only because I doubted my ability to carry out your father's wishes," Phillip defended. "I am not a free agent. I was afraid to make a promise I might not be able to keep . . . I'm a naval officer, Selina, and in command of one of Her Majesty's ships. I might receive orders when I reach Ghelenjik which would take me away from here for the duration of the war and which—"

"Yet you made my father a promise *this* evening," Selina

persisted. "Or you endeavoured to . . . and it was the same promise, was it not?"

Phillip sighed. It was proving much more difficult to explain his decision to her than he had anticipated it would be—perhaps because he had not made adequate allowance for her courage and her proud spirit. "Yes," he said, forcing himself not to sound impatient. "I endeavoured to set your father's mind at rest on your account because I—"

"Because you pitied him!" she accused. "For no other reason—because nothing has changed, has it? You are still not a—what did you call it? A free agent, are you? You are still an officer in the English Navy with a ship to command and a war to fight—and you must still obey your orders, you must go wherever your Admiral sends you. You cannot be responsible for me, for my future, can you?"

"In certain circumstances I can," Phillip asserted. "I wasn't thinking clearly last night but today I have had second thoughts. Please listen to me, Selina, because there *is* a way and I am in your father's debt, don't you understand?"

"Oh, I understand," she assured him. "And I am not ungrateful but"—her voice softened "Commander Hazard, you are, I believe, a good and honourable man and I respect you for what you are trying to do to ease my father's passing and give him peace of mind. You have discharged your debt to him—if you owe him one. But I—*I* do not want your pity and I will accept no sacrifices from you either. I am not a defenceless child, as surely you must have seen for yourself? I am not like your gentle English women . . . I can ride and shoot as well as any man and I do not need you to protect me." She was speaking the truth, Phillip was forced to concede, facing reality with pride and dignity but . . . "Selina, please," he begged, "Will you not listen to me?"

Selina waved him fiercely to silence. "You cannot change my mind. I have made arrangements for my own future. That is why I shall go to Ghelenjik, Commander Hazard—not in order to follow you, so that I may be sent to some place of safety in one of your ships or bundled off to my uncle, who does not want me. But because—"

"What arrangements have you made, Selina?" Phillip asked, in swift alarm. "For God's sake, *what* arrangements?"

"To stay in Circassia." Selina's dark eyes met his without flinching, bright with the same light of defiance that he had seen in Erikson's a little while ago. "These are my people and they, too, have a war to fight . . . a cruel and bitter war, against an enemy they—and I—have more reason to hate than you English have. I have been here for nearly two years and, had my father lived, I should have stayed, I should have gone on fighting with them. And I—"

"But you cannot stay! Your father—"

"My father is dying," she pointed out. "And Serfir has promised me his protection. Yusef also, of course." Her voice was flat but her eyes did not waver or lose their defiant gleam. "Yusef offered for my hand, some time ago, and my father refused. So did Serfir but . . . circumstances have changed now, have they not?"

Phillip stared at her in shocked disbelief. *"I do not want my Christian child in a Moslem harem,"* the old Colonel had said and he had added, *"But whilst she goes unveiled and accompanies me on these forays of theirs, there is always a terrible fear in my heart that, perhaps, she might let her eyes stray to one of them . . . as theirs stray constantly to her. They treat her with fitting respect, none would lay a hand on her but . . ."*

He drew in his breath sharply. "No!" he exclaimed angrily. "You cannot marry Yusef—he is a Mohammedan and you are a Christian, Selina. A Christian marriage is what your father wanted for you and I promised him that you should have one. For pity's sake, you—"

"And how," she demanded scornfully, "do you propose to keep your promise? Will you marry me to one of your sailors? Or to your young Mr Cochrane—does *he* feel such devotion towards you that, if you order him to, he will marry me?" Her anger flared, matching his. "I heard what my father said to you last night, Commander Phillip Hazard . . . he endeavoured to give me to you, did he not? *'I would give her to you more gladly than to any other man living . . .'* those were his words. I heard them, so do not trouble to deny it. *'She will make you a good and dutiful wife,'* he told you. *'As her mother was to me.'* But you did not want me, so you gave him no answer."

"I told you," Phillip began, making a great effort to control himself, "that last night I was not thinking clearly but today—"

"Today is too late," she said, with finality.

"No it's not, Selina." He attempted to take her hand but she wrenched herself free and stood up.

"I am sorry," she told him, but without contrition, her eyes still blazing as if from some inner fire. "I did not intend to let you know that I overheard what my father said to you last night, what he . . . what he offered you. I had hoped it would not be necessary . . ." she backed away as Phillip also got to his feet.

"Please, Selina . . ." she had never seemed more desirable than she did at this moment and, with the awareness of her attraction, he felt the blood pounding in his veins and was seized with a sudden longing to take her in his arms and crush the defiance out of her, with his mouth on hers and her soft, young body held against his own. But there were eyes watching them, he realized—Cochrane's, wide with astonishment, a few yards from him; Thompson's and Erikson's; a dozen pairs from beside the fire, including Yusef's—and the longing died as swiftly as it had been born. He let his arms fall to his sides and turned to meet Selina's gaze again, keeping a tight rein on his temper. "Won't you listen to me now?" he asked quietly. "Because I have a proposal to make to you."

"Of marriage?" she flung at him, her voice low. "Are *you* offering me marriage?"

"Yes," Phillip answered, "I am, Selina."

"So that you may keep your promise to my father?" she asked wryly. "Is that the only way you can keep it?"

He shook his head. "You know it's not."

"Yes, perhaps I do. I thought—oh, it does not matter what I thought, only that I am ashamed . . . you see, I—" The anger faded from her eyes and tears came to quench the smouldering fires of rebellion which had burned in them an instant before. She made no attempt to hide her tears but let them fall unchecked, to glisten on her smooth cheeks like raindrops in a summer storm. Phillip moved towards her but she stumbled back to her seat on the couch and let her head fall into her hands, weeping without restraint, as if all the grief she had held back for so long had been suddenly released. After a while, she raised her tear-wet face and said, very quietly, "I am honoured that you should offer me marriage, Phillip—honoured and grateful. But I—I must refuse."

"Why?" Phillip challenged, his throat tight as he stood looking down at her, forgetful now of those who might be watching him. "Why, Selina—why must you refuse?"

"For many reasons," she answered gravely. "First because I do not love you and because you do not love me . . . no"— she silenced his protest with a swift shake of the head—"that is the truth. But most important of all—because I am not the woman for you. I never could be."

"Should I not be the judge of that?" Phillip objected. In

response to her invitation, he seated himself once more beside her, conscious of a host of conflicting emotions as she laid her hand on his arm. The attraction which she had had for him from the moment he had set eyes on her was still there, as strong and disturbing as ever, and yet . . . he captured her hand and held it, feeling its unwomanly strength and roughness against his own, and was reminded forcibly of how she had fired her long flintlock rifle the previous day. She had fired to kill, coolly and accurately, without pity and when he had sought to dissuade her, she had been surprised . . . and the thought of his mother had come, unbidden, into his mind. He had wondered what his mother's reaction would be to a girl like Selina Gorak . . . "Well?" he prompted, with less certainty. "Should I not be the judge of whether or not you are the woman for me?"

"You cannot know," Selina told him. She smiled at him, the tears gone. There was a hint of mockery in her smile, as if she guessed his thoughts and understood—better than he did—his doubts and reservations where she was concerned. "I have watched you and *I* know. I confess there were moments when I regretted my knowledge and tried to tell myself that I was wrong . . . but I am *not* wrong. The fact that you have offered to marry me is proof that I am not." She took her hand from his and flashed him another smile, this time without mockery, a frank and trusting smile, completely without coquetry. "Oh, you are a man, with red blood in your veins, and I am a woman—in other circumstances, we might have been lovers. I might have been tempted to blind myself to the truth, even to have taken advantage of your—your chivalrous offer. But not here, with my poor father dying and the war—your people's and mine—yet to be fought to its bloody conclusion. We should have the truth between us—if that is all we may have.

No"—again she silenced him, her forefinger pressed to his lips—"there is nothing you can say. We are of different worlds, Phillip Hazard. And now, if you will forgive me, I must go back to my father. I have left him for too long and—"

"Erikson is with him," Phillip reminded her. "He'll call you if you are needed. Please don't go for a minute, Selina." He echoed her smile, feeling at ease with her for, perhaps, the first time since their return to the cave. "Will you not reconsider my proposal? Surely our worlds are not so different that they cannot be reconciled?"

"I fear they are, Phillip. And"—her voice was sad but devoid of the bitterness it had held a little while ago—"I am truly sorry. You are kind and compassionate and you try to hide it but I know very well that I have shocked you."

"Shocked me? You are mistaken, you—"

"Am I? I think not. In the world you come from women marry and bear children, they cook and sew and keep house for their husbands but they do not use a rifle or ride into battle—as I have done—when their country is at war." Selina spread her hands in a resigned gesture. "I cannot change what I am or what I have done, Phillip."

"I did not ask you to," Phillip pointed out.

"No, you did not," she allowed. "But could you forget it?"

Recognizing the logic of her argument, he frowned. Could he, he asked himself, in all honesty, could he?

"You could not," Selina answered for him. "You want, as your wife, a woman who is gentle, who loves and depends on you without question. One who is content always to stay at home, waiting for your return from whatever voyage you may be ordered to undertake or whatever war your English Navy may be engaged in, and in your absence, building her life round the children you will give her . . ."

Phillip made a wry grimace at the image her words conjured up although, he supposed, the description could—save for the addition of charm and tolerance and a never failing sense of humour—have fitted his mother. She, heaven knew, had faced years of separation during her long marriage, but she had faced them bravely, without complaint, and had brought up her large family virtually alone, when the old Admiral, as a junior officer, had been engaged in waging war under Nelson's and then Cochrane's command . . . Selina's voice broke into his thoughts, sounding suddenly strained and harsh.

"You do not want me, Phillip. I was born in an army camp and all my life I have been with soldiers, except when I was at the convent school . . . and even then the soldiers were seldom far away. And I—oh, don't you see, I need a man who is prepared to take me as I am? As life has made me, if you like— a man who will love me in spite of the fact that I have killed the Muscovs and have seen them kill and rape and torture innocent people. A man who will allow me to follow him, as I have followed my father. I . . . I have such a man in mind and I—"

"Yusef?" Phillip suggested accusingly. "Although you know that both your father and Serfir forbade it?"

"No, not Yusef," she denied. "I had thought of him but . . ." her expression relaxed and she went on, with a sincerity he could not doubt, "Do not concern yourself on Yusef's account. I am, as my father said, a dutiful daughter. I will obey his wishes."

Perhaps the young Irish officer, of whom the Colonel had spoken, was the man she now had in mind, Phillip thought, infinitely relieved. If he was serving with General Cannon, then he would be at Eupatoria and it should not be difficult to get in touch with him . . . "What do you mean, Selina?" he asked, anxious to make sure.

"That I will make a Christian marriage," she answered. "Or none at all—even if I stay with Serfir's people until the war ends. I . . . I give you my word and I will keep it, have no fear."

"What has caused your change of heart?" Phillip prompted curiously.

She sighed. "You have."

"*I* have? But—"

"I misjudged you and, perhaps, myself," Selina admitted. "I did not expect you to offer me marriage but you did and I . . . I no longer feel a desire to—to wound or humiliate you, such as I felt last night." It was a frank admission, made with the courageous honesty that was typical of this strange, unpredictable girl, Phillip thought, concealing his surprise. She added, at pains not to look at him. "I am truly ashamed, because I understand now why my father liked you so much and why he trusted you. He told me that you were an English gentleman and that I should be safe with you, no matter what the circumstances. He was always afraid for me, you know, my poor Papa."

"Yes, Selina, I know." She had paid him an odd compliment, Phillip reflected wryly, and one that, by some standards, might be said to call his manhood into question but—aware that she had intended it as a compliment—he voiced no protest. Looking up suddenly, he saw that Yusef's eyes were fixed on him with suspicious watchfulness and permitted himself a cynical smile. English gentleman or not, he told himself, it would be as much as his life was worth to lay a hand on Colonel Gorak's daughter at this moment and he decided that it might be as well if Yusef could be persuaded to accompany his father to Ghelenjik next day—if only for Erikson's sake.

"I must go back to my father," Selina said. She rose, shaking her head reprovingly when he endeavoured to get to his feet in order to take leave of her. "No, please—you are tired and you must rest your leg now, in preparation for tomorrow. Serfir intends to leave here soon after dawn, I think. But I—I shall see you before you go, Phillip, and we will say our farewells then."

She looked so lovely standing there, with the faint red glow of the firelight behind her, that Phillip was conscious of a feeling of agonized regret and with it a weakening of his resolve. But she did not linger, did not touch or even smile at him as she bade him sleep well and when he saw her, a moment or two later, bending once more over the old Colonel's couch, he knew that—as she had said—there had been the truth between them and was thankful that he had not yielded to the temptation to call her back.

It was a long time before he slept but when at last he did so, he slept deeply, with no dreams to trouble him and he wakened instantly, feeling refreshed and in good spirits, when a hand shook him by the shoulder.

"Coffee, Monsieur Hazard!" Yusef's voice said pleasantly. The Pasha's son was smiling as he set down the earthenware drinking vessel on the edge of the couch and his dark eyes, Phillip observed, no longer held even a hint of mistrust, as they met his own. He struggled into a sitting position and, taking out his watch, looked down at the engraved cypher on it, before opening the case. *"This . . . was my father's,"* Mademoiselle Sophie had written, on the card that had come with it, *"I send it to you with my gratitude . . ."* He snapped it shut and grinned back at Yusef in high good humour, the cares of the past few days suddenly lifted from his shoulders at the prospect of returning to his ship.

"Plunder?" Yusef suggested, leaning over to examine the handsome timepiece and expelling his breath in a gasp when he recognized the Imperial Russian cypher. "You took it, no doubt, from a very high ranking Muscov officer?"

There was envy in his voice, mingled with grudging admiration and Phillip shrugged, feeling his schoolboy French unequal to giving him a truthful explanation. "When do we start?" he asked, returning the watch to his pocket. "At what hour do we leave for Ghelenjik, Yusef?" He took a few sips of the hot, strong coffee and swung his legs to the ground, flexing the muscles of his heavily bandaged right leg cautiously. The leg was still a trifle stiff but gave him no pain.

"In half an hour it will be light," Yusef told him. "We leave then—but not for Ghelenjik. My father wishes me to tell you that—"

"*Not* for Ghelenjik?" Phillip echoed, in angry dismay. "But your father promised he would go, he—"

"He will go, Monsieur Hazard, do not fear. But our scouts have come in with word that the accursed Cossacks are out in force, searching for us. First we must deal with them"—there was a savage gleam in the young Circassian's dark eyes and he gestured expressively to the dagger in his belt—"it will not take long. Then we will go with you to Ghelenjik. The Muscovs must not find this cave, you understand . . . but you will be quite safe here, if you wish to stay and rest your wound. My father says we will come back for you in one or perhaps two days."

Phillip eyed him in exasperation. "I have no wish to stay here or to rest my wound," he began. "All I want is—"

"Good!" Yusef exclaimed, misunderstanding him but clearly delighted by his decision not to remain in the cave—presumably on Selina's account. "Then come with us, Monsieur

Hazard. This time we will show you how we fight the thrice-damned Muscovs!"

Phillip bit back an angry rejoinder and demanded with grim purposefulness, "Take me to His Excellency your father at once, please. I must speak to him."

"Certainly, if you wish," Yusef agreed. He added, his tone faintly malicious, "He will not listen to you, if you seek to dissuade him, I warn you."

CHAPTER EIGHT

Serfir, as his son had warned, refused to be dissuaded from his purpose. He was already buckling on his weapons in readiness for departure and it became evident, from the ill-concealed impatience with which he listened to Phillip's pleas, that he had no intention of leaving for Ghelenjik without having taken all possible steps to ensure the safety of his mountain refuge. And indeed, with Colonel Gorak still clinging tenaciously to life, Phillip found it difficult, in all conscience, to advocate any course which might permit a Cossack search party to ascertain the whereabouts of his hiding-place.

The cave obviously figured largely in the Circassian chief's scheme of things. Its value, he explained through the medium of his son's halting French, lay in its inaccessability and the care with which the approaches to it had been concealed, which meant that only a small guard need be left to keep watch on the place when an operation—calling for a large force—was in progress.

"Our people need this place," Yusef translated. "But let a Cossack patrol stumble on it—even by accident—and they will at once despatch a large raiding party to smoke us out. We dare not take the risk that they may find this cave after we have gone with you to Ghelenjik, so . . ."

Convinced, Phillip smothered his misgivings and ceased to argue. He was rewarded by a hearty slap on the back by Yusef, who eagerly launched into details of his father's plan of action. "We shall lead them away from this neighbourhood, you understand. First, we entice them to pursue us, then we lead them further astray and finally we turn on them. And, as I told you," the Pasha's son added, grinning gleefully at the prospect, "it will not take us long to deal with these Cossack swine. Two days, at most—you can surely allow us two days, can you not? The way we deal with them, as a rule, discourages them from sending out any more search parties for a long while. We will waste no time on this party, I promise you. But come with us, if you are up to it and then you can keep us to our promise . . . that is a fair offer, is it not?"

Having little choice, Phillip agreed. He did not relish the prospect of two long days in the saddle but he had been prepared to endure a day and a half, in order to reach Ghelenjik, and he could not reconcile his conscience to the alternative— which would be to allow Serfir to leave without him. There would be no chance of keeping the Circassian chief to his promise if he remained, nursing his wound, in the cave. It was going to be a pretty close-run thing in any case . . . but perhaps, as a precaution, he ought to send Cochrane to Ghelenjik ahead of him, to report that Serfir was on his way.

"Well?" Yusef demanded, noticing his hesitation. "What troubles you? Do you not wish to come with us after all?"

"Oh, I'm coming," Phillip assured him. "But . . ." he outlined the precaution he proposed to take and Yusef nodded approvingly. "Of course," he answered readily. "That is an excellent suggestion. We will provide your Monsieur Cochrane with an escort and he can leave when we do . . . which should be in a few minutes." He gestured to Serfir. "My father is losing patience. Give your orders swiftly, if you please, and join us outside. I will arrange the escort."

Anthony Cochrane received his new instructions with a pleasure he made no attempt to disguise. Phillip decided to send Gunner's Mate Thompson with him and, as the two were making their brief preparations, he called Erikson over. "You've heard what's afoot, Erikson?" The Norwegian seaman nodded. "Yes, sir, I heard. You are sending Mr Cochrane and the gunner's mate back to the ship and you want me to remain here with Miss Selina and her father."

"Oh—then she mentioned the possibility to you?"

"Yes, sir." Einar Erikson's blue eyes met his, innocent of guile, yet somehow oddly challenging. "I'll stay, sir. The Colonel's still breathing but that is about all. I do not think he can last much longer, sir."

"No." Phillip looked at him, puzzled by his attitude. But there was no time now to question him; he was a good man and could be trusted to obey orders. He gave these briefly and then, observing that Selina was asleep, added an equally brief message of farewell, which he instructed Erikson to give her when she wakened. "Remember," he added, "report to me at Ghelenjik as soon as you can and bring Miss Selina with you. I do not anticipate that we shall be there for much over a week, so you'll have to get to the port by then or—"

"Or be posted as a deserter, sir?" Erikson asked quietly. Phillip shook his head. "I shan't post you as a deserter," he returned. "But you'd have to stay here until we were able to pick you up . . . and that might mean a long stay."

"Aye, aye, sir," the young Norwegian acknowledged, smiling. "I understand. I . . . good luck, sir."

"And to you, lad." Phillip's gaze lingered for a moment on Selina's lovely sleeping face and then, smothering a sigh, he followed Cochrane and Thompson to the entrance of the cave.

During the next forty-eight hours, Phillip endured the most

intense discomfort he could recall ever having suffered on land. Serfir and his force of about a hundred horsemen rode hard and without respite and he, perforce, rode with them, lacking their skill on horseback but grimly determined, nonetheless, to stay with them. He saw, at first, no visible sign of the enemy they were trying to outwit—only the tracks of their horses and, in one place, a scant three miles or so from the cave, the ashes of their bivouac fires. The Cossacks were skilled horsemen, too, and initially matched skill with skill, cunning with cunning, refusing the feint attacks launched by small bodies of Circassians against them and disdaining to pursue those sent to lead them astray.

"They are well led," Yusef confided, at the end of the first day when, with the coming of darkness, his father at last ordered a halt. "But we shall settle that small problem tonight, do not fear, Monsieur Hazard."

"How?" Phillip asked wearily. He was so stiff and saddle-sore that he had to allow Yusef to help him dismount but shook his head impatiently to the young Circassian's concerned enquiries. "I am all right, just a trifle stiff, that's all. It will wear off." One of the men took his horse to tether it with the rest, and he started to pace slowly up and down, as the circulation painfully returned to his numb and swollen right leg. "How?" he asked again, seeking distraction from his pain. "How will you settle what you are pleased to call your small problem tonight, Yusef?"

Yusef put a friendly arm round his shoulders and matched his long, lithe stride to his guest's limping one. "The Cossacks light fires at night," he answered, smiling. "They post sentries and the rest sleep—the officers, almost always, apart from their men—and this is when we have the advantage over them. To our men, darkness is a friend, not an impediment . . . we like to launch our raids under its cover, stealing in silently, like a pack of hungry wolves, overcoming the sentries one by one." He laughed, a deep-throated, amused laugh. "Tonight, when they have settled down, some of us will raid their bivouac and whilst my men silence the sentries, I shall see to it that their commander does not live to see the dawn."

"You'll be taking the very devil of a chance," Phillip objected.

"Not so great," Yusef assured him confidently. "And it is necessary, if we are to keep our promise to deal with these Muscovs in time for my father to meet Mustapha Pasha at Ghelenjik, within the limit set by your Admiral. We Circassians are men of our word, Monsieur Hazard."

"I would not want you to keep any promise at the risk of your life, Yusef . . ." Phillip halted and turned to face the Pasha's son uneasily. "Please understand that." He had to search for the words he wanted, stumbling, as Yusef did, to make his meaning clear in a language in which neither was really fluent and, not for the first time that day, he found himself wishing that Selina had been there to interpret for him.

Yusef's smile widened. "It is good of you to concern yourself for my life, Monsieur Hazard, but you need not. These Cossacks are swine and I hate them; it is for myself, for my own—how do you call it?—satisfaction that I intend to outwit them. I would take you with me, so that you might see that I make no idle boast, but with that leg of yours, you would make too much noise." He pointed to a hollow in the ground and, divesting himself of his heavy sheepskin riding cloak, laid it across Phillip's shoulders. "I shall not need this, for I go on foot. Wrap it round you and sleep, Monsieur Hazard . . . we light no fires, and you might be cold."

"The men who slept on the bare ground without fires," Selina

had called them, Phillip reminded himself and took the cloak reluctantly. "Come and claim this, will you?" he suggested. "When you return from your raid?"

Yusef eyed him for a moment with raised brows and then, laughing aloud, enfolded him in a bear-like hug. "Very well," he replied. "I will do as you ask. You are a friend, Monsieur Hazard—a true friend, just as the Colonel was to us. At first I was not sure—I saw your eyes on Selina but now I understand and I trust you. If your heart desires her, she is yours . . ." he did not wait for Phillip's reply but left him, gliding like a shadow into the darkness and making no sound.

He returned, in the same cat-like silence sometime later and Phillip, roused from his chilled and uneasy slumber on the bare ground, felt a round, smooth object thrust into his hand. "I bring this as proof," Yusef whispered, "It is a watch, like yours."

"Like mine? But—"

Yusef gave a dry chuckle. "It has no crest but it belonged to a pig of a Cossack officer who will not need it any more. We took some of their horses also—they will give us little trouble tomorrow, you will see."

His forecast proved uncannily accurate. Without their experienced commander, the hunters became the hunted and, where before they had been elusive, they now showed themselves with increasing frequency, committing blunder after blunder and finally allowing their force to be split up. One party of about thirty strong, finding itself cut off from the main body, took refuge in ignominious flight, after glimpsing Dafir and a mere half dozen Circassians on a ridge above them and, although Dafir did not bother to pursue them, they were not seen again.

A second and bolder group, seeking to ride down a small

decoy party led, with consummate skill, by Yusef, was attacked from the rear by the Circassians in roughly equal strength and routed with the loss of almost a third of its number, after a brief and bloody battle. The fighting, when it became hand-to-hand, was fierce and savagely brutal, with no quarter given or asked by either side and no prisoners taken. Phillip, riding with Serfir, was sickened by the spectacle, although he could not but admire the tactical skill which the Circassian leader displayed and the manner in which he controlled his wild, brigand horsemen, wheeling them this way and that and making use of the natural cover afforded by trees and hills.

The fighting, however, obeyed no civilized rules of warfare and once, after a successful encounter when the Circassians were systematically slaughtering and plundering the wounded, Phillip was driven to voice a protest, which was received with surprise and then ignored. Later, having evidently been told of his protest by Serfir, Yusef took him to a small clearing among the trees, a mile or so from where they had camped the previous night, and pointed to the bodies of three of his men. All three, Phillip saw with horror, had been hideously mutilated and Yusef said harshly, "These men were with me last night and they were taken alive."

"Alive? But—"

The young Circassian shrugged. "Monsieur Hazard, we kill but we do not torture. The Cossacks have never shown us mercy; they have no pity even for our women and children and we have been fighting them for thirty years. So . . ." he gestured with his blood-stained scimitar to the burial party which had accompanied him and Phillip turned away, unable to reproach him or to offer any reply.

By mid-afternoon what, in his ignorance, he had thought of as Serfir's cat and mouse game was virtually over and, to his intense relief, the scattered remnants of the Cossack search party were permitted to make their escape, miles from where they had begun their search and, Yusef assured him solemnly, in order that his father might adhere to his promise and waste no time on them.

"We start now for Ghelenjik, Monsieur Hazard," the Pasha's son added. "And we will ride as long as it is light."

They covered eight or nine miles before nightfall, made camp—this time with cooking fires—and were off again at first light, riding at a steady, loping canter among seemingly trackless and thickly wooded foothills in a westerly direction, with occasional glimpses of the sea.

It was almost dusk when, at last, the harbour and the huddled rooftops of Ghelenjik came in sight, dwarfed by height and distance but nevertheless unmistakable. Phillip, by this time exhausted and unshaven and in considerable pain, breathed a prayer of thankfulness to his Maker as they descended and he was able to make out the riding lights of three ships through the gathering darkness. All three lay at anchor close inshore but he was considerably disconcerted when he took out his Dollond and saw that two of the anchored ships were paddle-wheel vessels and the third a steam-screw gunboat which he recognized as the *Viper*. Of his own *Huntress* there appeared to be no sign and, in his exhausted state, he became a prey to the most alarming misgivings, which were only relieved when Dafir, who had galloped ahead to the fort, returned from it, ten minutes later, bringing Lieutenant Roberts with him.

"How are you, sir?" the young Marine officer greeted him cheerfully, reining in his horse to the slow gait of Phillip's weary, mud-spattered mount. "You look pretty done up, I must say. Perhaps you'd care to come to the fort for a meal and a tub, before you report to Commander Osborn?"

Osborn . . . so the *Vesuvius* was here, Phillip's mind registered; the second paddle-wheel steamer was probably Mustapha Pasha's Turkish transport. "Yes," he said, "thank you, Mr Roberts, I should . . . I haven't shaved for three days. But tell me, where is the *Huntress*? And did Mr Cochrane and the gunner's mate, Thompson, reach here safely a couple of days ago?"

Roberts nodded. "Oh, yes, sir, they both turned up all right and they're back aboard the *Huntress* now. She sailed early this morning for Soujak and Anapa, sir, with Emin Bey and some of the other Circassian leaders on board. I understand that, on orders from Commander Osborn, she was to throw some shells into the shore defence, sir—though I don't exactly know with what object, unless it was a cover for a survey or something. The Turkish Pasha—Mustapha, sir—got here the day before yesterday and I believe he went along too. The Circassian chiefs evidently don't trust him further than they can see him because they've been sticking to him like glue, sir, ever since he arrived." The young Marine officer grinned as he added, "The *Huntress* is expected back at this anchorage tomorrow morning, I understand."

Phillip, his fears for his ship allayed, gave vent to a deep sigh of relief. He took his leave of Serfir, who was to make camp with his men outside the town and, after passing on the news Roberts had given him to Yusef, continued on his way to the fort. Here, he discovered, Roberts and his Marines had made themselves very comfortable and he was pleased to notice that the Bey's *redifs* appeared to be on excellent terms with their British allies.

"We've got them fairly well organized, sir," Roberts told him, with pardonable pride. "But I imagine, now that you've brought the Bey's men back, we shan't be here much longer, shall we?" He opened the door to his own quarters, standing aside for Phillip to precede him. "Here we are, sir. Please make use of anything you need. I'll get my servant to bring you some hot water."

An hour later, freshly shaven and the stains of travel removed from his person, Phillip sat down to a meal with his host. "Ship's rations, sir, I'm afraid," Roberts said apologetically. "But I've managed to get hold of some quite pleasant local wine."

"After a diet of goats' meat, Mr Roberts, I shall welcome anything," Phillip assured him. "And you can bring me up to date with what's been happening in my absence, if you will. But first—has Mustapha Pasha brought any troops with him, do you know?"

"He's brought two field batteries and four hundred men, I believe, sir," Roberts answered promptly. "But so far he hasn't landed them."

Four hundred men, Phillip thought . . . it was not a generous contribution, in view of what the Turks had promised and he—heaven help him—had led Serfir to expect. But the field-guns would be useful and if Serfir and the other chiefs could raise twenty or thirty thousand Circassians of the calibre of those he had spent the past few days with, then an assault on Anapa and Soujak would not be beyond the bounds of possibility. He questioned Roberts minutely as he ate and learnt that Emin Bey was confident that, with the force he could raise allied to Serfir's, Anapa could be taken without difficulty.

"In his view, sir," the Marine Lieutenant said earnestly, "The Russians won't put up any resistance, if they are seriously threatened. Emin Bey thinks they will evacuate both Anapa and Soujak and retreat to the Kouban . . ." he went into details and ended, "But the Bey says he must have guns, sir."

"And two field batteries won't be sufficient for his purpose?"

"Hardly, sir. He's had one conference with the Turkish

Pasha already, sir, on board the Turkish frigate and I think it went quite well. But they were waiting for Serfir, of course, and now that you've delivered him there shouldn't be any holdup. You had quite a job getting him here, did you not, sir? Or so I gathered from Mr Cochrane—he had a meal and a bath here, too, sir, so I heard his news."

Phillip frowned into his wine glass. Quite a job, he thought wearily . . . well, perhaps it could be thus described. He looked up to meet Roberts's grave-eyed scrutiny, remembering the conversation they had had before he had left the *Huntress* to go in search of Serfir. "Tell me, Mr Roberts," he asked curiously, "how did you get on when you called at Soukoum? Did you see the—er—the Georgian girl?"

Young Roberts flushed to the roots of his thick, fair hair. This, obviously, was a question he did not relish but he answered it, after a moment's embarrassed hesitation. "No, sir, I did not see her. She was married, sir, and . . ." he choked with suppressed indignation. "Married to a man old enough to be her father! I saw him and I . . . well, to tell you the truth, sir, I don't mind all that much. Not now, I mean—it was a bit of a shock when I first found out but it wouldn't have worked, I realize that now I've had time to think about it . . . if I'd married her, I mean. We come from different worlds, sir, and if I'd had to bring her home and introduce her to my family . . . well, it would have upset them quite a bit, I'm quite sure."

Selina had spoken of different worlds, Phillip thought, with a twinge of sadness. Brave, beautiful Selina! Like young Roberts he might—had circumstances been different—have married her. And such a marriage, as Roberts had said, would probably have upset his family also . . . he sighed and took a deep draught of his wine, as Roberts talked on about the *Huntress's* visit to Soukoum Kaleh.

"The men behaved admirably, sir," he said. "There were no incidents and no one made trouble ashore. Er—some more wine, sir? It's not bad, is it, sir?"

"It's extremely pleasant, Mr Roberts," Phillip assured him warmly. "And I am most grateful for your hospitality. I think, though, that I had better report my arrival—and Serfir Pasha's—to Commander Osborn now. Have you any means of communication with the *Vesuvius*—could you ask them to send a boat for me?"

"Yes, of course, sir." Roberts rose at once. "I'll tell my sergeant to signal for a boat. Er—shall we report to you aboard the *Huntress* when she returns to the anchorage tomorrow, sir?"

"I'll let you know, Mr Roberts, when I find out what orders Commander Osborn has for me."

"Aye, aye, sir."

Phillip reached for his cap. "I shall probably sleep on board the *Vesuvius*. The *Viper*'s here, too, is she not?"

"Yes, sir," Roberts confirmed. "She arrived from Kazatch just before you did."

Then she would have had latest news from the Fleet, Phillip thought and, eager to hear it, he donned his torn and mud-stained sheepskin cloak from sheer force of habit, only realizing how odd he looked when the midshipman in command of the boat from *Vesuvius* eyed him with unconcealed distaste before enquiring haughtily if he spoke English.

"Well enough to command Her Majesty's ship *Huntress*, youngster," he replied with pretended asperity and grinned at the boy's open-mouthed astonishment. "All right," he added, as the midshipman started to stammer an apology. "It's an understandable mistake. I shan't mention it to your Captain."

He received a much warmer welcome when he stepped on board the *Vesuvius*, to be met by both her commander, Sherard

Osborn, and Lieutenant William Armytage of the *Viper.* Both had served with distinction in the China War of 1842, when Armytage had been one of Captain Henry Keppel's junior officers in the *Dido,* and Osborn in the *Clio,* under Captain Edward Troubridge. They were old friends of Phillip's midshipman days—Sherard Osborn was, in fact, only two years his senior, although he had been promoted to his present rank soon after joining the Black Sea Fleet.

"Well, Phillip," Osborn said, when greetings had been exchanged. "Have you eaten? Good—then come along to my cabin and we'll have a drink. Unless you'd like our surgeon to look at your leg? Your young Second Lieutenant—what's his name? Cochrane, isn't it? He told me that you got a spent musket ball in it and I see you're limping." Phillip shook his head and Sherard Osborn smiled. "See the surgeon before you turn in, then, because I expect you are anxious for news and we've got quite a lot to tell you, haven't we, Willie? As no doubt you have to tell us." Reaching his day cabin, he waved a hospitable hand. "Sit down and make yourself at home. I'll fix you up with a cot for the night, of course—sorry I had to send your *Huntress* off without you but in view of the Admiral's specific instructions, I had no choice . . . and she'll be back here by tomorrow. In any case, your brother's a pretty experienced First Lieutenant, isn't he? Indeed he's . . . what? Seven or eight years senior to me. I was glad to hear he'd had his commission restored. Now . . . what will you have!"

"Brandy, I think, thanks. I've been most royally entertained at the fort by my Marine officer, so make it a small one, would you?" Phillip lowered himself into a chair, stretching his injured leg out in front of him. It was not so swollen as it had been, he noticed—evidently Roberts's tub had done it some good. Sipping his brandy, he gave a brief report of his stay with

Serfir Pasha—Cochrane had already reported on this, so that it was necessary only to fill in such gaps as he had left. Both Osborn and Armytage listened with interest and when he had done, Osborn asked thoughtfully, "They're pretty formidable fighting men, these Circassians, wouldn't you say?"

"I would indeed," Phillip agreed, remembering the past two days.

"Do you consider that this fellow Serfir is a man of his word, Phillip?" Sherard Osborn pursued.

"I do," Phillip assured him unhesitatingly.

"And do you think he really can raise about twenty thousand of his countrymen for an assault on Anapa and Soujak?"

"Yes, I do—if he says he will. But he *will* need help from the Turks and I hope Mustapha Pasha realizes this—I hear he's only brought four hundred men with him, and a couple of batteries of field-guns—"

"Six hundred," Osborn corrected. "Or so he told me." They discussed the situation at some length and then, when Osborn rose to refill their glasses, Phillip turned to Armytage. "What is the latest news from the Fleet, Willie? Has the Admiral managed to persuade Canrobert to agree to a second attempt to put a squadron into the Sea of Azoff?"

Armytage chuckled. "Better than that, my dear fellow—he's persuaded Pélissier to agree to it and with enthusiasm! Canrobert has resigned the French Supreme Command, in favour of Pélissier—on the grounds of ill-health, it is believed."

"You mean that Pélissier is the French C-in-C?" Phillip was staggered, unable to believe his ears. "Good Lord, when did this—this miracle happen?"

"Just before I left Kazatch. There were rumours floating about for days but this one was definitely confirmed yesterday. I can vouch for it." Armytage smiled. "Our Chief, as you may imagine, has taken on a new lease of life . . . and small wonder! Canrobert has been like a millstone round his neck throughout this war. They say that Bruat is delighted, too."

"And what is even more important," Sherard Osborn added, putting Phillip's refilled glass into his hand, "is that a conference has been called to plan the capture of Kertch. There seems, indeed, every reason to hope that the second expedition will leave Sebastopol within the next four or five days. The Admiral is only waiting confirmation—which Willie will deliver to him the instant Serfir and the other chiefs reach agreement with Mustapha—of a simultaneous uprising in Circassia and an attack on Anapa and Soujak."

"Then," Phillip suggested, elated by this news, "let's drink to that, shall we?" He raised his glass.

"Let us drink to it by all means, my dear chap. But"—in the act of drinking the toast, Osborn frowned and lowered his glass—"I was on patrol off Kertch until thirty-six hours ago, Phillip, and every day adds to the accumulation of impediments which the enemy are placing in the deep water channel off Yenikale which may well impede even ships of very shallow draught, like your *Huntress*."

"Does the Admiral know this?"

"Oh, yes, I've kept him informed—Willie has been back and forth carrying reports to him. We shall have to send a ship in to test and buoy the channel, I imagine."

Phillip met his gaze in swift understanding. "Do you want a volunteer?" he asked. "How about the *Huntress?*"

"Well, that sounds a fair offer, Phillip. You draw less water than any of us, I fancy."

"Then I'll be happy to volunteer. When do you want to make the test run?"

Osborn smiled. "When I receive definite word that the expedition is on its way—not before, because we don't want to alarm the enemy prematurely." He laid a friendly hand on

Phillip's shoulder, "I've received no instructions yet, so we'll wait and see what transpires, shall we?"

"Very good," Phillip agreed. He shook his head to the offer of another drink. "No, thanks, I think I'll turn in fairly soon, if you don't mind, Sherard. How about tomorrow? You're not leaving here yet, I take it?"

"No, not yet . . . though I can't stay more than a day or so. Tomorrow I'd like to arrange a meeting between Mustapha Pasha and your chap Serfir Pasha, Emin Bey and Najib Bey and the rest of the Circassian leaders and, if it's possible, get them to commit themselves. If and when they do, Willie can dash back to Kazatch to inform the Chief—I hope by tomorrow evening at the latest—and bring us back our orders. I think you'd better attend the conference tomorrow, Phillip, if you don't mind, because you know Serfir and you might be able to tip the scales if he's reluctant."

"I'll do my best," Phillip promised. "But he doesn't speak English—you realize that, don't you?"

Osborn sighed. "I'd forgotten, I confess. I tell you what, then—we'll get the conference organized as soon as your *Huntress* delivers Mustapha Pasha and Emin Bey, and leave them to it until about mid-afternoon. Then all three of us could go along to hear what they've decided. Bring that Turkish interpreter of yours—the little fat fellow—will you please? He can translate for us." His expression relaxed in an amused smile. "I don't wonder that you decided not to take him mountaineering with you, though—he's hardly what one would describe as an athletic sort of chap, is he?"

Phillip laughed. "Not really, no. I hope he's been useful to you?"

"Oh, yes, he has." Sherard Osborn rose. "Well, I think we've covered the essentials and I don't want to keep you up . . . you look as if you could do with a good night's sleep."

"I could," Phillip admitted. He followed his host to the cabin which had been set aside for his use and Osborn said, "I'll send my surgeon along to look at that leg of yours before you turn in, Phillip. If he can do nothing else, he can dress it for you."

"Thanks, Sherard . . . also for your hospitality."

"He's young but he's quite good at his job," the *Vesuvius*'s commander added, brushing aside Phillip's thanks. "And take advantage of my hospitality—get yourself some rest, old man, please. I'll have you called the minute your *Huntress* comes to anchor. Good night—and sleep well."

The young assistant-surgeon made his appearance a few minutes later. As his commander had said, he was good at his job—unlike poor young Brown, the *Huntress*'s assistant-surgeon, Phillip thought wryly, this boy had obviously had a good deal of experience and knew exactly what he was about. He spent a long time cleaning and probing the wound made by the spent musket ball, asking diffident questions concerning its removal and the old shrapnel wound above it as he worked.

"All things considered, sir," he said when—apparently satisfied—he started to apply a fresh bandage, "it's remarkably clean and should soon start to heal if you are able to rest your leg for the next day or so. You've been very fortunate in that no infection has set in—whoever took the ball out was—well, a trifle ham-fisted, I'm afraid."

Remembering Erikson's reluctant efforts, Phillip permitted himself a brief smile. "That," he returned, "is no exaggeration, Doctor. One of my seamen removed the ball with his clasp-knife—and I had to order him to do it."

The young surgeon looked shocked. "Then you are even more fortunate than I had supposed, sir," he said, finishing off his bandaging with a neat knot. "However," he qualified, "at least you're better off than you would have been had the ball been left in until now. If it had, I'd have been taking your leg off, instead of dressing it, I think. If I may presume to advise you again to rest as much as you can, you should have no more trouble with this wound. I'll look in again tomorrow. Good night, sir."

Phillip thanked him and, left alone, wasted no time in undressing and getting into his cot. He was asleep almost instantly and did not waken until a steward called him with breakfast and the news that the *Huntress* had been sighted, entering the bay.

It was with a keen sense of pleasure and relief that he boarded his own ship, an hour later. The Turkish and Circassian passengers were already on their way ashore when his boat tied up to the starboard chains and Graham met him with a restrained, "Welcome aboard, sir," and a rueful smile that told more than words could have done. In the privacy of his day cabin, the efficient Higgins served them both with coffee and when he had gone, Phillip said, eyeing his brother quizzically, "You're glad to be rid of your passengers, I gather?"

Graham sighed. "I don't know how you guessed but . . . yes, I am. Oh, it was quite a successful trip, Phillip, you need have no anxiety on that score. We made a useful reconnaissance of both Soujak and Anapa and young Grey's gunners made excellent practice on the forts at both places—I'll give you full details in a moment. But the language difficulties have been, to say the least of it, a strain for all concerned and—"

"What about the corpulent Aslam? Isn't he on board?"

"Oh, yes, he's on board—but currently indisposed. To tell you the truth, he's no sailor. No doubt he's recovering now."

"It's to be hoped he is," Phillip said. "We shall require his services this afternoon, when Sherard Osborn and I are to attend the Turkish-Circassian conference . . ." he brought Graham up to date with the plans Osborn had made and the latest news from Kazatch and saw his brother's expression becoming more cheerful.

"Cochrane got back to you all right, I hear, and the gunner's mate with him?" Phillip said.

"Indeed, yes. Young Tony Cochrane has been regaling us, ever since his return, with the most fantastic tales of your adventures among the Circassians. I confess to a certain scepticism, though."

"Oh—on what account, pray? He's a truthful young man as a rule."

Graham refilled his coffee cup. "So I had always believed. But his stories of the beautiful Circassian girl—or was she Polish?—took some swallowing."

"She's Polish—that is to say, on her father's side. Her mother was English, a sister of General Guyon's, apparently . . ." Phillip's thoughts went back, almost against his will, to Selina. How was she faring, he wondered anxiously, she and Erikson and the poor old Colonel? He had to make an effort to take in what his brother was saying.

"According to Cochrane, she's quite an Amazon. He said she was shooting better than any of you when you ambushed that Russian supply train."

"She was," Phillip confirmed, his voice flat. "With a flintlock rifle, against our Miniés."

Graham's dark brows lifted in astonishment. "Well, of course, if *you* say so, then I believe it. Cochrane also said that you were hit in the thigh by a spent musket ball . . . is that true? And if it is, how are you?"

"It's true—but I am perfectly all right, or shall be if I can rest the leg for a day or so. The *Vesuvius*'s surgeon has given me a clean bill of health."

"I'm immensely relieved to hear it," Graham said dryly. "I'll grant you look quite fit, although I should not have thought that the best cure for a bullet wound in the leg was to spend—how long? Three or four days on horseback, with a Circassian raiding party!"

Phillip shrugged. "It was kill or cure, I think . . . although honestly, I hadn't much choice. If I had let Serfir out of my sight, I should never have got him here. But God preserve me from ever taking part in such an operation again!"

"What was it like?" Graham asked curiously.

"The fighting was—oh, my God, Graham, it was quite horrifying. I did not think I was squeamish but it turned my stomach, I must admit . . ." He gave a strictly factual account of what he had witnessed and saw his brother's eyes widen in shocked surprise.

"In defence of the Circassians though, they have suffered appalling oppression for thirty years and their hatred is directed mainly against the Cossacks, who have apparently been used as the instruments of that oppression . . ." he repeated the account Selina had given him, of the Cossacks' behaviour when sent to occupy an undefended Circassian village and added, an edge to his voice as he recalled the terrible wounds inflicted on Selina's father, "The Cossacks caught Colonel Gorak—the girl's father—did Cochrane tell you? I saw, with my own eyes, how little mercy they showed *him* . . . and he was quite obviously a European and a Christian, like themselves."

Graham nodded. "Yes, Cochrane told me about the Colonel—said he was a fine old man. He—I gather he was mortally wounded?"

"I'm afraid so," Phillip confirmed. "I had to leave him where he was—in the cave, which Serfir uses as his mountain headquarters and field hospital. His daughter stayed with him and I left Erikson to look after her—I couldn't leave her by herself, you see." He explained the orders he had given Erikson and went on, aware that he looked and sounded embarrassed, "The poor old Colonel made me responsible for his daughter, Graham. It was his—I suppose it could be called his dying request, although he was still just about alive when I left him, so I could hardly refuse, could I?"

Graham sighed. "No," he said, with conviction, "You could not have refused in such circumstances. One has obligations to one's allies . . . how do you propose to carry out the Colonel's dying wish in regard to his daughter? Cochrane seemed to think . . ." he broke off and Phillip demanded harshly, "For God's sake, what *did* Cochrane think? I'd like to know."

"Well, he said you'd told him nothing and that he was only guessing but he thought that the Colonel had asked you to marry her. I found that hard to believe, Phillip, I must confess, but . . ." Graham eyed him speculatively.

"It is true, nevertheless," Phillip told him.

"Well, Cochrane said that she's a really beautiful girl. Did you propose marriage to her, Phillip?"

"I did," Phillip confessed. "And she refused me."

"*Refused you,* by heaven!" Taken by surprise, Graham stared at him incredulously. "I suppose, in a way, I should be relieved for you . . . the Old Man wouldn't have liked such an alliance, would he? And, I fear, neither would Mother but—did you *want* to marry her, Phillip? Did you fall in love with her?"

Phillip hesitated, a trifle resentful of the question yet seeking an honest answer to it. Remembering Selina's fearless honesty, he finally shook his head. "No," he said. "No on both counts . . . but I would have married her, for all that, if she had accepted my proposal. And you may call me every sort of a fool, if you like—I shall not deny it."

His brother was silent, subjecting him to a thoughtful

scrutiny. "In the circumstances," he said, frowning, "I think you did the only thing possible, my dear Phillip. Indeed, I cannot see what else any man—with half a heart—could have done. But you're not yet free of your promise, are you, even though she refused your proposal? How will you keep it?"

"I don't know, Graham—in truth I don't know." Phillip spread his hands in a despairing gesture. "When she arrives here—as I trust she soon will and Erikson, too—I shall have to try to arrange a passage for her either to Batoum, in Mustapha Pasha's ship, to join her uncle or, perhaps, to Eupatoria in one of ours. There's an East India Company officer there, serving under General Cannon, who, her father told me, offered for her hand some time ago. Selina said that she would obey her father's last wish—she gave me her word that she would make a Christian marriage or not marry at all—and she did mention that she had someone in mind. I can only suppose that it was this Indian Army officer, Captain O'Hay, whom she meant."

"A passage to Eupatoria should not be too hard to arrange, Phillip," Graham observed.

"No, I trust not. But I can arrange nothing until I see her again and . . . we may not be here for more than another day or two. If a second expedition to Kertch and the Sea of Azoff *is* agreed to by the new French Commander-in-Chief, I imagine it will be launched without delay, if the Admiral has anything to do with it." Phillip took out his watch. "I promised Sherard Osborn that I would attend the conference on shore with him this afternoon and he wants me to bring Aslam, to interpret for us. If all goes well, Willie Armytage will sail this evening, to inform the Admiral . . . and if there is to be a second attempt to enter the Sea of Azoff, we may be required to make a survey of the deep water channel and buoy it, before Jack Lyons's squadron reaches the Straits. Osborn says he has seen the enemy endeavouring to block it."

"Then we've no time to spare, have we?" Graham suggested.

"No, we have not." Phillip got to his feet. "I think I had better pay a call on the Captain of the Turkish frigate, don't you? In case Selina does not reach here until after we've sailed, I could ask him to give her passage—if she wants it—to Batoum. She did tell me that she would like to stay with Serfir's people but it's possible she may change her mind. Erikson, I'm afraid, will have to wait here until we can pick him up but I imagine that Najib Bey could accommodate him at the fort and—" he was moving towards the cabin door but Graham forestalled him.

"A moment, Phillip." He stood with his back to the door. "You ought to rest that leg of yours. I can quite easily call on the Turkish Captain on your behalf and, if I rout out Aslam and take him with me, I can be every bit as persuasive as you could. And as to Erikson, can you not have a word with Najib about him, when you're ashore this afternoon—the conference with the Pasha is being held at the fort, is it not?"

"Yes, it is. But—"

"Then there's no earthly reason that I can see to prevent you taking a couple of hours on your cot," Graham interrupted firmly. "For pity's sake, Phillip, I'm not Ambrose Quinn—you can delegate chores like this to me and stop driving yourself into the ground, surely?"

Phillip gave in with a good grace. He duly rested his leg until his brother returned, to tell him that the Turkish commander had willingly agreed to provide General Guyon's niece with a passage to Batoum, if she required one. "He's under Mustapha's orders, of course, but he expects eventually to return to Batoum, since the Pasha has his headquarters there," Graham added.

And this, Phillip thought, was all he could do, until Selina reached Ghelenjik. He dined with his officers in the gunroom and, at five bells of the Afternoon Watch, a signal from the

Vesuvius requested his presence, and that of the *Viper*'s Captain, on shore. Leaving Midshipman O'Hara at the now familiar fish quay, with orders to occupy the time of waiting by taking off Lieutenant Roberts and his Marines, Phillip joined his two fellow commanders and, with Aslam trotting breathlessly after them, walked at a leisurely pace to the fort.

The conference, surprisingly, appeared to be almost over. Mustapha Pasha, a fine-looking man, whose age was difficult to guess, was addressing the assembled Circassian chiefs when the three British officers entered the room and, from Aslam's rapid translation, it looked and sounded as if he were willing to offer them more assistance than they had expected.

"His Excellency is saying, sir," Aslam repeated in a hoarse whisper, "that he cannot spare more than two or three thousand regular troops from Abassia and this only with some risk. But he is proposing to establish a military post here, at Ghelenjik, within two or three weeks and he says that he has already established one at Ponahs, which is sixty miles from here . . ." he paused for breath and then went on, "His Excellency is thanking you for having given him the opportunity to make a reconnaissance of both Anapa and Soujak Kaleh in one of Her Britannic Majesty's ships . . . if you would bow, gentlemen, this would be a pleasant compliment." All three officers gravely bowed and the Pasha responded with a dignified smile.

Serfir Pasha rose when, after more courteous bows, the Turkish General resumed his seat on a pile of cushions. "His Circassian Excellency," Aslam stated, "is saying that a spy, who returned here yesterday from Soujak, has told him that the Russians observed the presence of His Excellency Mustapha Pasha on board the British ship and they are now offering large rewards, in gold, to anyone who can tell them when and in what manner the Ottoman forces will attack them." There was a deep roar of amused laughter and even the plump little Turkish interpreter was smiling as he explained that the spy had shown Serfir two pieces of gold, given him for the information that Mustapha Pasha and a large army were close at hand.

Serfir's speech was brief, but well received by his fellow chiefs and, it seemed from his expression, also by Mustapha. "He is promising a general uprising throughout Circassia," Aslam translated. "Which will include every Circassian soldier in Russian employ in the Kouban and elsewhere. Within twenty days, His Excellency is confident that he can collect a force of between twenty and thirty thousand armed men, both horse and foot. And now, your honour"—the swarthy little Turk turned excitedly to Phillip—"His Excellency is paying a tribute to you in person, sir, for having risked your life to seek him out in the mountains."

Phillip flushed scarlet with embarrassment, suddenly aware that he had become the centre of attention and Sherard Osborn whispered, lips close to his ear, "A speech is now called for from you, I fancy, Commander Hazard. Come on, old man—don't lose your nerve, with the honour of the Service at stake!"

"Tell His Excellency, if you please, Mr Aslam," Phillip said, after a moment's anxious thought, "that it was a privilege, as well as a—a valuable experience, to serve under his command. I am only deeply sorry that my presence with His Excellency's forces should have cost the life of the brave man who guided me to him, Colonel Gorak . . ." Aslam got no further with his interpretation, for Serfir crossed the room, both hands outheld, and laying them on Phillip's shoulders, embraced him warmly.

"His Excellency Serfir Pasha wishes me to tell you," Aslam said delightedly, "that your honour will be welcome at his campfire for as long as Allah shall spare you both. He takes leave of your honour with regret but trusts that the English Admiral Commander-in-Chief may, when your honour shall report to him, send you back with your ship to assist His Excellency's attack on Anapa. In this hope, he bids your honour farewell."

"The shrewd old devil!" Sherard Osborn observed, as Serfir returned to his place. "Doesn't miss a trick, does he? But well done, Phillip . . . well done on all counts, not least for getting him here. You've created much goodwill for us all and your speech was excellent—brief and to the point. I can see you're wasted in the Royal Navy—you should be in the Diplomatic Service!"

"Heaven forbid!" Phillip retorted. "Don't wish that on me, I beg you."

Osborn laughed. "Well, the meeting appears to be breaking up. Could you lend me your Mr Aslam for half an hour or so? I want to have a word with both Mustapha and Serfir before they leave—I'll write my report here, I think, and read part of it to them both, so that they know exactly what they've committed themselves to. And then you can get under way, Willie my friend, and deliver the good news to our Commander-in-Chief."

"Aye, aye, sir," Lieutenant Armytage acknowledged. "Whenever you're ready."

The *Vesuvius*'s commander went off with Aslam, and Phillip felt a touch on his arm. Turning, he recognized Yusef. "They have returned, Monsieur Hazard," the young Circassian announced.

"They, Yusef? Do you mean Selina Gorak and my seaman, Erikson?" Phillip questioned, conscious of relief when Yusef inclined his dark head in assent. "Are they here?"

"At the camp," Yusef answered. "I have horses outside—will you ride back with me? It is no distance and will not take you long."

Puzzled by his manner, Phillip hesitated and Willie Armytage, who had followed the conversation in their still somewhat hesitant French, offered helpfully, "Go with him, if you want to, Phillip. We'll be here for at least an hour, I imagine—Sherard is a very conscientious fellow, as you know, when it comes to writing reports. I'll tell him you'll be back, shall I?"

"All right—thanks, Willie. I won't be any longer than I can help." Phillip nodded to Yusef and followed him outside to the waiting horses. He asked, as they rode, "What news of Colonel Gorak? He's dead, I take it?"

"Yes, he is dead. My people gave him a Christian burial, as he would have wished."

"A Christian burial? But—"

Yusef smiled. "There are Christian priests in the villages in the mountains—not many, but a few. One of them came to—how do you call it? Administer the last rites to our good friend the Colonel. Rest assured, Monsieur Hazard, we shall not forget him."

Phillip felt curiously warmed by these words and, turning in his saddle, he echoed Yusef's smile. "That was good of you."

"My people are not savages," the young Circassian told him quietly. "True, we hunt down and kill our enemies but we respect and are loyal to our friends." He was silent for the rest of the short ride to where Serfir's men had made their camp but, when they pulled up close to the main camp-fire, he said, "Monsieur Erikson has a favour to ask of you. My father and I would be very happy if you will grant it."

"Of course," Phillip began uncertainly, "if it is within my power, I—"

"It is within your power, Monsieur Hazard," Yusef assured him. "I will tell Einar Erikson you are here."

Erikson appeared instantly in response to his summons and came to attention, freshly shaven and spruce in a change of clothing which, Phillip noticed, must have been borrowed from one of the Circassians. He made his report in a flat, expressionless voice, repeating in more detail what Yusef had said concerning the Colonel's death, the brightness in his intelligent blue eyes somehow belying the carefully controlled voice and disciplined manner. Phillip listened in some bewilderment, sensing the man's tension but at a loss to know what could have caused it.

"Thank you, Erikson," he said, after being assured that Selina had borne up bravely after her father's death. "You have done well, very well indeed. I shall see to it that you are given the first vacancy that arises in a higher rank, because you've more than earned it. You had better report back on board at once and—"

"Commander Hazard"—Erikson's voice was no longer flat—"I beg to make a request, sir."

The favour Yusef had mentioned, Phillip's mind registered the favour that was within his power to grant and which . . . light dawned on him suddenly as Erikson said urgently, "I wish to request leave of absence, sir."

"You mean you want to remain here, with the Circassians?"

"Yes, sir. If you could second me—I believe that's the official term, sir—for service under Serfir Pasha, I'd be very grateful indeed, sir."

Was it within his power to grant the man's request, Phillip asked himself and then decided that, in certain circumstances, it might be. He would have had to leave Erikson here indefinitely, had his sailing orders come before the seaman reported his return to Ghelenjik and he had not, as yet, reported back to the *Huntress* . . .

"I've been offered the rank of captain, sir," the Norwegian added. "By the Pasha himself and I'd be fighting the war—I mean I'd go on fighting the war with them, sir, would I not? Perhaps more usefully than I could as a member of your ship's company. But I don't want to be posted as a deserter, sir, if it can be avoided, although I . . . well, sir, you see—"

"Are you trying to tell me that you'll desert if I do *not* grant you leave of absence?" Phillip asked, his tone quite mild.

The seaman reddened. "I . . . yes, sir. But I don't want to, believe me. And I do have a very—a very good reason for making this request, on my word of honour."

There was a soft footfall, coming from behind him and Phillip spun round, guessing who would be there and—when he saw her face—intuitively aware of why she had come.

"Is this to be your Christian marriage, Selina?" he asked her softly. "And is Einar Erikson the man you have chosen to be your husband?"

Her lovely face was raised to his and he saw that it held a warm glow of happiness and pride. "Yes," she answered simply and, smiling, held out her hand to Erikson. "But we are already married. The priest, the one they brought for my father, married us before he returned to his village. And now my—my husband requests that you will permit him to stay here, if only for a little while. Please, Phillip . . . you have many sailors, surely you can do without one of them?"

And that one, Phillip recalled, not really a sailor at all but a schoolteacher and a mountain man, who felt at home here and to whom Serfir had offered a command of his own . . .

"Your request is granted, Erikson," he said formally and was conscious of a feeling almost of release as he realized that he need no longer let the promise he had made to Colonel Gorak weigh upon his conscience, since Erikson had kept it for him. "My sincere congratulations to you—you have a wife to be proud of, one in a million, I think."

"Thank you very much indeed, sir," Einar Erikson acknowledged. "Have you time to eat a meal with us? We—"

Phillip shook his head regretfully. "No, I must get back to the ship, I'm afraid. But we shall meet again—your leave is not permanent, you know, and you'll want a passage back to England for your wife when the war is over, I imagine. I—I'd better be on my way. Farewell to both of you and . . . may God be with you!"

"And with you, sir."

They stood, hand in hand, as Phillip mounted his shaggy Circassian horse, and watched him go into the gathering darkness, with Yusef again at his side.

"You will permit us to keep Einar Erikson?" Yusef asked.

"Yes, I have given him leave of absence and I shall record it in my ship's log."

The Pasha's son grunted his approval. "Good," he said. "He will help us to capture Anapa." His hand rested lightly on Phillip's shoulder and then he raised it in salute, swung his horse around, and was gone.

At the fort, Osborn and Armytage were waiting, but Mustapha Pasha and the Circassian chiefs had gone.

"Emin Bey and several of the others are to accompany the Pasha to Soukoum Kaleh in the Turkish frigate," Osborn volunteered. "To raise more troops—and Serfir is to have the field-guns he wanted, so that he may, in the meantime, harass the enemy and keep them guessing. I gather that command of the artillery is being given to the boy you had with you—Najib Bey's son, isn't he?"

"Dafir—yes, that's right," Phillip confirmed "He's a trifle young but as brave as a lion."

"There's some other fellow they're hoping will share the command with him—a fellow with a Scandinavian name. A mercenary, I suppose, although I didn't think they had any Scandinavian mercenaries, did you?"

Phillip smiled. "Einar Erikson?" he suggested.

"Yes, do you know him?"

"I do indeed." Phillip's smile widened. "He is one of my Jacks—a Norwegian mountaineer, well educated, completely trustworthy. At Serfir's request I've just given him leave of absence to serve with the Circassians."

"Ah—the one you said was adrift? That's fine then—you can sail for the Straits of Kertch with me tomorrow, can't you?"

"Yes, of course, if you want me to."

Osborn sighed. "I need you, Phillip, if we're to survey that channel. McKillop's *Snake* is the only other ship we've got with as light a draught as your *Huntress* and she's still with the Fleet at Kazatch. You said you were low on coal, didn't you? Well, the *Prompt* should be back in the Straits by tomorrow—she'll supply you. Just one other thing—how about the girl you mentioned, the Polish Colonel's daughter? Have you been able to make satisfactory arrangements for her?"

Phillip inclined his head. "Yes, I have—most satisfactory arrangements. There's nothing to keep me here now, Sherard."

Sherard Osborn subjected him to a searching glance and then gestured to the papers in front of him. "Splendid," he said, "and there's nothing to keep me here either, once I finish this despatch to the Admiral. I'd like you to read it, Phillip, before Willie takes it for delivery. I have not mentioned your exploits but rest assured that I shall, when I report to the Chief in person, and you'll be making your own report to him in any case,

I imagine." He held out the despatch. "This is simply an account of this afternoon's proceedings and I've set out the promises made by Mustapha and Serfir with regard to Anapa, and Soujak. I hope you'll agree that it is accurate."

Phillip read through the short, two-page report and returned it with a nod of approval.

"Completely accurate, in my view, Sherard."

"Thanks, my dear chap. Well, here you are then, Willie. I need not tell you to get this to the Chief as speedily as you can."

"You need not," Armytage confirmed. "I have steam up, so I'll get under way at once." He smiled, offered his hand first to Osborn and then to Phillip and, with a quiet, "Good luck to you both," took his leave.

Sherard Osborn rose, stretching his cramped limbs. "Come back to the *Vesuvius* for a meal and a yarn, Phillip, will you? We probably shan't have much chance of a peaceful chat once we return to Kertch . . . and if our blockading squadron becomes the Sea of Azoff squadron, then we probably won't even have time to eat."

Phillip thanked him. "I hope like the very devil there will be no last minute hitch on *this* occasion, though," he added gravely. "I hope that with all my heart."

"So do I," Osborn agreed, with equal gravity. "Like our revered Commander-in-Chief, I am quite certain that, if we can cut the enemy's supply routes from the Sea of Azoff, we shall take Sebastopol and win the war . . . and with half the losses and in half the time it might otherwise take us. Dear God, when you think how many lives have been lost in the siege this winter, it makes you sick, doesn't it? And they've been thrown away, with nothing to show for their sacrifice— at least if we take Kertch and Yenikale and if the Circassians capture Anapa and Soujak, we shall be on our way to victory."

He gathered up his writing materials and put his arm round Phillip's shoulder. "Oh, well . . . I'm ready. Shall we go back to where we belong?"

They left the fort and walked down towards the fish quay in companionable silence. Feeling the cool touch of a fresh, offshore breeze on his cheeks, Phillip's gaze went to where his ship lay at anchor, her riding lights gently rising and falling on the slight swell which lapped against her stout wooden sides. He was pleased to be going back to her, excited by the prospect of action, for which the Fleet had waited for so long, and thankful that he could leave Ghelenjik—and the Circassians—with a clear conscience and no serious regrets.

He did not think of Selina, as he set his face once more towards the sea and, although he thought of Mademoiselle Sophie, it was fleetingly, and no tantalizing vision of her came to haunt him. Instead it was a vision of his *Huntress* that he saw and he was, he realized, content that this should be so. As Sherard Osborn had remarked a few minutes before, he was going back to where he belonged and instinctively he quickened his stride.

APPENDIX

SOURCES

Despatch from Commander Sherard Osborn to Rear-Admiral Sir Edmund Lyons.

Vesuvius, off Ghelenjik   19th May, 1855.

Sir,

I reached this place last night and had an interview with His Excellency Mustapha Pasha, as well as with Serfir Pasha (the Circassian). The information I have gleaned, as well as what took place between His Excellency and myself, is as follows:

The Circassians of Soujak, Anapa, and the Kouban have repeatedly requested Mustapha Pasha to visit them, in order that they might be assured he was desirous of their co-operation, and to arrange some future plan of proceedings against the Russian posts.

The Pasha had now done so, and although his force of regular troops is small, he has, he assures me, every certainty of collecting around this neighbourhood, in about twenty days, a force of not less than twenty thousand or thirty thousand armed Circassians, horse and foot.

Upon my expressing doubts as to the Circassian assistance being much to be relied on, Serfir Pasha as well as the General declared that there was no doubt now of a general rising, and that they held documents from almost every Circassian officer in Russian employ in the Kouban, declaring that they were ready when the opportunity was offered them to show that they were still Circassians.

Mustapha Pasha said his plan was to carry on a purely guerilla warfare, to blockade and harass Soujak and Anapa, and to occupy two small posts which lie between these two towns. I strongly concurred in the wisdom of his employing his men in a manner best adapted to their roving and predatory habits, and assured His Excellency that you would be highly pleased to see his plans carried out to the letter, moreover that I was sure he would best serve the plans you had in mind against Kertch, by keeping up the impression, among the Russians, that an attack of a serious nature was contemplated upon Soujak and Anapa.

Having heard that the Pasha had eleven battalions of regulars under his command, I asked him, in the event of your desiring to join him in any operations against the Russians in this neighbourhood, what was the actual number of troops he could move up from Abassia without weakening his position there. His reply was that he could not spare more than two thousand or three thousand regular troops, and that only with some risk—indeed, His Excellency appeared rather to avoid the question.

However, he promises to establish a military post here within twenty days, and so anxious are the

Circassians that he should do so, that several chiefs have gone with him to Soukoum Kaleh (whither he sailed this morning) to insure his returning among them. At Ponahs, about sixty miles S.E. of this place, the Pasha has already established a post.

Mustapha Pasha is, as I dare say you are already aware, Sir, the son of the 1st Turkish Governor of Anapa. He is evidently well known and liked here, and his visit has caused considerable excitement . . .

All my information goes to confirm the fact of the great strength of Anapa as a fortified place, but that the want of water within the works renders it incapable of withstanding a rigid blockade by land and sea, a fact that Mustapha Pasha insists on. At Soujak, five more heavy guns have been mounted.

The despatches for yourself, Admiral Bruat, Omar Pasha and the Porte, will be taken by that zealous officer, Lieutenant Armytage who, having been present and heard all that passed between the Pashas and myself, will be able to give you, Sir, all further information that you may require.

The *Vesuvius* will leave this place in two hours' time for Kertch, visiting the coast on the way up.

I have, etc.,

(Signed) Sherard Osborn.

Despatch from Captain John Moore to Rear-Admiral Sir Edmund Lyons.

Highflyer, off Kertch   2nd June, 1855.

Sir,

I have the honour to inform you that, in obedience to your orders, I have visited various points on the Circassian coast, as far as Soukoum Kaleh, and everywhere the news of the occupation by the Allies of the Straits of Kertch and Sea of Azoff was received with the greatest joy.

At Soukoum, I found Mustapha Pasha . . . he appeared to find the operations at Kertch of the utmost importance, and to be most anxious to second them, by appearing himself in the neighbourhood of Anapa with a small Turkish force, and a *levée en masse* of the Circassians, which he seemed very confident of being able to effect. He informed me that, during his late absence in Circassia, the Russians had made an attack on Redoute Kaleh, which had been repulsed, and that they also threatened his positions at St Nicolai and Chorouk-sou, and that . . . he found it necessary to visit his army before again proceeding to Circassia which, however, he would certainly do as soon as circumstances allowed. He hoped to be at liberty in about ten days to bring up two or three Turkish battalions and several light field-pieces, and he hoped you would be able to assist him in transporting them . . .

In the meantime, I took charge of a letter from him to Serfir Pasha (who is in the neighbourhood of Ponahs) containing a proclamation calling on the Circassians to rise and complete the success of the Allies in cutting off the Russian communications in all directions. On reaching Ponahs and finding that Serfir Pasha was at some distance in the country, I was obliged to despatch the letter to him by a Circassian messenger, as I did not feel justified in awaiting his return, which was very uncertain . . .

This morning I reconnoitred Anapa and I perceived convoys leaving in the direction of Kouban Lake, which confirms what I have heard from the Circassians, that they are sending away the inhabitants and their property from the town.

> I have, etc.,
> (Signed) John Moore.

NOTE

Captain Moore landed at Soujak on 28th May, following its evacuation by the Russians. He found it in the possession of the Circassians and landed Captain Hughes (liaison officer) there.

From *The Russian War, 1885:* edited by Captain A. C. Dewar, O.B.E., B.Litt., F.R.Hist.S., R.N., and published by the Navy Records Society.

Also details from: *A History of the War Against Russia,* E. H. Nolan (2 vols., 1857).

Mustapha Pasha distinguished himself at the Battle of Oltenitza (Nov., 1853) and in the Danube campaign of 1854, under Omar Pasha. He succeeded Selim Pasha as Turkish Commander-in-Chief at Batoum in August, 1854, after the for-mer—suspected of having been bribed by the Russians—sustained a heavy defeat at Karaboulah, near Bayazid, and fled from the battle at the head of the Turkish reserve, which he did not bring into action. Twenty-five hundred Turks were taken prisoner and at least twice this number killed or wounded.

Richard Debaufre Guyon was born on 31 March, 1813, at Walcot near Bath, the son of a Commander, R.N. He entered the Austrian service in 1831, played a distinguished part in the Hungarian war of independence under Kossuth (1848) after which he fled to Turkey. He was appointed a General in November, 1853, in the Army of Asia Minor and was one of the few European officers who refused to embrace the Mohammedan faith. He died of cholera in 1856.

BOOKS CONSULTED
ON THE CRIMEAN WAR

GENERAL

History of the War Against Russia, E. H. Nolan (2 vols., 1857)

History of the War With Russia, H. Tyrell (3 vols., 1857)

The Campaign in the Crimea, G. Brackenbury, illustrated
    W. Simpson (1856)

The War in the Crimea, General Sir Edward Hamley (1891)

Letters from India and the Crimea, Surgeon-General
    J. A. Bostock (1896)

Letters from Headquarters, by a Staff Officer (1856)

The Crimea in 1854 and 1894, Field-Marshal Sir Evelyn Wood
    (1895)

The Destruction of Lord Raglan, Christopher Hibbert (1961)

Battles of the Crimean War, W. Baring Pemberton (1962)

The Reason Why, Cecil Woodham Smith (1953)

Crimean Blunder, Peter Gibbs (1960)

The Campaign in the Crimea, 1854–6: Despatches and Papers,
    compiled and arranged by Captain Sayer (1857)

Letters from Camp During the Siege of Sebastopol, Lt.-Colonel
    C. G. Campbell (1894)

The Invasion of the Crimea, A.W. Kingslake (1863)

With the Guards We Shall Go, Mabel, Countess of Airlie (1933)

Britain's Roll of Glory, D. H. Parry (1895)

Henry Clifford, V.C., General Sir Bernard Paget (1956)

BIOGRAPHIES

The Life of Colin Campbell, Lord Clyde, Lt.-General
L. Shadwell, C.B. (2 vols., 1881)

A Life of Vice-Admiral Lord Lyons, Captain S. Eardley-Wilmot,
R.N. (1898)

NAVAL

The Russian War, 1854 (Baltic and Black Sea), D. Bonner-
Smith and Captain A.C. Dewar, R.N. (1944)

Letters from the Black Sea, Admiral Sir Leopold Heath (1897)

A Sailor's Life Under Four Sovereigns, Admiral of the Fleet the
Hon. Sir Henry Keppel, G.C.B., O.M. (3 vols., 1899)

From Midshipman to Field-Marshal, Sir Evelyn Wood, V.C.
(2 vols., 1906)

Letters from the Fleet in the Fifties, Mrs Tom Kelly (1902)

The British Fleet in the Black Sea, Maj.-General W. Brereton
(1856)

Reminiscences of a Naval Officer, Sir G. Gifford (1892)

The Navy as I Have Known It, Vice-Admiral W. Freemantle
(1899)

A Middy's Recollections, The Hon. Victor Montagu (1898)

Medicine and the Navy, Lloyd and Coulter (vol. IV, 1963)

The Price of Admiralty, Stanley Barret, Hale (1968)

The Wooden Fighting Ship, E.H.H. Archibald, Blandford (1968)

Seamanship Manual, Captain Sir George S. Naes, K.C.B., R.N.,
Griffin (1886)

The Navy of Britain, England's Sea Officers, and *A Social History of the Navy,* Michael Lewis, Allen & Unwin (1939–60)

The Navy in Transition, Michael Lewis, Hodder & Stoughton (1965)

Files of *The Illustrated London News* and *Mariner's Mirror*

Unpublished Letters and Diaries

The author acknowledges, with gratitude, the assistance given by the Staff of the York City Library in obtaining books, also that given by the Royal United Service Institution and Francis Edwards Ltd.

The Alexander Sheridan Adventures

BY V. A. STUART

FROM THE Crimean War to the Sepoy Mutiny, the Alexander Sheridan Adventures deftly combine history and supposition in tales of scarlet soldiering that cunningly interweave fact and fiction.

Alexander Sheridan, unjustly forced out of the army, leaves Britain and his former life behind and joins the East India Company, still in pursuit of those ideals of honor and heroism that buoyed the British Empire for three hundred years. Murder, war, and carnage await him. But with British stoicism and an unshakable iron will, he will stand tall against the atrocities of war, judging all by their merit rather than by the color of their skin or the details of their religion.

1 Victors and Lords
ISBN 0-935526-98-6
272 pp., $13.95

2 The Sepoy Mutiny
ISBN 0-935526-99-4
240 pp., $13.95

3 Massacre at Cawnpore
ISBN 1-59013-019-7
240 pp., $13.95

4 The Cannons of Lucknow
ISBN 1-59013-029-4
272 pp., $14.95

5 The Heroic Garrison
ISBN 1-59013-030-8
256 pp., $13.95

"Stuart's saga of Captain Sheridan during the Mutiny stands in the shadow of no previous work of fiction, and for historical accuracy, writing verve and skill, and pace of narrative, stands alone."
—*El Paso Times*

V. A. STUART wrote several series of military fiction and numerous other novels under various pseudonyms. Her settings span history and the globe. Born in 1914, she was in Burma with the British Fourteenth Army in WW II, became a lieutenant, and was decorated with the Burma Star and the Pacific Star.

Philip McCutchan
The Halfhyde Adventures

Set at the turn of the 20th century,
Philip McCutchan's 15-book
Halfhyde Adventures Series promises
a witty, adventurous outing as
Lieutenant St Vincent Halfhyde plies
the seas in Her Majesty's Royal Navy.

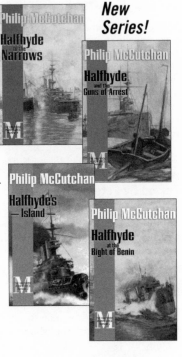

**New
Series!**

The Halfhyde Adventures
Series follows the remarkable,
rollicking adventures of the head-
strong Royal Navy Lieutenant
St Vincent Halfhyde. Acting as
a virtual Agent 007 in the early
years of the 20th century,
Halfhyde's forté is performing
risky special missions for the
Admirality. In action set against
a background of rapidly shifting
alliances, Lieutenant Halfhyde
triumphs as the Royal Navy
challenges Russia, Japan, and
Germany for control of the seas.

**"Halfhyde is a fine hero, insubordinate
and ingenious."**
—*The New York Times*

"Riveting and authoritative, with flashes
of dry humor and bawdiness to lighten
the strain."
—*Savannah News*

1 Halfhyde at the Bight of Benin
ISBN 1-59013-078-2
224 pp. • $13.95 pb.

2 Halfhyde's Island
ISBN 1-59013-079-0
224 pp. • $13.95 pb.

3 Halfhyde and the Guns of Arrest
ISBN 1-59013-067-7
256 pp. • $13.95 pb.

4 Halfhyde to the Narrows
ISBN 1-59013-068-5
240 pp. • $13.95 pb.

The Nelson and Emma Trilogy
by David Donachie

PART ONE
On a Making Tide

NEW!

Young Nelson and Emma begin to make their ways in the world with corresponding recklessness and precocious ambition: Nelson enters the Royal Navy at the age of twelve and quickly develops a reputation as a daring yet benevolent leader. At the same time, teenage Emma rises quickly up the ranks from bawdy house prostitute to noblemen's courtesan to celebrated artist's model.

ISBN 1-59013-041-3
416 pages, maps • $17.95

PART TWO
Tested by Fate

In a string of spectacular naval battles—Cape St Vincent, Tenerife, the Nile—the ravages of war take their physical toll on Nelson, even as he gains the fame and honour he desperately craves.

Emma, now Lady Hamilton, meets the mercurial Nelson in Naples, and she is inexplicably drawn to the brash sea captain. All the doors of Europe are open to her—but how can she forget Nelson when he has not forgotten her?

ISBN 1-59013-042-1
416 pages, maps • $17.95

PART THREE
Breaking the Line

Nelson sets sail for Copenhagen, Trafalgar, and glory. To a nation consumed by war, Admiral Horatio Nelson is a hero. Nelson's lover, the disreputable Lady Emma Hamilton, is another matter. Yet the two are inseparable, and defy friends and enemies alike to stay together. Fate has other plans, however, as Nelson moves inexorably toward the stunning conclusion of his career.

ISBN 1-59013-090-1
368 pages, maps • $16.95

The 3-part biographical novel that chronicles the rise of Horatio Nelson, Great Britain's greatest naval hero, and his legendary mistress, Lady Emma Hamilton.

"The strength of Donachie's writing lies in his convincing dialogue that brilliantly conveys the personalities of Nelson and Hamilton. The author certainly has done his homework . . . historical facts are very cleverly intertwined into the story."

—*Bookpleasures.com*

Available at your favorite bookstore, or call toll-free:
1-888-BOOKS-11 (1-888-266-5711).

To order on the web visit **www.mcbooks.com** *and read an excerpt.*

More Action, More Adventure, More Angst . . .

This is no time to stand down! McBooks Press, the leader in nautical fiction, invites you to embark on more sea adventures and take part in gripping naval action with Douglas Reeman, Dudley Pope, and a host of other nautical writers. Sail to Trafalgar, Grenada, Copenhagen—to famous battles and unknown skirmishes alike—and find out why nautical fiction is the next best thing since sliced bread with weevils.

All the titles below are available at bookstores. For a free catalog, or to order direct, call toll-free 1-888-BOOKS-11 (1-888-266-5711). Or visit the McBooks website, www.mcbooks.com, for special offers and to read excerpts from McBooks titles.

ALEXANDER KENT
The Bolitho Novels

___ 1 Midshipman Bolitho
0-935526-41-2 • 240 pp., $13.95

___ 2 Stand Into Danger
0-935526-42-0 • 288 pp., $13.95

___ 3 In Gallant Company
0-935526-43-9 • 320 pp., $14.95

___ 4 Sloop of War
0-935526-48-X • 352 pp., $14.95

___ 5 To Glory We Steer
0-935526-49-8 • 352 pp., $14.95

___ 6 Command a King's Ship
0-935526-50-1 • 352 pp., $14.95

___ 7 Passage to Mutiny
0-935526-58-7 • 352 pp., $15.95

___ 8 With All Despatch
0-935526-61-7 • 320 pp., $14.95

___ 9 Form Line of Battle!
0-935526-59-5 • 352 pp., $14.95

___ 10 Enemy in Sight!
0-935526-60-9 • 368 pp., $14.95

___ 11 The Flag Captain
0-935526-66-8 • 384 pp., $15.95

___ 12 Signal – Close Action!
0-935526-67-6 • 368 pp., $15.95

___ 13 The Inshore Squadron
0-935526-68-4 • 288 pp., $13.95

___ 14 A Tradition of Victory
0-935526-70-6 • 304 pp., $14.95

___ 15 Success to the Brave
0-935526-71-4 • 288 pp., $13.95

___ 16 Colours Aloft!
0-935526-72-2 • 304 pp., $14.95

___ 17 Honour This Day
0-935526-73-0 • 320 pp., $15.95

___ 18 The Only Victor
0-935526-74-9 • 384 pp., $15.95

___ 19 Beyond the Reef
0-935526-82-X • 352 pp., $14.95

___ 20 The Darkening Sea
0-935526-83-8 • 352 pp., $15.95

___ 21 For My Country's Freedom
0-935526-84-6 • 304 pp., $15.95

___ 22 Cross of St George
0-935526-92-7 • 320 pp., $16.95

___ 23 Sword of Honour
0-935526-93-5 • 320 pp., $15.95

___ 24 Second to None
0-935526-94-3 • 352 pp., $16.95

___ 25 Relentless Pursuit
1-59013-026-X • 368 pp., $16.95

___ 26 Man of War
1-59013-091-X • 320 pp., $16.95

___ 26 Man of War
1-59013-066-9 • 320 pp., $24.95 HC

DOUGLAS REEMAN
Modern Naval Fiction Library

___ Twelve Seconds to Live
1-59013-044-8 • 368 pp., $15.95

___ Battlecruiser
1-59013-043-X • 320 pp., $15.95

___ The White Guns
1-59013-083-9 • 368 pp., $15.95

Royal Marines Saga

___ 1 Badge of Glory
1-59013-013-8 • 384 pp., $16.95

___ 2 The First to Land
1-59013-014-6 • 304 pp., $15.95

___ 3 The Horizon
1-59013-027-8 • 368 pp., $15.95

___ 4 Dust on the Sea
1-59013-028-6 • 384 pp., $15.95

Historical Fiction Published by McBooks Press

DUDLEY POPE
The Lord Ramage Novels

___ 1 Ramage
    0-935526-76-5 • 320 pp., $14.95

___ 2 Ramage & the Drumbeat
    0-935526-77-3 • 288 pp., $14.95

___ 3 Ramage & the Freebooters
    0-935526-78-1 • 384 pp., $15.95

___ 4 Governor Ramage R. N.
    0-935526-79-X • 384 pp., $15.95

___ 5 Ramage's Prize
    0-935526-80-3 • 320 pp., $15.95

___ 6 Ramage & the Guillotine
    0-935526-81-1• 320 pp., $14.95

___ 7 Ramage's Diamond
    0-935526-89-7 • 336 pp., $15.95

___ 8 Ramage's Mutiny
    0-935526-90-0 • 280 pp., $14.95

___ 9 Ramage & the Rebels
    0-935526-91-9 • 320 pp., $15.95

___ 10 The Ramage Touch
    1-59013-007-3 • 272 pp., $15.95

___ 11 Ramage's Signal
    1-59013-008-1 • 288 pp., $15.95

___ 12 Ramage & the Renegades
    1-59013-009-X • 320 pp., $15.95

___ 13 Ramage's Devil
    1-59013-010-3 • 320 pp., $15.95

___ 14 Ramage's Trial
    1-59013-011-1 • 320 pp., $15.95

___ 15 Ramage's Challenge
    1-59013-012-X • 352 pp., $15.95

___ 16 Ramage at Trafalgar
    1-59013-022-7 • 256 pp., $14.95

___ 17 Ramage & the Saracens
    1-59013-023-5 • 304 pp., $15.95

___ 18 Ramage & the Dido
    1-59013-024-3 • 272 pp., $15.95

DEWEY LAMBDIN
Alan Lewie Naval Adventures

___ 2 The French Admiral
    1-59013-021-9 • 448 pp., $17.95

___ 8 Jester's Fortune
    1-59013-034-0 • 432 pp., $17.95

JAMES L. NELSON
___The Only Life That Mattered
    1-59013-060-X • 416 pp., $16.95

ALEXANDER FULLERTON
The Nicholas Everard WWII Saga

___ 1 Storm Force to Narvik
    1-59013-092-8 • 256 pp., $13.95

PHILIP McCUTCHAN
The Halfhyde Adventures

___1 Halfhyde at the Bight of Benin
    1-59013-078-2 • 224 pp., $13.95

___2 Halfhyde's Island
    1-59013-079-0 • 224 pp., $13.95

___3 Halfhyde and the Guns of Arrest
    1-59013-067-7 • 256 pp., $13.95

___4 Halfhyde to the Narrows
    1-59013-068-5 • 240 pp., $13.95

DAVID DONACHIE
The Privateersman Mysteries

___ 1 The Devil's Own Luck
    1-59013-004-9 • 302 pp., $15.95
    1-59013-003-0 • 320 pp., $23.95 HC

___ 2 The Dying Trade
    1-59013-006-5 • 384 pp., $16.95
    1-59013-005-7 • 400 pp., $24.95 HC

___ 3 A Hanging Matter
    1-59013-016-2 • 416 pp., $16.95

___ 4 An Element of Chance
    1-59013-017-0 • 448 pp., $17.95

___ 5 The Scent of Betrayal
    1-59013-031-6 • 448 pp., $17.95

___ 6 A Game of Bones
    1-59013-032-4 • 352 pp., $15.95

The Nelson & Emma Trilogy

___ 1 On a Making Tide
    1-59013-041-3 • 416 pp., $17.95

___ 2 Tested by Fate
    1-59013-042-1 • 416 pp., $17.95

___ 3 Breaking the Line
    1-59013-090-1 • 368 pp., $16.95

JAN NEEDLE
Sea Officer William Bentley Novels

___ 1 A Fine Boy for Killing
    0-935526-86-2 • 320 pp., $15.95

___ 2 The Wicked Trade
    0-935526-95-1 • 384 pp., $16.95

___ 3 The Spithead Nymph
    1-59013-077-4 • 288 pp., $14.95

C. NORTHCOTE PARKINSON
The Richard Delancey Novels

___ 1 The Guernseyman
  1-59013-001-4 • 208 pp., $13.95
___ 2 Devil to Pay
  1-59013-002-2 • 288 pp., $14.95
___ 3 The Fireship
  1-59013-015-4 • 208 pp., $13.95
___ 4 Touch and Go
  1-59013-025-1 • 224 pp., $13.95
___ 5 So Near So Far
  1-59013-037-5 • 224 pp., $13.95
___ 6 Dead Reckoning
  1-59013-038-3 • 224 pp., $15.95

V.A. STUART
Alexander Sheridan Adventures

___ 1 Victors and Lords
  0-935526-98-6 • 272 pp., $13.95
___ 2 The Sepoy Mutiny
  0-935526-99-4 • 240 pp., $13.95
___ 3 Massacre at Cawnpore
  1-59013-019-7 • 240 pp., $13.95
___ 4 The Cannons of Lucknow
  1-59013-029-4 • 272 pp., $14.95
___ 5 The Heroic Garrison
  1-59013-030-8 • 256 pp., $13.95

The Phillip Hazard Novels

___ 1 The Valiant Sailors
  1-59013-039-1 • 272 pp., $14.95
___ 2 The Brave Captains
  1-59013-040-5 • 272 pp., $14.95
___ 3 Hazard's Command
  1-59013-081-2 • 256 pp., $13.95
___ 4 Hazard of Huntress
  1-59013-082-0 • 256 pp., $13.95
___ 5 Hazard in Circassia
  1-59013-062-6 • 256 pp., $13.95
___ 6 Victory at Sebastopol
  1-59013-061-8 • 224 pp., $13.95

Military Fiction Classics

R.F. DELDERFIELD
___ Seven Men of Gascony
  0-935526-97-8 • 368 pp., $16.95
___ Too Few for Drums
  0-935526-96-X • 256 pp., $14.95

NICHOLAS NICASTRO
The John Paul Jones Trilogy

___ 1 The Eighteenth Captain
  0-935526-54-4 • 312 pp., $16.95
___ 2 Between Two Fires
  1-59013-033-2 • 384 pp., $16.95

Classics of Nautical Fiction

CAPTAIN FREDERICK MARRYAT
___ Frank Mildmay OR
  The Naval Officer
  0-935526-39-0 • 352 pp., $14.95
___ The King's Own
  0-935526-56-0 • 384 pp., $15.95
___ Mr Midshipman Easy
  0-935526-40-4 • 352 pp., $14.95
___ Newton Forster OR
  The Merchant Service
  0-935526-44-7 • 352 pp., $13.95
___ Snarleyyow OR The Dog Fiend
  0-935526-64-1 • 384 pp., $16.95
___ The Phantom Ship
  0-935526-85-4 • 320 pp., $14.95
___ The Privateersman
  0-935526-69-2 • 288 pp., $15.95

RAFAEL SABATINI
___ Captain Blood
  0-935526-45-5 • 288 pp., $15.95

WILLIAM CLARK RUSSELL
___ The Yarn of Old Harbour Town
  0-935526-65-X • 256 pp., $14.95
___ The Wreck of the Grosvenor
  0-935526-52-8 • 320 pp., $13.95

A.D. HOWDEN SMITH
___ Porto Bello Gold
  0-935526-57-9 • 288 pp., $13.95

MICHAEL SCOTT
___ Tom Cringle's Log
  0-935526-51-X • 512 pp., $14.95